A FINAL
REGRET

A FINAL REGRET

JEFF WARREN

Independently Published

ACKNOWLEDGMENTS

My thanks go to my wife and sons, to whom I am forever grateful for their patience and understanding, for their detailed feedback, and for pointing out my numerous typos and other errors. If you notice any, I must have introduced them after they read it.

Thanks to Martin, Linda and Pam, who read 'A Final Regret' and who provided helpful suggestions, and to Hannah, who helped me avoid some major pitfalls.

The cover was created from photos of a Pwll Deri Sunset by Daniel Morris and Rame Head by Vinzling, downloaded from Unsplash and Pixabay respectively.

PROLOGUE

Wind and spray lashed Rianna's face and body as she pounded the coast path. A hundred feet below, giant breakers battered the rocks.

Drizzle and mist rolled in clouds across the cliff tops, one moment blotting out the landscape, then clearing to reveal the gorse-clad hillside and the boiling seas below. Between wave crests, the waters looked as grey and greasy as liquid slate.

Rianna's resolve to complete her early morning runs never faltered. She was determined to get back into shape.

She turned up the volume on her phone. The clamour of the wind and waves battled with "Pray for the Wicked". She smiled at the album title. She didn't need anyone to pray for her. She could look after herself.

The mists ahead parted briefly and, for a moment, Rianna thought she saw a figure on the path ahead of her. Then the vision was gone, hidden in the swirling mist.

Getting the occupation order against Dylan, Meg's father, had been ridiculously easy. He'd begged and pleaded for Rianna not to take him to court, not to have him excluded from his own home. Then, predictably, he'd lost his temper, giving her all the justification she'd needed.

Now for the first time in her life she had a place of her own, a space that she happily shared with her daughter.

Meg was developing fast. She could already raise her head and shoulders off the floor. Rianna thought she could see signs of Meg's first tooth. She'd be crawling soon.

Since she'd embarked on her mission, the pain of her morning runs had diminished. Her muscle tone and the contours of her body improved day by day.

She was looking forward to the end of her run. It was Tuesday and that meant college. A quick shower back at the flat, hair and makeup, then the bus into town. Her first class was with Ross. It hadn't taken her long to twist him around her little finger. He had a small cottage on one of the tiny back roads close to Merlin's Bridge, just a short walk from the college.

Ross was fit, truly fit. In his classes she'd often lose the thread of what he was saying, letting her eyes devour every inch of his body. He was by far the best lover she'd ever known. She lusted after him with a passion that no previous lover had ever provoked.

Her knees grew weak at the thought, and she stumbled on the uneven surface, nearly flying headlong on the slippery path. She righted herself and ran on, her pulse pounding, her body stirring at the memory of Ross's caresses.

Could she tempt Ross away from college during his lunch break? Not if that witch Wendy had her way. Rianna couldn't understand what Ross saw in the woman. Okay, she was brainy, but she didn't qualify as pretty, not remotely attractive.

The mists parted again, and this time Rianna was certain someone was standing on the cliff top ahead. Was it a bird-watching nut? Was he holding binoculars to his eyes? Not that there were many birds flying in this early morning murk. What was he up to?

A gust of wind buffeted and moulded Rianna's top to her body. Her leggings were icy cold against her skin, and water infiltrated her clothes and tricked down her back. She licked salt from her lips and took a drink from her water-bottle as she ran. The path was uneven, rock strewn and constantly changing gradient, but she was used to it.

She thought of Meg as she ran, occasionally slipping and stumbling, but driving herself on. She was amazed at the bond that they'd formed. She hadn't expected to feel it so strongly. Now she had to succeed. She'd pass her college course with Ross's connivance, despite his distractions, and get a better job for both Meg and herself. Maybe she could become the manager, instead of being a waitress on the minimum wage at the Madoc's Bay Hotel.

Griff Llewellyn. Now he'd be a catch. Not that she wanted a man as a permanent feature in her life, not yet. But Griff Llewellyn, the hotelier's son. Decidedly dishy. Last Saturday night, after her shift at the hotel, he'd given her a lift in his Porsche.

He'd stopped in a gateway on a narrow, deserted country lane. He was all over her, but she'd fought him off, not because she didn't want him – her whole body tingled at his touch. He'd just have to wait. It would make him more eager. Could he be a more skilful lover than Ross? She'd lead him on, stoke his ego and find out. She needed someone rich to give her the gifts that she and Meg deserved.

The swirling mists closed in as Rianna ran along a section of path close to the edge of the cliff. Below her the waves crashed and thundered on the rocks.

She smiled to herself. If she played her cards right, maybe her new project would pay off. She'd need to go carefully. She'd never done anything like it before. She didn't know how much to demand.

A short flight of steps descended into a gully notched in the cliff top. Careful not to slip, Rianna told herself. Ahead the path looped around the gully and then turned sharp right around a fence post, right on the edge of the cliff.

Too late she sensed movement behind her. As she turned, a dark clad figure rose from the gully, a rock in its raised hand. Rianna tried to dodge, but she was off-balance, powerless to prevent the rock from smashing down on her skull.

She screamed. An image of a motherless Meg flashed through her mind. A split second of agony as shock waves obliterated her thoughts, her being. Then nothing.

*****

The murderer pushed Rianna's body over the edge before it had time to hit the ground. It bounced and cartwheeled down the steeply sloping cliff-face before landing in a crumpled tangle of limbs among the wave-washed boulders below.

The murderer threw the rock after it. The rapidly rising tide would soon wash the body out to sea. No one would even know where she'd died. A perfect murder with no incriminating evidence.

CHAPTER 1

'It's disgraceful, that Rianna's gone off and left Meg with a friend all day long, and hasn't even bothered to turn up and collect her.' Gemma Rogers radiated anger and disapproval, her features contorted with rage.

'So, who was that on the phone?' Alys asked. 'Dylan?'

'What that court did was outrageous,' Gemma continued, 'kicking my poor Dylan out of his own home.'

Alys suspected that once Gemma started, she'd be difficult to stop. But Alys couldn't help feeling sympathy for her. Gemma positively doted on her baby granddaughter.

Then Alys's police training kicked in. 'So what's happened to Rianna? Who's looking after Meg?'

'That Vicky Morgan. Her and Rianna Hughes are two of a kind. Both as bad as each other. And to think they took Meg away from my Dylan. They call that justice?' Tears welled up in Gemma Rogers' eyes. Then she glared at Alys and stabbed her finger at her, 'You should do something about it,' she said accusingly. 'That's what you're for isn't it?'

'That's not the police's job,' Julie Bowen said. 'It was the family court's decision to grant the court order against Dylan.'

'You didn't do much good either,' Gemma said, her voice getting louder and rounding on Julie. 'Always going on about what a caring mother she is. You didn't tell them what Rianna's really like, cheating, lying schemer that she is.'

The other members of the Madoc's Haven Historical Society stopped talking among themselves and were now all listening to the developing argument. The local vicar, Cedric Davies, came over and put a comforting hand on Gemma's arm.

'Julie was only telling the court what she saw as the district nurse,' Cedric said. 'She put in a good word for Dylan too, told them what a good father he was. Said she'd never seen him raise a hand against either Rianna or Meg.'

'Much good it did my poor Dylan,' Gemma said, truculently. 'It's weeks since I last saw Meg.'

'So, was that Dylan on the phone?' Alys tried again. 'What exactly did he say? Who told him that Rianna hadn't turned up?'

Gemma dabbed her eyes with a tissue. 'Dylan,' she said. 'Seems that Vicky's calling around trying to find out what's happened to Rianna. Probably shacked up with some man, knowing her. I told Dylan she was no good, but he wouldn't listen. My Huw, he's tamping mad. Says she should be locked up. Doesn't know what the world's coming to, when a father's kicked out of his home and not allowed to look after his own kid.'

'Do you know who else Vicky's contacted?' Alys asked, wondering why Vicky was looking after Meg all day.

'Oh Goodness,' Julie Bowen said. 'Look at the time, Cedric. We'll have to get the meeting started.'

As well as being the district nurse, Julie Bowen was the Historical Society's secretary, Cedric its chairman.

Cedric clapped his hands and shouted, 'Sorry everyone. I wasn't watching the clock. Can you all take your seats?'

As the session got under way, the minutes of the previous meeting and matters arising faded into the background. Alys focussed her thoughts on the conversation they'd just had. Could Rianna have had an accident? Had Vicky called the hospital in Haverfordwest? Perhaps she'd follow up when the meeting was over.

She couldn't help thinking that the family court had it wrong about Dylan. Okay, he had a fiery temper and was prone to angry outbursts, but he wasn't violent by nature. She hadn't been to the hearing, so she didn't know what evidence was presented.

Alys didn't know Rianna well. She'd seen her around the village since the young woman had started working at the Madoc's Bay Hotel the summer before last. She was attractive, but there were rumours that she slept around, even after she'd moved in with Dylan and given birth to his child. Rianna claimed that Meg was Dylan's daughter, and he seemed to accept it. Alys suspected that Rianna was manipulative and used her looks to get what she wanted from men. If she'd been Dylan, she'd have demanded a paternity test.

Alys pulled her thoughts back from Rianna's disappearance and discovered that she'd missed an entire agenda item, something about a planning application and the need for a dig at Clebaston Manor.

Cedric announced the next topic, 'Rediscovering Ancient Connections – The Saints', a project investigating links between West Wales and Southern Ireland during the dark ages.

But Alys found it difficult to concentrate on what the speaker was saying, or the following discussion. If Rianna truly was missing, where could she be? Had Vicky phoned it in?

*****

'What's this I hear about Matt Vincent moving back into the area?' Julie Bowen asked.

The thought of meeting Matt after all these years boosted Alys's heart rate into orbit. It had been a traumatic time, that last summer. How would he cope with returning? It was odd that they'd both decided on careers in the police.

'Moved back, actually,' Alys said, refocusing on Julie Bowen's question. 'A couple of months ago. Matt's a Detective Inspector now, or so I heard on the grape-vine. He's hoping to get a promotion to Detective Chief Inspector by moving here.'

The Historical Society meeting over, its members were drinking tea and coffee and chatting. Gemma Rogers, Dylan's mother, didn't stay, so Alys hadn't been able to ask for more information about the missing Rianna.

'I haven't seen him around,' Julie said. 'Where's he based?'

'At Police HQ over by Carmarthen, 'Alys said, 'I doubt if he'll come this far west, unless someone commits a crime that's serious enough for the Major Crime team to be involved.'

Memories of that tragic summer came flooding back. She was surprised Matt had returned to West Wales. His parents had moved to Aberdeen earlier the same year and he had no relatives in the area, few other ties, just heart-breaking memories.

'What do you think's happened to Rianna?' Alys asked, dragging her mind back from the past.

'Hopefully she's just delayed getting home,' Julie said. 'I know she has a bit of a reputation, but she genuinely cares for little Meg. What I can't understand is why she did what she did to poor Dylan. He seems like a caring father. I'm sure what was said in court blew matters up out of all proportion.'

Alys avoided commenting on the court order against Dylan, As sergeant in charge of the Madoc's Haven neighbourhood policing team, she was willing to listen to gossip, but she wasn't going to add to it.

'Yes, probably just delayed,' Alys said. 'She could have turned up by now. If I knew her well, I might have given Vicky a call, but since we moved to Llanbrioc, I've not got to know Madoc's Haven's newer inhabitants at all well. Any idea why Vicky was looking after Meg?'

'She has a toddler of her own, Dafi he's called,' Julie said. 'Cute little lad. Vicky and Rianna help each other out when either of them has to work.' She frowned as if racking her brains, then she suddenly smiled. 'I think Rianna goes into Haverfordwest by bus every Tuesday. She's studying at the college.'

'So maybe the bus has broken down.'

At that moment Alys's phone started to vibrate in her pocket. She glanced at the screen, then said, 'Sorry, I have to take this.'

She stepped outside into the corridor and answered the call. 'Sergeant Carey,' she said.

'Duty sergeant here. We've had a missing person's report from Madoc's Haven. Been classified as high risk. Are you anywhere near?'

'Yes. I'm in Madoc's Haven right now.'

'I know you're off duty, but can you meet DI Vincent there in about thirty minutes? Says he knows you from the past.'

Alys's throat and chest constricted. She hadn't expected to meet Matt at such short notice. Her pulse raced.

'Certainly. We can meet in our office at the fire station. I'll get over there and put the kettle on.'

The estates department had closed Madoc's Haven police station, like many other smaller stations across the county, and arranged shared facilities with the fire brigade. Yet one more of the many economy measures that were sweeping through the force like a chill wind. Perhaps it was more like a winter gale, Alys thought bitterly. Now there were plans to close down their little office, even though it had only been in existence for a couple of years, and replace it with a mobile police station, an office in the back of a van. How the higher ups expected the clear-up rates to improve when their main priority was cuts, she couldn't understand.

She didn't know if Matt expected her to be in uniform. Well, she couldn't go home to Llanbrioc, get changed, and get back to Madoc's Haven in time to meet him. Thank heavens she'd put on a smart top and her best jeans for the Historical Society meeting and that she'd had her hair trimmed the previous week.

The wind whined through the telegraph wires and chimney pots and drove rain into Alys's face as she walked down the High Street to Cross Square to the fire station. It was a miserable night to be out. She didn't doubt that the missing person was Rianna Hughes. She just hoped that Rianna would turn up safe and well, but grim foreboding gripped her heart.

Alys punched the entry code into the lock on the fire station door. The building was dark, cold and deserted. She punched another code into the lock on the room that her team used as an office and let herself in. The infrared wall heater would take the chill off the air. She filled the kettle and set it to boil.

How long ago was the last time she'd spoken to Matt? It must be ten years. How much had he changed in the intervening period? For that matter, how much had she changed? She checked her hair and makeup in the mirror. Her hands shook as she took two cups from the cupboard. She smiled in disbelief. She was acting like an immature schoolgirl.

CHAPTER 2

'Mr Llewellyn wants to see you, Cassie, in his office,'
Penny told Cassie. 'Now!'

Cassie was about to back through the swing door
into the dining room of the Madoc's Bay Hotel, her
arms laden with artistically arranged, but minimalistic,
starters.

'I'll have to finish serving table eight. I can't just
serve half of them.'

'I'll get Ellie to finish the table,' Penny told her. 'You
can't keep him waiting, he'll go ape. He's furious
enough as it is. I did warn you.'

Cassie served four of the diners on table eight,
moved swiftly back through the kitchen to check that
Ellie was collecting the remaining starters and then
hurried through to Rhodri Llewellyn's office with dread
clutching her stomach.

The man was a tyrant with an absolute lack of care
for his staff. It was bad luck he'd been in the hotel
when Dylan's call had come through. Usually he was
off elsewhere doing whatever it was he did to make
other people's lives a misery.

She knocked on his private office door. He barked
'come' like some yapping little dog. She opened the
door, stepped inside, closed it gently behind her and
stood stiffly to attention in front of his massive antique
desk. The room's opulent furnishings must have cost
more than her student loan for the full three years of
her degree, yet all she was earning was the minimum
wage, and that was paid begrudgingly.

Cassie waited while he studied something on the

screen of his computer. She suspected he was making her wait deliberately to rack up her unease.

Rhodri Llewellyn was running to fat, the result of too much gracious living, Cassie suspected. His face was rounded and double-chinned. His hair was thinning and turning to grey. From his deeply tanned skin it was obvious that he spent much of the winter in a sunnier climate. His shirt was pristine white and appeared freshly ironed. Gold cuff-links gleamed at his cuffs, and his watch looked seriously expensive.

Finally Llewellyn turned his attention to her.

'I thought it was made clear to you when you were employed, that you were not to make or receive personal telephone calls while you were on duty. Yet I understand that you received one this evening while you were on duty, strictly against your terms of employment.'

Was the pompous old windbag going to fire her just for taking one call? Cassie began to feel sick. She couldn't afford to lose this job, even with the pay as lousy as it was.

'Well?' Llewellyn demanded. 'What have you to say for yourself?

'I'm sorry sir,' Cassie said, despising herself for apologising so subserviently, 'but I was told it was urgent, an emergency.'

'What could be so urgent that you would place it above your duties here at the hotel? This is a five star establishment with a well-deserved reputation. I'll not have my staff put that reputation at jeopardy.'

Cassie thought it wisest to say nothing. She'd already apologised. Wasn't that enough?

'Who was the call from?' Llewellyn demanded. 'Come on girl, speak up.'

Should she tell him? If she did, it would probably make matters worse. If she didn't and he already knew, he'd definitely fire her. She wanted to tell him to get stuffed, but she didn't dare. The man was a bully. She hated him.

She didn't dare look him in the eyes. He'd see that she despised him. She kept her gaze focused on the desk. 'Dylan Rogers, sir.'

'Rogers?' Llewellyn said angrily. 'I gave that man the sack for bringing the name of the hotel into disrepute. What on earth could he want that was so urgent that you'd ignore your duties to speak to him?

Cassie was in a dilemma. She guessed he knew that Dylan had had an injunction granted against him, but did he know that it involved Rianna too? What gossip had the man heard? Cassie didn't want to say anything that could lose Rianna her job too.

Cassie crossed her fingers behind her back and said, 'His child's mother has disappeared. He asked if I knew where she was.'

She could feel Llewellyn's eyes boring into her. She held her breath and kept her eyes averted, hoping that he wasn't aware that Rianna was the mother of Dylan's child. She waited. Why didn't the damned man say something?

'You'll be docked an hour's pay for the time that you've wasted,' he finally said. 'Think yourself lucky that I haven't fired you, but consider yourself on warning. Now get back to work.'

'Yes sir,' Cassie said meekly. 'Thank you, sir.'

Cassie stepped out into the corridor, closed the door quietly behind her, and burst into tears.

*****

'What's the matter, Cassie bach?' Bill Symonds asked. 'Let's not stand here in the corridor. Come along with me to the scullery.' He put his hand on Cassie's shoulder and propelled her along to his domain, the scullery, where he spent his days operating the potato peeling machine, scraping plates into the pig bins, loading the dishwashers and doing other menial chores. 'Don't you upset yourself. Come and sit on my stool.'

Bill Symonds was the hotel's kitchen porter, odd job man and general shoulder to cry on. He acted as an uncle to Cassie and the other youngsters who waited table and acted as maids throughout the year. He had a soft spot for Cassie. She'd returned to Madoc's Haven to help look after her dying mother. Cassie had stayed on, comforting her grieving father. It was a shame. The poor girl should be away in Swansea or Cardiff enjoying herself and working at a job better suited to her talents.

'Dylan called to ask if I knew where Rianna is,' Cassie sobbed, 'and I got it in the neck for taking the call. That miserable old bastard's docking me an hour's pay and talking about firing me.'

'Ssssh,' Bill said. 'Don't let anyone hear you calling him that, or we'll both get the sack.'

'I don't know how you can stand working here as long as you have,' Cassie said. 'It's like being in purgatory without any chance of salvation.'

Bill was amused. It wasn't many of the young folks who'd be speaking of purgatory and salvation, but she was the vicar's daughter. Some of her father's religion had obviously rubbed off.

'It's not so bad, if you keep your head down,' Bill said. 'It was far better when Mr Rhodri Llewellyn's's father was alive. He ran a tidy ship. It was a pleasure to work here then.'

Cassie wiped her eyes and blew her nose.

'So what's this about Dylan asking after Rianna?' Bill asked.

'Seems that Ree left Meg with Vicky Morgan this morning, and hasn't been seen since. Both Vicky and Dylan are phoning around, trying to find out where she is.' Cassie frowned with concern. 'I hope nothing's happened to Ree. Vicky's phoned the hospital to see if she's been in an accident, but they don't know anything. Now she's thinking of phoning the police.'

Bill shook his head. 'I don't know what got into that girl's head, making those complaints against Dylan. He's a good lad. Mind you, bit of a temper, but he wouldn't hurt a fly. But look, you'd better get back to work, or you will be getting the sack.'

*****

Cassie ploughed through the rest of service like an automaton, but her mind was on Dylan, Rianna and Meg. What could have happened to Ree? She was lucky to have Vicky as a friend. From what Cassie gathered, baby Meg often slept over with Vicky when Ree had the evening shift.

Cassie doubted that Rianna was faithful to Dylan. She'd heard too many rumours. Only two nights ago after work, she'd seen Ree getting into Griff's posh new Porsche.

Griff was Rhodri Llewellyn's son. While all the other children in Madoc's Haven had gone to secondary school in Haverfordwest, the nearest large town, Griff had gone away to an expensive boarding school in Surrey.

Most of Cassie's school friends who'd gone to university went to either Swansea or Cardiff. She'd been an exception, going to Bristol to study archaeology and anthropology. Griff went to Oxford.

Cassie helped the other girls clear the dining room and lay up for breakfast, still wondering what had happened to Rianna, whether she'd turned up. She'd find out in the morning. Rianna was on the rota to serve breakfast.

'Hello gorgeous. Can I give you a lift home?'

Well, Ree couldn't be with Griff, Cassie thought. She turned to Griff and forced a smile. She didn't enjoy his cheesy chat-up lines, even though they boosted a girl's ego. 'No thanks. I doubt if my bike would fit in your Porsche, and I'll need it to get to work in the morning.' She was glad she wasn't wearing her Lycra cycling gear. His eyes would have been peeling her out of it, like they did during last summer's warm weather. 'Kind of you to offer though,' she said, with a total lack of sincerity.

Cassie wondered if Rianna had gone back to the Llewellyn family mansion the other night. Or did Griff have some secret hideaway where he took his sexual conquests? Cassie had no intention of finding out.

She let herself out of the hotel's back door and put on her cycling helmet. Where to goodness was her bike? Oh, over there. Odd, someone must have moved it. She set out on the dark lonely ride back to the vicarage, humming to keep herself company. Shame it was such a miserable night. No moon or stars. Maybe she'd see a fox or a badger.

CHAPTER 3

Returning to Madoc's Haven would reopen old wounds but that was inevitable, once he'd applied for the transfer back to Dyfed-Powys. Matt took the decision with mixed feelings, but he saw it as his best route to the promotion he deserved. He was determined to reach the rank of Detective Chief Inspector before he turned thirty. Besides, he missed the countryside, the wildlife and the sea.

He parked the pool car, a Ford Focus that had seen better times, on the forecourt of the single-engine fire station where the neighbourhood policing team had their bolt-hole. There were no other cars, but lights showed inside the building. Alys must have walked there to meet him. Did she still live in the village?

Matt remembered Alys as 'The Pest', a gawky young teenage girl with braces on her teeth who followed Matt and his friends around wherever they went. What would she look like now? She was listed as Sergeant Alys Carey so, unless she was married but still using her maiden name, she was single.

The wind howled down the High Street, driving sheets of rain before it. It was as if beaded curtains were being dragged through the cascades of light cast by the street lamps.

Matt pulled his coat more tightly around him as he climbed from his car and dashed for the door. It opened as he reached for the bell push.

'Come along in, it's miserable out there,' Alys said. 'Saw you arrive on the CCTV.

Matt glanced at her as he stepped into the entrance

corridor. Alys closed the door behind him and turned to face him. Wow, she had changed. The harsh lighting of the entrance hallway revealed an attractive young woman in her mid-twenties, five or six years younger than he was. Her figure had filled out and her hair had darkened to a rich chestnut hue. He'd forgotten the intensity of her cornflower blue eyes.

Matt held out his hand.

Alys forestalled him by stepping forward and hugging him hard. He stiffened in surprise as her body pressed against his. His emotions plunged into free-fall as the scent from her hair filled his nostrils.

He was briefly at a loss for words and the ability to breathe as he processed what had just happened, but he recovered quickly, putting his hands on her shoulders and gently easing himself out of her embrace. He touched his cheek against hers in what he intended to be a far less sensual form of greeting.

'I wasn't expecting such a warm welcome,' he said, as he struggled to marshal his thoughts.

'I always wanted to do that when we were younger, but I never had the courage,' Alys said with a smile as she let go of him and stepped back. 'I promise not to do that again,' adding, 'Sir.' as an afterthought. Her cheeks blushed pink and her eyes sparkled as they locked on to his, connecting with his emotions in a way no one else had done in years.

'Don't hang around out here, go straight along in,' Alys said. 'The second door on the right.'

Matt went ahead in a welter of chaos and confusion. He could still feel the pressure of her body, warm and yielding, against his.

'We'll have to catch up some other time,' he said, attempting to sound efficient and business-like. 'We have a missing person to find.'

'I'm making coffee,' Alys said, still smiling. 'White and two sugars?'

'I've cut out the sugar, white would be great,' Matt said, amazed that Alys remembered. 'Control received a 101 call from a Vicky Morgan earlier this evening, reporting Rianna Hughes missing.' Matt said, uncomfortable and determined to reset the tone of their meeting. 'Do you know either of them?'

Alys's eyes flicked over his face as if probing his thoughts. 'Not that well. I know them both by sight, but they both arrived after we moved to Llanbrioc a couple of years ago.' She passed Matt his coffee and took a sip of her own, gazing at him over the rim. 'Isn't it rather soon for this to be high risk? She's only a few hours late turning up, probably delayed getting back from Haverfordwest.'

'What have you heard?' Matt asked, wondering where Alys's information came from.

'There was some discussion at the Historical Society meeting,' she said. 'Vicky was ringing around. What did she tell Control that made this a priority?'

'Let's go hear what Vicky says,' Matt said. 'Then we can judge for ourselves.'

*****

Matt drove them both to the small back street where Madoc's Haven's affordable housing was hidden away.

Alys had certainly changed. He could still feel the imprint of her body against his. No longer was she the gawky, reticent teenager whom he'd known. Now she was decisive, assertive and attractive. He hoped she hadn't metamorphosed into an adult version of 'The Pest'. The last thing he needed was a stalker.

What was it she'd said? '...we moved to Llanbrioc two years ago.' Who was 'we'? Was she married? Still living with her parents?

They arrived at the block of flats. Vicky answered the entry phone and buzzed them in straight away. Her flat was on the ground floor. She ushered them in and quickly closed the door behind them. She pushed a draft excluder in the form of a snake across the bottom of the door. It was snug and warm inside.

A toddler stood watching them, sucking his thumb, clutching a teddy bear and dressed in grey pyjamas with a picture of a mechanical digger emblazoned across his chest. A baby lay on her back on a yellow woollen blanket, sucking on a feeding bottle that was clasped between her hands and her feet.

Vicky was young for a mother, barely out of her teens. She looked worried and frazzled. She gestured for them to sit on the small, two-seater settee.

Alys took out her phone and settled back to take notes.

'I'm Detective Inspector Matt Vincent,' Matt told Vicky, 'and this is Sergeant Alys Carey. I expect you've seen her around. She's in charge of the neighbourhood policing team.'

Vicky nodded distractedly to Alys. 'I can't think what's happened to Ree, she's never been late like this before. She should have been here around five. What is it now? Nearly ten,' she said, glancing at the wall clock. 'Dafi and Meg can sense there's something's wrong. I can't get either of them down.'

Dafi, the toddler, clutched Vicky's leg and peered out from behind it. Vicky picked Dafi up and sat on the armchair, settling her son on her lap.

'I know you explained everything when you called 101,' Matt said, 'but can you take us through it all again, please? From when Rianna left Meg with you this morning? What she was intending to do, where you think she might have gone?'

'Ree goes to college in Haverfordwest every Tuesday,' Vicky said, bouncing Dafi gently on her knee, 'but first she goes for a run along the coast path towards the Madoc's Bay Hotel and back. She's desperate to get back into shape after having Meg.'

'Did she do that this morning'? Matt asked.

'Must have. She was dressed for running when she dropped Meg off. That was about 7 o'clock. It was just getting light. I didn't see her again after that. What do you think's happened to her?'

'Do you think she returned safely from her run?'

Vicky shrugged. 'I dunno. She'd usually have a shower, catch the bus to H'west and go to her classes. Studying hospitality management or some such.'

'Has anyone checked her flat?'

'I went round earlier this evening and rang the bell, knocked on the door. Before I called you lot. There weren't any lights on and she didn't answer or anything.'

'Do you have a key?'

Vicky shook her head.

Meg threw her feeding bottle away and started grizzling, waving her arms and legs in the air. Vicky sat Dafi on the floor and picked Meg up, resting the baby on her shoulder and patted her back until she burped. 'There, there. That's better out, isn't it?'

'We need to know if she caught that bus,' Matt said. 'Does anyone from the village travel in with her? Someone we can ask tonight?'

'Dunno. Must do I guess, but I dunno who.'

While they were talking, Dafi crawled over and lay down on Meg's blanket, still sucking his thumb.

'Do you know the names of any of her lecturers at the college?' Matt asked. 'I'd like to find out if she attended classes today.'

'I think there's one called Ross,' she said.

A fleeting smile passed across Vicky's face, so quickly that Matt wondered if he'd imagined it.

Matt decided that he'd need to follow up on lecturer Ross. That transient smile must have meant something, but he let it go for the moment, wanting to create empathy, not engender resistance. 'You don't know his surname, do you?'

Vicky shook her head.

'After classes finish, Rianna catches the bus back to Madoc's Haven and collects Meg?' Matt asked. 'Has she ever been late before?'

'Maybe half-an-hour. Never anything like this.'

Meg had fallen asleep on Vicky's shoulder. Vicky gently lay the baby down on the blanket beside Dafi, who was now gently snoring.

'Does she have any friends in Haverfordwest she could be visiting?'

There was an almost imperceptible pause before Vicky said, 'Not that I know of.'

Matt suspected that Vicky was lying. He had a shrewd idea why, but he'd leave it for the moment, return to it later.

'Tell me about Rianna and Meg,' he said. 'Who's Meg's father?'

Again Vicky hesitated before answering, doubtless considering how much to tell him.

Unexpectedly Alys looked up from her phone and said, 'Dylan Rogers. There was a problem between Rianna and Dylan. Rianna took Dylan to the family court and obtained an occupation order against him. I don't know the full details, but I believe it was mainly verbal abuse.'

Wow, Matt thought. That adds a whole new dimension to the case. He wondered how long it would have taken for him to find out about Dylan Rogers and the court order if Alys hadn't been with him. 'Thank you, Sergeant. That's very helpful.'

'Dylan had to move out of the flat they shared,' Alys continued, 'but he still has to pay half the rent. There's also a child arrangements order. He can only see Meg in the presence of a member of social services or a person nominated by them, usually only at the supervised contact centre.'

Matt was impressed. Sergeant Alys Carey was definitely an asset, but had 'The Pest' persona been totally banished?

He turned back to Vicky and asked who she'd contacted before calling 101.

'I was afraid she'd had an accident or something, so I called the hospital in H'West, but they didn't know anything. Then I tried some of the crowd she goes around with. None of them knew anything either, so I called Dylan. He was at work. He went spare when I said Ree hadn't turned up. Said he'd come round when he'd finished service. I tried to tell him not to, but he wouldn't listen.'

Alys said quietly to Matt, 'He'll be breaking the terms of the injunction if he does.'

At that moment there was a furious buzzing noise that woke Dafi and Meg. They both started crying.

Vicky leapt up and dashed to the entry phone. Pressing a button, she asked, 'Who is it?'

'Dylan,' came the distorted reply.

'Go away, you can't come in. The police are here,' Vicky shouted.

CHAPTER 4

Both Alys and Matt jumped to their feet as Dylan pushed past Vicky into the room, wild eyed, his sandy coloured hair dishevelled. He dashed straight to Meg, who was lying on her back on the blanket, crying.

Alys put her hand on Matt's arm, willing him not to intervene. She was sure Dylan didn't mean his baby daughter any harm. She didn't want them adding to the drama.

'You poor little thing,' Dylan said, scooping Meg up in his arms and hugging her. 'Has that naughty mummy gone and deserted you?'

Vicky pushed the draft excluder back in place, then knelt on the floor comforting Dafi, soothing him with gentle words.

They could be a family group, mother, father and two young infants, Alys thought. She wondered what the relationship was between Dylan and Vicky.

Dylan had grown up in the area, went to the same schools as Matt and herself, although she didn't know him well. She was three or four years older than he was. Vicky was a relative newcomer to the area, arriving at the same time as Rianna as part of the annual influx of seasonal hospitality workers.

Alys and Matt sat back down on the small settee, waiting for Dylan and Vicky to settle their offspring. Meg's hair was much darker than Dylan's, but it wasn't unusual for a baby's hair to lighten as it grew older. Alys wondered again if Dylan really was Meg's father. He didn't seem to have any doubts.

Alys was eager to start questioning Dylan, but as Matt was the detective inspector, while she was only a sergeant, she knew she shouldn't jump in first. She was also unsure of their relationship. They'd only just met, after years of not knowing each other. They had a lot of catching up to do. She wondered how Matt was going to play it. She knew how she wanted to.

Dylan looked up from comforting Meg, staring straight at Alys. 'What are you doing here? Have you found out what's happened to Ree?' he demanded.

She and Matt stood up again. 'Dylan,' she said, 'I don't know if you remember Matt Vincent. He's Detective Inspector Matt Vincent now. Vicky was so worried about Rianna that she put in a call to the police. That's why we're both here.'

'Hello, Dylan,' Matt said. 'Sorry to meet you again in such worrying circumstances. I can remember travelling into school on the bus with you. That was several years ago, before I went away.'

Alys desperately tried to push the memories of that last summer from her mind. It was the summer that Hannah Andrews had died.

'Yes, I remember you too,' Dylan said, staring at him. Then, after a pause, 'What are you doing about Ree?'

'We've contacted the hospital, the ambulance service, the coastguard, all the usual people,' Matt said, 'but so far we've drawn a blank.'

The coroner too, Alys thought, but didn't say.

'We're tracing Ms Hughes's last movements,' Matt continued, 'but as she's not long been reported missing, we're not as far advanced with our enquiries as I'd have liked. Ms Morgan, Vicky, last saw Rianna when she left Meg here with her this morning. Have you seen, or been in contact, with Rianna today?'

Alys thought Matt was doing well. He hadn't jumped in, telling Dylan that he shouldn't be holding baby Meg in his arms. She wondered how Dylan was coping, banned from his own home, unable to see his baby daughter whenever he wanted.

Dylan stared at Matt, while gently rocking Meg in his arms. Alys guessed he was trying to work out if Matt knew about the injunction. She wished she hadn't allowed Matt to rush into visiting Vicky before she'd had time to fill him in on the background. She should have guessed that Dylan would barge into Vicky's flat unannounced.

'Sergeant Carey told me that Ms Hughes had an occupation order and a child arrangements order granted against you,' Matt told Dylan. 'We'll worry about that later. It's more important that we discover what's happened to Ms Hughes first.'

It sounded bizarre, Alys thought, Matt calling her Sergeant Carey. It made her sound like a stranger, reinforcing the gulf that now separated them.

Matt held Dylan's gaze, obviously waiting for an answer to his question.

Dylan kissed Meg's forehead before answering. 'Of course not,' he said. 'I don't want to make matters worse. Ree can have the lousy flat for all I care. I just want my kid back, be able to see her when I want. She was lying in court, what she said about me. I don't know why she did it. I loved her. I never did the things she said I did. I...' Dylan choked and a tear ran down his cheek.

Vicky stood up, holding Dafi on her hip, and brushed the tear from Dylan's cheek. 'Don't fret yourself Dyl, I'm sure things'll come out right in the end.'

Matt waited a few moments for Dylan to calm down, before continuing.

'Do you have a key to the flat? I'd like to check if Ms Hughes returned there after her morning run.'

Dylan shook his head. 'She changed the locks, right

after she kicked me out.'

Frustrating, Alys thought. We can hardly go breaking into her flat. She's been missing for less than a day.

'Can you tell me where you're living and working?' Matt asked. 'I don't think we have your address.'

Dylan's face contorted and went red. 'That miserable bastard Llewellyn gave me the sack from the Madoc's Bay,' he said angrily. He took several deep breaths before continuing. 'I was lucky to get another job. It's hard finding work here in winter. I'm chef at the Black Boar over at Brannock's Cross, sleeping in a crappy old caravan out the back. Lucky the landlord was a friend of my dad and that his wife got fed up cooking. Previous chef drank himself to death. Cirrhosis. Occupational hazard, I guess.'

Alys hoped for Dylan's sake that Rianna turned up alive. If she didn't and foul play was suspected, Dylan was setting himself up as prime suspect.

'Ms Morgan tells me...' Matt started, but Vicky butted in.

'For goodness sake, call me Vicky,' she said, glaring at Matt. 'You make me sound like some old crone.'

A smile flickered across Matt's face. He started again, 'Vicky tells me that Rianna goes to college on a Tuesday in Haverfordwest. Do you know the names of her lecturers or if she has any friends there she might be visiting?'

Alys noticed Dylan stiffen and clench his teeth. Vicky looked at him anxiously.

'I dunno,' he said sullenly. 'She's a law unto herself. Never tells me anything.'

The entry phone buzzed, causing everyone to flinch. Vicky answered it, Dafi still held on her hip. 'Yes?'

'Caitlin Gray and Viv Perry, social services. Can you let us in, please?'

'Who the hell invited them here?' Dylan shouted.

'Don't let them in, Vicky.'

Vicky shrugged apologetically and pressed the button. Seconds later she was letting a slight woman, mid-fifties with short curly brown hair, through the door, accompanied by a younger woman, in her thirties.

'What are you doing here?' Dylan asked aggressively, disturbing the two infants.

The woman glanced at Meg and Dafi, before turning to Matt and Alys. 'Good evening. I'm Caitlin Gray, senior social worker with the child care assessment team. This is Viv Perry. I've met Vicky, Dylan and the children before, but I don't believe we've met.'

'Detective Inspector Vincent,' Matt said, stepping forward and shaking her hand, 'and this is Sergeant Carey from the neighbourhood policing team.'

Alys shook the social worker's hand while studying her face. Not someone she'd like to go up against. There was steely determination in the woman's eyes.

Caitlin Gray turned to Dylan. 'I wasn't expecting to see you here. You're only supposed to see Meg at the family contact centre.'

'What d'you expect me to do? Ree's disappeared. Someone has to look out for Meg.'

'That's what social services are for.'

'I'm her dad. She's my baby. I'll take care of her.'

'I'm sorry Dylan, the family court decided against that.'

'That was before Ree walked off and left her.'

Vicky stepped forward. 'Meg can stay here with me until Ree turns up. I've been looking after her all day. She sometimes stays overnight anyway.'

The social worker turned to Vicky. 'I'm sorry, that won't do. You're not a registered child minder. I checked that before we came out.

'Have you made any progress in finding out what's happened to Meg's mother?' the social worker asked, turning to Matt.

He shook his head. 'Not yet. We're still trying to track her movements after she left Meg with Vicky this morning.'

'In that case I'll have to take Meg into care. I've alerted some very good emergency foster parents and they're prepared to take Meg in until you discover what's happened to her mother.'

'No!' Dylan shouted. 'You can't take Meg away and put her with strangers. My parents can look after her. They know her. They love her.'

Meg woke and started crying.

The social worker shook her head. 'That might be possible if it wasn't for the court orders against you. Ms Hughes's parents could, but I understand that she's an orphan.'

She turned to Vicky. 'Please pack Meg's things. It would be helpful if you made up a bottle of formula. We need to take Meg with us now.'

'I won't let you,' Dylan said defiantly, his face bright red. Disturbed by the shouting, Meg woke up fully and started crying, which set Dafi off too.

Alys stepped forward and put her hand on Dylan's forearm. 'You need to calm down,' she said, moderating her voice, making it as soothing as she could. 'You're upsetting Meg; not doing yourself any favours. You said yourself you're living in an old caravan. That's no place for Meg. The best thing you can do for Meg is to help us find Rianna.'

She turned to Vicky. 'Let me take Dafi while you get Meg's things together.' She reached out for Dafi. After a moment's hesitation, Vicky passed Dafi to her.

'There, there little fellow. Weren't they all making a noise?' Alys said. She sat down on the settee, with Dafi on her lap.' His thumb was back in his mouth and he wasn't crying. She smiled at him. He stared at her with big, round eyes.

'Dylan,' she said, softly. 'Sit down with Meg and give her a cuddle. Ask Ms Gray when you'll be able to see her again.'

Alys gave a silent sigh when Dylan and Vicky did as she directed, and both Meg and Dafi stopped crying. Result. She was desperate to find out what had happened to Rianna. She gave Dafi a cuddle. He felt warm and snug in her arms. Perhaps she did want children of her own after all.

CHAPTER 5

'Where are you, Rianna?' Matt asked himself rhetorically. He was staring at the photos that Dylan had reluctantly shared from his mobile phone the night before.

'What was that, sir?'

Matt looked across at his sergeant, Beth Francis. He shook his head. 'Sorry, Beth. I didn't realise I'd said that out loud. Just looking at the pictures of Rianna Hughes and wondering where she is now.'

'Attractive, that's for sure,' Beth said, her fingers flickering over her keyboard and looking at her screen.

Alys had uploaded Dylan's photos to the police computer system along with her notes of the previous night's meeting.

Social services pulling little Meg away from Dylan was one of the more heart-rending scenes that Matt had experienced during his police career, and there'd been plenty of those. He knew Caitlin Gray had only been doing her job, but that hadn't made it any better. It was as if baby Meg realised that she was being taken away from everyone and everything that she knew.

'I've checked with the hospital, emergency services, coastguard, the coroner,' Beth said. 'No reports of anyone answering Rianna's description as yet.'

'Have you heard back from the bus company or the college?' Matt said. 'We need to know if she caught the bus into town and if she went to lectures.'

'The bus company's still trying to contact their driver, and it's too early to get through to the college. Want another coffee, sir? You look like sh..., you need it.'

It was midnight before he'd got home after interviewing Vicky and Dylan. He'd stuck a ready meal in the microwave and gobbled it down.

Dreams that he'd suppressed for ten years came bubbling back, disrupting his sleep, waking him at intervals in an icy sweat-soaked panic.

Matt was up again at 5:30 and sitting at his desk in police headquarters by 7:00, feeling like he had sand under his eyelids.

'You must have been on that new tact and diplomacy course, Beth,' he said, then thought he'd better take the sting out of his remark with a smile. 'Yes please. Only managed a few hours' sleep last night.'

He stared at his surroundings. It was as if he was still with the Avon and Somerset force. Nowadays it seemed like all police headquarters were built in out-of-town locations and furnished and equipped by the same suppliers. The only difference was the lilt of the Welsh accents from the officers around him.

New job, new team. He'd not had time to settle in and get to know them. Bethan Francis, Beth, was in her early to mid-thirties, a few years older than he was. He wondered why she was still a sergeant. She seemed competent enough. Perhaps it was a lack of ambition.

The kitchen was at the far end of the office, so it took a while for Beth to come back with his coffee. They should have provided scooters or skateboards when they built the place.

Matt went back to studying Rianna's face on the screen.

'What d'you think's happened to her, sir?' Beth asked, as she put Matt's coffee down beside him.

'Depends whether she caught that bus into town, and whether she attended her course at the college.'

The phone on Beth's desk rang. She answered it,

speaking in Welsh. Matt listened, catching the gist of the conversation. He needed to brush up on his Welsh. There was a push for more officers in Dyfed-Powys to be bilingual now.

Beth put down the phone. 'That was the bus company. They've spoken to the driver. He knows Rianna by name, knows her well. She wasn't on any of the early morning buses yesterday. He's certain of it.'

'She could have had a lift from a friend,' Matt said. 'Try the college again.'

Matt was frustrated. His instincts told him that Rianna was missing and that the sooner he launched a search, the better. But he also guessed that the chief superintendent would never sign off on a search based on the evidence he had now.

While Beth was on the phone to the college, Matt messaged Alys. 'Any news?'

A sudden memory of her body pressed against his flashed through his senses as he hit send.

Seconds later his phone pinged. 'No sighting since she left Meg with Vicky.'

He messaged back, 'No news here. Seeking approval for search.'

'Struck lucky, sir,' Beth told him, as she came off the phone. 'Woman on the switchboard checked the register for the class. Rianna wasn't marked as present. Doesn't guarantee she wasn't there though. Some of the lecturers are rubbish at keeping their registers up to date.'

'Okay, here's what we'll do, Matt said. 'Alert the police search advisor. Tell him we may have to search the coastline around Madoc's Haven. Alert the coastguard too. Give them what we know so far. Then draft a missing person's report for the media office. Have them ready to send it the moment we have authority from the super.'

*****

'There's insufficient evidence to launch a search at this time,' Detective Chief Superintendent Norman Stone told Matt. 'From what you've told me the woman's promiscuous. She's been missing for what, 24 hours? She could be shacked up with some lover, and you want me to authorise a search? I don't think so.'

Matt forced himself to relax, unclench his fist, stop the fingernails from cutting into his palms.

'She's devoted to her baby daughter, and there's no evidence that she's done anything like this before,' Matt said, keeping his tone neutral, despite his growing frustration. 'She's always collected her daughter from the child minder when she said she would.'

'Could be suffering from post-natal depression,' DCS Stone said. 'Have you checked with her GP?'

Matt swore under his breath, his hopes plummeting. Stone would do anything to save money. What sort of officer had he been before he'd morphed into a bureaucrat? Why would anyone have promoted him?

'No sir, I'll get onto it right away. But the balance of evidence suggests that she's had an accident on the coast path, or it's a case of foul play. If she's lying somewhere, injured or unconscious, it's vital we find her immediately. If she's been abducted or murdered, the longer we leave it, the more likely the evidence is to vanish.'

'You've had my decision, inspector. Come back when you have something more substantial.'

Matt clamped down on his anger. He could see that the man's mind was made up, that he wasn't open to persuasion. Matt closed the door carefully behind him as he exited the DCS's office, as if that would seal the parsimony behind it.

Well, if the DCS wouldn't approve an official search, he'd just have to implement an unofficial one of his own. He'd make use of Alys Carey and her contacts in the local community. Could he persuade her to have her team join in the search too?

*****

Alys had no intention of waiting for any approval. She'd set out along the coast path at first light. Luckily she'd been on one of the higher points on the cliff tops when Matt messaged asking if Rianna had been sighted. Radio and mobile phone reception was iffy, the signal strength poor. If she'd been in some of the dips on the coast path, it would have been non-existent.

It was a miserable, gusty morning, with sea mist rolling up over the cliffs. Not quite as bad as the previous morning, but still unpleasant. The straggly gorse bushes whipped backwards and forwards in the wind, and sea-spray lashed her face. Despite the discomfort, she loved it.

The wind whined through the fence wire separating the path from the field, where sheep grazed apathetically. Down below, waves crashed against the base of the cliff.

After answering Matt's message, Alys slipped her phone back into the pocket of her waterproofs, and continued her slow trek along the cliff top. She scanned the ground at her feet and the vegetation to either side of the path, unsure what she was looking for. Periodically she peered over the cliff-edge. In some places there was a sheer drop to the churning waters below. In others, steep rocky slopes covered with clumps of grass, thyme and squill descended into the sea. Alys saw nothing unusual, nothing out of the ordinary. Where fields nestled up to the path, low banks topped with fences kept the livestock from straying into danger. At intervals, Alys stepped to the bank, often having to push aside the gorse, and checked on the other side in the fields.

Her progress was slow and methodical. Maybe Rianna had had an accident or something worse had befallen her. If she'd fallen into the sea, her body would have been swept away by the currents, which were strong between the coastline and the off-shore islands. That would be a job for the coastguards.

Alys was determined to find evidence, assuming it existed, of what had befallen Rianna. But how many walkers had traversed the coast path since Rianna was last seen? They could have obliterated vital pointers to what had happened. If she'd slipped, would there be marks where her feet skidded on the wet surface? If there had been a struggle, what traces would it have left?

She progressed slowly along the path with grim determination, moving ever closer to the Madoc's Bay Hotel.

*****

Matt returned to his desk, angry and frustrated that the DCS had refused his request. The more he thought about Rianna and her disappearance, the more he felt sure she'd come to harm.

Dylan had reason to hate her, assuming that the reasons she'd given to obtain the court orders against him were false. Could he have killed her?

Matt guessed that Rianna was playing the field. She was a woman who would attract many admirers and that could lead to jealousy. Had she pushed one of her lovers beyond the limit, made him angry enough to kill her?

'Without more evidence, the DCS isn't prepared to sign off on a search,' Matt told Beth. 'Phone the GP practice in Madoc's Haven. Find out if Rianna was suffering from post-natal depression or anything that might affect her state of mind. I'm going to pay another visit to the area. I'll start at the Madoc's Bay Hotel where Rianna worked. Ask around, find out what anyone knows.'

How would he feel, returning in broad daylight when he could see the coastline, the sea? He'd have to face it, sooner or later. Rianna's disappearance had simply brought it forward.

He ignored Beth's raised eyebrows. Did she know he'd grown up in Madoc's Haven? What did she know of his history? He guessed there would be gossip in the kitchen by the drinks machine, certainly down at the Major Crime team's favourite pub, the Forge Tavern.

'I want you to follow up in Haverfordwest. Interview her lecturers at the college. There's one called Ross. I've a suspicion Rianna's having an affair with him. Let me know what he says.'

CHAPTER 6

Beth was doubly disappointed. She'd expected to go to Madoc's Haven with Matt. Instead, he'd tasked her with interviewing one of Rianna's lecturers at the college, forename Ross. Okay, maybe Rianna was having an affair with him, but as far as they knew, Rianna hadn't left Madoc's Haven the previous day, the day she'd disappeared. Surely, Madoc's Haven was the place to be asking questions.

She needed to find out more about Matt Vincent, CID's newest detective inspector. He'd transferred in from Avon and Somerset Police just a few weeks before, taking the DI vacancy that should have been hers. Damn it, she'd worked for that promotion. Why couldn't he have stayed where he was? He was already a DI. Why did he have to move?

She couldn't find out much about DI Matt Vincent when she'd first been assigned to his team, except that he'd grown up in Madoc's Haven. His LinkedIn page showed the barest outline of his career.

She tried Googling 'Matt Vincent Madoc's Haven.

Matt's name appeared in a local news item from ten years back, concerning the death of a teenager called Hannah Andrews. She was eighteen, about the same age as Matt at the time. The girl died in a freak accident on the coast near Madoc's Haven. Matt Vincent and the girl had been coasteering at the time – it sounded a crazy activity to Beth, scrambling over wave-beaten rocks and leaping into the sea. The coroner returned a verdict of accidental death. Could there be more to it than that?

*****

Beth parked in a visitor's parking space in front of the college buildings. They hadn't changed much since she'd been a student there studying for her A-levels. It seemed an eternity ago. Fifteen years. Where had the time gone?

Beth had phoned ahead and made an appointment to see the principal and discovered that the lecturer's full name was Ross Keely. She'd looked at the college prospectus online and Googled Ross Keely before leaving the office. He was a lecturer in travel and tourism. His Facebook page showed hundreds of friends, more women than men. His photos included many of him posing with attractive, young women.

After an aggravating wait, the principal's PA ushered Beth into his office.

The principal was in his late fifties or early sixties, greying hair, looked after his clothes better than his body. Beth thought she remembered him as Head of Business Studies when she'd been a student there. A local man. He'd spent his energies climbing the promotion ladder and was now coasting downhill to retirement.

'A young woman, one of your part-time students, has been reported missing,' Beth told him, after the initial pleasantries were over. 'Rianna Hughes, studying hospitality management. I need to interview her course leader, Ross Keely.'

'I don't know the student, but I do know Mr Keely,' the principal said. 'He's not involved in any way, is he?'

There was something slightly odd about the principal's intonation, and he looked uncomfortable. Beth wondered what the man knew.

'Not that I'm aware of,' Beth said. 'We're just trying to trace Ms Hughes' last known movements.'

The principal visibly relaxed. 'I can have the class register checked. That should indicate if she was here.'

'I called earlier. She wasn't marked present, but I understand that the lecturers aren't always as diligent as one might hope.'

The principal grimaced, but didn't deny it.

'Anything more you can tell me about Mr Keely?' Beth said. 'Like his relationship with his students?'

He dropped his gaze and started fiddling with the papers on his desk.

Finally his hands stilled and he looked up. 'Anything I tell you is in strictest confidence,' he said.

'Of course,' Beth said, adding in her thoughts, I'm a detective sergeant, not some bloody newspaper reporter.

There was a long pause before he replied. When he did, he leaned forward and spoke in a low voice, a confidential whisper. 'A young female student's parents made a formal complaint against Mr Keely last year. Claimed he used his position to make improper advances. Said he'd had an intimate relationship with the girl.'

Beth thought back to her time at the college. There was one lecturer who was decidedly dishy. If he'd asked, she'd have willingly jumped into bed with him. She banished the thought from her mind.

'I'm assuming she was over the age of consent, or she wouldn't have been here at the college. Did you investigate the complaint?'

'Of course,' the principal said, pompously, sitting back up straight. 'The good name of the college was involved.'

Covering your back, more like, Beth thought. 'So what did your investigations conclude, and what action was taken?'

'The girl was interviewed. She claimed that she'd entered into the relationship willingly. We instituted a disciplinary panel, and Mr Keely was issued with a formal warning.'

'Was it just the one young woman?' Beth asked.

The principal visibly squirmed. 'There were unsubstantiated rumours that she wasn't the first.'

'And that was the end of the matter? Beth asked. 'Are you aware of any incidents since?'

'He's very popular with the students, particular with the young women, but if he has transgressed, he's being more discreet.'

The principal looked at his watch. 'You'll have to excuse me, but I have a meeting starting in a few minutes. Please have my PA find you an empty tutorial room and ask Mr Keely to see you.'

*****

'What's all this about?' Ross Keely demanded, as soon as he'd banged the door shut behind him. 'It's not that blasted girl again, is it? I thought that was all cleared up ages ago.'

Beth wondered what his female students would make of him, if they could hear him now. She could see they might find him good looking, when he didn't have that snarl on his face.

'I'm Detective Sergeant Beth Francis, Dyfed-Powys CID,' she said, holding out her warrant card for him to see. 'And you are Ross Keely, lecturer in travel and tourism. Is that correct?'

'Yes,' he said, sullenly.

'Please take a seat. I'm sure this won't take long.'

'It had better not. I have lectures to prepare.'

Beth sat and waited for him to do the same. She took out her phone, ready to take notes. Was his angry attitude the normal reaction that some people have when questioned by the police, or did he have something to hide?

'It's about one of your students, Rianna Hughes.'

Beth watched him carefully as she spoke.

He looked relieved and momentarily confused.

'What about her? She's not been making complaints too, has she?'

'Did she have reason to?' Beth asked.

'Of course not,' he said, tersely.

'Can you tell me when you last saw Ms Hughes?'

'Rianna? She wasn't in class yesterday. Perhaps that kid of hers was sick or playing up?'

'So when did you last see her?' Beth persisted.

'Why? Has something happened to her?'

'If you could just answer the question, please?'

'Must have been last week. She was in class then.'

'And you haven't seen her since?'

'That's what I said, wasn't it?

Had Vicky Morgan or Dylan Rogers contacted him last night to ask him about Rianna? If they had, he was ace at disguising it, but why would he pretend ignorance?

'Can you tell me your movements yesterday?' Beth said. 'Starting from the time you woke up in the morning.'

Beth's thumbs flickered over the screen of her phone as she noted times and locations. 'Do you share a flat or a house with anyone?' Beth asked. 'Can someone vouch for your movements between you waking up and arriving at the college?'

'Blood hell, what is this? Do I need a lawyer or something?' Ross was on his feet now, red-faced, angry, or was it scared? 'What's happened to Ree? Is she okay?'

Beth noted that Ross had called Rianna, Ree. Interesting.

'You shouldn't need a lawyer, not unless you have something to hide,' Beth told him. 'Were you with anyone between waking and arriving at the college?'

Ross sank back on his chair and raked his hand through his hair. 'I rent a flat in town. Well, it's not more than a couple of rooms really. I live by myself. I didn't see anyone until I got to college. You'll just have to take my word for it.'

Beth wasn't sure that she could. Was he 'entertaining' another of his young, female students, or did he have something more sinister to hide?

'Can you tell me more about your relationship with Ms Hughes?' Beth asked. 'I gather that it's more than the normal lecturer-student relationship?'

'How d'you know about that?' Ross demanded, then realised what he'd said. His face turned red again. 'It was just a harmless fling. Just a bit of fun. Neither of us meant anything by it. You don't have to tell anyone, do you? It's private and it's over now.'

It certainly is, Beth thought, if her suspicions were correct.

'Ms Hughes hasn't been seen since yesterday morning,' Beth told Ross. 'She was reported missing last night. If you hear from her, I'd be grateful if you could let me know. Here's my card. You can call that number, any time, day or night.'

Beth stood up to indicate that the interview was over. 'Thank you for your help and cooperation. I'll be in contact if I have any further questions.'

Beth was sitting in her car outside the college buildings when Ross Keely walked out, pursued by a dark-haired woman, early thirties, slim build. She was angry. Staff, not a student? Beth powered down her window hoping to hear what was said. She couldn't make out any words. Frustrating.

After Ross turned his back on the woman, one of the students said something to her which she briefly acknowledged before storming off.

Beth hopped out of her car and asked the student who the woman was. The student replied Wendy Pryce, a lecturer at the college.

Could Wendy Pryce be a jilted lover? Beth smiled. Mr Keely leads an interesting life.

CHAPTER 7

Matt could get no answer, either from Alys's phone or from her police radio. Damnation. Matt wanted to tell her he was on his way, and that they should meet at the Madoc's Bay Hotel.

The Pembrokeshire coastline might be beautiful, but in some locations it was the back of beyond as far as communication was concerned. Would the new emergency services network ever be rolled out? It was yet another of those ill-fated government projects, massively over-budget and running years late. Even when it was, would there still be areas with worse reception than the most backward of developing nations?

It was an hour's drive from police HQ to the Madoc's Bay Hotel.

A quarter of a mile short of his destination he joined the narrow road that ran parallel to the sea. Today was his first proper view of the coastline that he'd turned his back on it ten years before. It had been too dark the previous evening.

Icy fingers gripped his heart. Hannah! In the distance he could see the rocky inlet where she'd died. He pulled into the tiny cliff-top car park and stopped. Unwanted memories came flooding back. He struggled to suppress them, to focus on the happier times that they'd shared.

The mist was clearing; the sky looked less gloomy and forbidding. Matt forced his thoughts back to the present. With luck it would turn into a bright, sunny day. He stood by his car, stretched, inhaled the fresh, clean air, and suddenly realised how much he'd missed the rugged cliffs and the sea.

Below, the waves crashed against the rocks, adding salty sea-spray to the air. A pair of birds landed twenty feet away and started pecking around in the clumps of thrift. For a moment Matt thought they were jackdaws, but then he saw their sharp, bright red, downward curved beaks, red legs and feet. Choughs! Amazing! They were the first he's seen in ten years.

It was good to be back after his self-imposed exile. He would never forget Hannah, her smile or her care-free laughter, but that was the past. The future was now.

He tried calling Alys again, but without success.

He'd remembered Alys as a fifteen year old girl with braces on her teeth, too young for an eighteen year old lad to consider. Now she was a confident, attractive, self-assured young woman. Probably married and besides, she was a junior colleague, he told himself firmly. He was here to progress his career. Having a romantic relationship with Alys could be a career-limiting distraction, one he certainly didn't need. But the memory of her body pressed against his bubbled up in his mind. It was hard to forget.

The sun was breaking through the mist as Matt continued on his way.

A little further on he turned down the steeply sloping driveway.

The Madoc's Bay Hotel was built from grey local stone and was perched in a dramatic cliff-top location overlooking the sea.

Even the car park had great views. Matt's pool car looked a poor relative beside the guests' Mercedes, BMWs and Jaguars.

Matt gazed around him as he stepped into the entrance hall. It was unrecognisable from when he'd last walked through the doors. The make-over was drastic and not to his taste. It was dark and claustrophobic, but maybe that was how a posh boutique hotel was supposed to look.

The receptionist was an attractive blonde dressed in a black business suit. About his age? A newcomer. He'd have remembered her if she was local.

She gave him a swiftly appraising once-over, flashing him a warm, welcoming smile. 'Can I help you?'

'I'd like to see the owner,' he said, holding up his warrant card. The name on her badge was Penny Evans. 'It's still Mr Rhodri Llewellyn, is it?'

'Has she been found yet?' Penny asked. 'It's about Rianna, isn't it?

Matt inwardly smiled. News travels fast in rural communities. He raised one eyebrow and waited.

'I'm sorry, Inspector,' Penny said, suddenly flustered. 'You've just missed Mr Llewellyn. He's had to travel to Swansea on business.'

'What is it, Penny?'

The voice made Matt start.

Turning, Matt found himself face-to-face with Griff Llewellyn, the hotel owner's son. Matt hadn't heard Griff walk in behind him, or perhaps he'd emerged silently from the dining room or the lounge.

Griff's jaw clenched and his fists bunched as he recognised Matt. 'What are you doing here?' he demanded.

Matt disliked Griff. The antipathy was mutual. Griff grew up the pampered and privileged son of one of the wealthiest families in Pembrokeshire. Matt's father worked as an engineer at the oil refinery in Milford Haven.

Matt and Griff had come to blows over Hannah Andrews when she told Matt that Griff had tried to force himself on her. Griff's face still bore a faint scar where Matt had split his lip during the ensuing fight.

It was the only time that Matt had been in a fight, if you didn't count the various scraps accompanying contested arrests during his time on the force.

'Good Morning, sir,' Matt said, hating himself for calling Griff Llewellyn 'Sir'. I'm Detective Inspector Vincent.'

'Yes, I know who you are. I'm not a bloody idiot,' Griff snapped.

'I'm investigating the disappearance of Rianna Hughes,' Matt said, determined to keep his tone calm and professional. I wonder if we could have a word in private.'

'I've nothing to tell you, except she didn't show for work this morning, leaving us short-handed,' Griff said angrily. 'A confounded nuisance. She's unreliable. We'll have to let her go.'

A middle aged couple, presumably guests, stared at Griff and hurried out of the hotel.

Anger and outrage cascaded adrenaline into Matt's veins. 'The woman is missing, sir. We're attempting to discover if any harm has befallen her.'

Matt knew he sounded pompous, but he was having difficulty controlling himself. Memories of the fight and what had sparked it sprang into his mind. Much as he wanted to floor Griff again, he wouldn't risk his career over the man. He wasn't worth it.

'I need to interview those of your hotel staff who were closest to Ms Hughes. It's imperative that we trace her movements and find her.'

Griff glared at Matt.

Matt held his gaze, remembering Beth's warning when he told her that he intended to visit the hotel, 'Old man Llewellyn's buddies with the Chief Constable and several government ministers. Best not to cross him, or his son.'

Beth wasn't aware of the past history.

Griff looked away first.

Matt was disappointed. He knew it would have been stupid, but he'd have loved to book Griff for obstruction.

Griff turned on his heel and stalked off into the inner recesses of the hotel.

Penny watched him go before gazing curiously at Matt and saying quietly, 'I'd start with Bill Symonds. There's not much goes on here that he doesn't know about.' She glanced behind her furtively, before adding. 'He normally nips out behind the bins for a smoke about now.'

*****

Matt went in search of Bill Symonds.

A collection of aging vehicles occupied a roughly surfaced area to the back of the hotel, doubtless belonging to those staff who could afford to run cars.

An aging pickup truck was parked beside them, with "H Rogers Building Services" in bold lettering along its mud-splattered sides.

Dylan's dad was a jobbing builder, Matt remembered. The H stood for Huw. The sound of a power tool came from a cluster of decrepit buildings up a short track, possibly once a stable yard or the like.

Matt found Bill Symonds hidden behind the bins where he couldn't be seen. A puff of cigarette smoke gave away his location.

'I recognise you!' Bill said, shaking Matt's hand and clapping him on the shoulder. 'You're Phil and Terry Vincent's son! Matt, isn't it? I haven't seen you in ages, not since...'

His voice tailed off and the smile vanished from his face. 'Sorry business,' he said, shaking his head. 'Hannah Andrews. Lovely young thing. You were sweet on her too, weren't you?'

'Yes,' Matt said tersely, his insides knotting with pain.

After an awkward pause Bill said quickly, 'I've not heard tell of Phil since he finished that job at the refinery. What's he doing now?'

'Up in Aberdeen,' Matt said. 'More opportunities in the oil industry up there.'

Matt was anxious to move the conversation on.

'I'm a detective inspector now with the Dyfed-Powys police. We're investigating the disappearance of Rianna Hughes.'

'Aye, I heard she's gone missing,' Bill said. 'Dylan was phoning around last night and she didn't show for work this morning.'

'Who did he speak to?' Matt asked.

'Young Cassie Davies, the vicar's daughter. Dropped her right in it. Staff aren't supposed to take personal calls.'

'So what happened?' Matt asked, curious.

'Old man Llewellyn gave her a right dressing down, put her on warning and docked her an hour's pay. Reduced the poor lass to tears.'

Matt filed the information away. It all helped build up a picture of how things worked in the community around Madoc's Haven.

'Have you any idea what might have happened to Rianna?' Matt asked. 'Heard any rumours? She's not been seen since yesterday morning when she left her baby with Vicky Morgan to look after. We think she was planning to run along the coast path in this direction and back again.'

Bill Symonds shook his head. 'Taking a chance she was then, running along the coast path in that weather. Easy enough to trip or slip and go over the edge. It was a miserable morning, yesterday. Blowing half a gale.'

Matt was still furious that Detective Chief Superintendent Stone had refused to authorise a search. As soon as he could, he'd begin that unofficial search of his own, preferably with Alys. He wondered where she was.

'Which of the girls working with Rianna should I talk to?' Matt asked. 'Who do you think knows her best?'

Bill smiled. 'They're all a bit wary of her. Think she'll steal their boyfriends, and they're probably right. It's happened to one or two of them.'

'Anyone in particular?'

'I wouldn't rightly know,' Bill said, 'but I think Penny was sweet on Dylan, before Rianna gobbled him up and spat him out.'

'Why did Ms Hughes take out the court order against him? Matt asked. 'Did he treat her or the baby badly?'

Bill took a last drag on his cigarette, pinched it out and threw the butt into one of the bins. He rubbed the stubble on his chin. 'This is only a hunch,' Bill said, 'so don't take it as gospel. I'm guessing it was her way of getting a place of her own. She's a cunning little jezebel. No morals. Attractive though. She can twist most men around her little finger. If you do get to meet her, never lend her anything. From what I've heard, you'll never get it back.'

'Do you think any of the girls are jealous enough of Rianna to wish her harm?' Matt asked.

'Plenty of them are certainly jealous, but I can't think any of them would be that jealous,' Bill said. He looked cautiously around and leaned in closer to Matt. 'If it's foul play you're thinking, you could try looking at Griff Llewellyn. I hear things from the girls about him. He's always trying to get them into that flash car of his, and you can guess why. He's none too happy if they won't give him what he wants.'

Bill dropped his voice to a whisper, so quiet that Matt had to lean closer to hear.

Matt's nose twitched at the smell of stale tobacco smoke on the man's clothes.

'After you'd gone off to university, there was a man came snooping around, asking questions about Griff. Seems there was a girl that Griff knew, died. I think the man was the girl's father. Old man Llewellyn saw him off. Threatened to set your lot on him.' Bill shook his head. 'Never heard anything more of it.'

CHAPTER 8

Alys's pockets contained evidence bags and disposable gloves, in case she found traces on the coast path linked to Rianna's disappearance. She knew that if she did, she shouldn't touch them. That would be a job for the Scenes of Crime Officers and CID, but having them in her pockets made her feel hopeful.

Alys's attempts to move back into CID had so far been unsuccessful. Maybe if she proved her worth to Matt Vincent, he'd put in a good word, but somehow it felt wrong to pin her hopes on Rianna's possible misfortune. Alys walked slowly onwards, scanning the ground, looking into the fields and over cliff edges. Nothing.

The mist was clearing and the wind dropping. The scenery was stunning when the sun shone down from cloudless blue skies. Only a few weeks now and the cliff-top sward would burst into flower. Alys loved the springtime.

A shout and the bark of a dog made her turn and look back towards Madoc's Haven. A distant figure was waving. Who was it? Then Alys recognised Cedric Davies, the local vicar, walking towards her with a sheepdog at his heels.

'I didn't expect to catch up with you,' he said as he closed the distance between them. 'You youngsters tend to walk faster than us older folks.'

'Hello gorgeous,' Alys said, bending down and making a fuss of Cedric's dog. 'What's your name?'

The dog was a Welsh Collie, unusual because it had one blue eye while the other was brown. Its colour was striking too. The fur around its eyes and ears was a bright orange-brown, as if it had some fox in its ancestry. For the rest it had a typical Welsh Sheepdog's appearance.

'He's called Whiskey,' Cedric said. 'What were you doing? Day-dreaming?'

Alys grimaced. 'If you must know, I was searching for clues that might explain Rianna Hughes's disappearance.'

'So she hasn't turned up yet?'

'She hadn't when I set out along the coast path.'

'Strange business,' Cedric said, shaking his head sadly. 'In many ways I can't approve of the young lady, but I've heard that she's a good mother to young Megan. To be honest, I was surprised when she and Dylan asked me to christen her. Precious few of my parishioners ask for that these days, but I suspect that was Gemma's doing.'

'Dylan's mother?' Alys said. 'She was certainly upset at Rianna taking out that court order against Dylan. What do you make of that?'

'I don't know, to be honest, but there are rumours that Dylan cramped her style. She's a flighty young woman, if what people are saying is true.'

Alys raised her eyebrows. Not being a churchgoer, she didn't know Cedric well.

Whiskey sat, then lay down on the ground. Alys guessed he wasn't a young dog. Probably retired from life on a farm.

'What do you think could have happened to Rianna?' she asked.

'Much the same as you do, I expect,' Cedric said. 'She's probably had an accident, but if that's the case, it's odd that you and the other emergency services haven't heard about it. Unless she fell in the sea and was swept away by the tide.'

He looked into Alys's eyes, probing. 'I'm surprised

that there aren't more people out looking. Are you the only one?'

'Just me at the moment,' she said. 'Often times people reappear and there's a perfectly reasonable explanation for their disappearance.' Alys didn't like to say that she thought Matt's super was being irresponsible. If Rianna was lying injured and out of sight, she could be dead before he approved a search. And if she'd been killed, valuable forensic evidence could be lost.

'You don't think Rianna's run off with a man?' Alys asked.

Cedric shook his head. 'Not if I've judged her correctly, but that's what some of the villagers are saying.'

Alys didn't think so either. From what she'd learned, Rianna genuinely cared for her daughter

'I hope I'm not delaying you,' Cedric said. 'I only go another few hundred yards before I turn back. May I walk with you?'

Alys agreed, thinking it would useful to get to know the man better. He could provide interesting insights into what had gone on in the local community since she'd moved to Llanbrioc.

They walked slowly on in silence except for the squawks of the gulls and the sounds of the sea and the wind. Whiskey followed at their heels.

Alys dimly remembered an item from the previous night's historical society meeting. It was mentioned when she was thinking of Rianna's disappearance. It was only later, when she'd arrived home, that she'd thought about it.

'What was that about Clebaston Manor, last night?' she asked. 'I'm afraid I wasn't paying attention.'

'There's talk of Rhodri Llewellyn rebuilding and extending it,' Cedric said. 'He wants to create the Clebaston Manor Resort. It's a very grandiose scheme.

He wants it to rival the Celtic Manor Resort over by Newport.'

'So what's the historical society's interest?'

'There's some evidence that where he's planning to build the new accommodation block and spa is the site of a monastery built by Saint Egwad in the 7th century. He can't just go ahead and destroy a potentially important archaeological site. There has to be an exploratory dig at a minimum.'

'There's a problem with that?'

'Rhodri Llewellyn's dead set against it. Says his scheme will bring jobs into the area, revitalise the local tourist industry. Says if there's any delay, he'll lose his backers. We want the county archaeology advisor to insist on a dig before a planning application can be considered.'

'Surely he will, won't he?'

'It's a she, not a he.'

Cedric put his hand on Alys's arm and stopped. He looked all around, as if he was afraid of being overheard. There was no one else in sight. Alys was amused by the vicar's sudden furtive behaviour.

'Do you remember my daughter Cassie? She's working as a waitress at the Madoc's Bay Hotel. She's friendly with Rianna.'

He continued looking around and lowered his voice.

'She told me an interesting piece of information last week.'

'What did she tell you?' Alys prompted.

'Aled Ingram, the Welsh government minister who deals with planning appeals, was dining with Rhodri and Griff Llewellyn at the hotel. They were on very friendly terms.'

'And?'

'Rianna was serving them, not Cassie. Later that evening, Rianna was excited. Cassie thinks she overheard something the three of them were saying.'

'About the Clebaston Manor Resort?'

'Cassie doesn't know. Rianna wouldn't tell her.'

Interesting, Alys thought. What had Rianna overheard, and what did she intend to do with the information? And how far would the Llewellyns go, to stop their plans from being thwarted?

'Thank you for that,' she said. 'Let me know anything else you hear and you think might be helpful.'

They walked slowly on. The mists were clearing now, and the sky was definitely brighter.

Ahead of them, a short flight of steps descended into a gully notched in the cliff top. At the bottom, the path looped around the gully and then turned sharp right around a fence post, right on the edge of the cliff.

As they neared the bottom of the steps, Whiskey became lively and excited and started barking. He ran forward into the gully and started sniffing around.

'Heel, Whiskey,' Cedric said. 'I don't know what's got into him. It's the liveliest I've seen him all week.' Cedric caught hold of the dog's collar, pulled him back and snapped on his lead. 'He's getting old. I don't think he would, but I don't want him going over the edge in his excitement.'

Whiskey strained forwards, looking eager.

'What is it old boy? Can you smell a fox, or a nice plump pheasant? Anyone would think I don't feed you.'

Alys looked where Whiskey had been sniffing. The vegetation was broken and appeared to have been trampled down near the mouth of the gully. Odd. I wonder who or what did that, and why, she thought.

She turned and looked over the cliff edge. It was a near vertical drop to the wave-lashed rocks below. A small fluttering movement caught her eye from part-way down. It looked like a piece of fabric, snagged on a stunted gorse bush desperately clinging to the rock face.

Alys pulled out her phone and photographed it. She

doubted that the image would show more than a few blurred pixels, certainly not enough to identify the fabric. She wished she'd brought her camera with her. How long had the fabric been there, and for how much longer would it remain? There was no way she could clamber down to take a closer look or retrieve it.

Frustrated, she turned and photographed the trampled vegetation in the gully, then cursed when she noticed the total absence of any signal on her phone.

She turned and noticed Cedric watching her, an appraising expression on his face. Suddenly she realised the precariousness of her situation, standing on the cliff edge, with nothing between her and eternity.

CHAPTER 9

Matt was frustrated. He wanted to meet up with Alys, but he still couldn't get a signal on his mobile phone. He had better luck with his police radio, but Alys wasn't answering on that. Unobtainable.

He tried Beth instead. She answered and quickly filled him in on her conversations with the college principal and Ross Keely.

'I want you to follow up on the woman who had the heated exchange with him outside the college,' Matt said. 'What did you say her name was? Wendy Pryce? If Rianna's the victim of foul play, jealousy must feature high on the list of possible motives.'

Matt drove swiftly along the narrow country lanes back towards Madoc's Haven. He had to pull into passing bays twice to give way to oncoming cars, and then he was held up by a farmer driving his herd of cows back to their field, presumably after milking time. Matt curbed his impatience. There was nothing he could do but sit and wait.

He tried to reach Alys again, but still without success.

He decided to visit Vicky, to see if she'd heard from Rianna, and to probe further into her knowledge of Ross Keely.

Vicky started speaking as she opened her door. 'Any news of Rianna?'

Disappointment clouded her face when he shook his head. 'That's what I came to ask you. Is it okay if I come in?'

Dafi, her toddler, was sitting in a play pen,

surrounded by toy farmyard animals. He stood up and stared, round-eyed, at Matt as he entered the room. Vicky was in a dressing gown and had a towel wrapped around her hair. Her face looked pink and was free of make-up.

'I hope I'm not disturbing you?' Matt asked. 'Are you getting ready to go out?'

Vicky looked embarrassed. 'I couldn't get to sleep, worrying about Ree and Meg. Then, when I finally did, I overslept. Can I get you a tea or a coffee?'

'No thanks. I had some follow-up questions about Rianna. Is it convenient if we talk now?'

Matt sat on the small two-seater settee. Vicky sat in the single arm chair. It was a nuisance that he didn't have Beth or Alys with him to take notes. He'd just have to remember what Vicky told him and enter it later. Thankfully he had a good memory.

'It would help if you could tell me a little more about the men in Rianna's life,' Matt said. 'I already know about Dylan. Last time we spoke, you mentioned one of Rianna's lecturers at the college, Ross.'

Vicky suddenly looked wary. Why, Matt wondered, was it just that she didn't want to discuss Rianna's colourful private life, or was there a more interesting reason?

'Was there anything going on between Rianna and Ross?'

'What d'you mean,' Vicky shot back quickly.

'Look, I know you don't want to betray any confidences, but the more I know about Rianna's private life, the more chance we have of finding her and getting everyone's lives back to normal.'

Vicky avoided his gaze.

'The sooner Rianna's back, the less time little Meg has to stay with her foster carers.'

Vicky clenched her fists but remained silent.

Was it just because she was reluctant to talk to the

police. He'd come across many people with that attitude. Bizarrely it made some people feel like informers, coppers' narks.

'Was she having an affair with Ross, sleeping with him,' he asked.

'Yes,' Vicky finally answered.

Vicky told Matt that the affair had started soon after Rianna had joined the course, and that once or twice Rianna had slept over at his flat while Vicky took care of Meg.

'Was this before or after the occupation order against Dylan?'

Vicky looked distressed. 'She took up with Ross before that happened. They had a few quickies during lunchtime. Ross has a place close to the college.'

'Did she stay overnight with Ross while Dylan was still living with her?'

Vicky laughed. 'No, that only happened after. She wasn't that stupid.'

'Did Dylan know about Rianna's affair with Ross?'

Vicky's eyes narrowed and she didn't answer immediately. Matt waited. Was she trying to defend Dylan? Was there a relationship between her and Dylan?

'Have you asked Dylan that?'

'I'm asking you.'

'He guessed,' she said, hesitantly. 'Lost his rag. That's what started the arguments that got him thrown out.' Then, 'He never hit her though,' she said defiantly. 'He had a temper, but he wouldn't hurt a fly.'

Matt wondered if that was true. Had he finally lost it and killed her? It was time to change tack.

'Were there any other men in Rianna's life?'

'What, recently d'you mean, since she moved here?'

'Yes.'

Vicky shook her head. 'Not that I know of. Possibly she had a couple of one-nighters with hotel guests the first summer she came, but not after she took up with Dylan.'

'No one else?' Matt asked.

Vicky shook her head.

'What about Griff Llewellyn?'

Matt's mobile buzzed before she had time to answer. He glanced at the screen. It was the police command and control centre.

'I'm sorry, I'll have to take this,' he said, getting to his feet. He let himself out of Vicky's flat before he answered.

'DI Vincent,' he said.

'There's been a body found. A young woman. On the beach at Petroc Sands. It's just north of the Madoc's Bay Hotel.'

'Yes, I know where it is,' Matt said, his pulse racing. 'Do you have any details?'

'That's all we have.'

'I'm on my way.'

Matt pushed the door open and called out to Vicky, 'Sorry. I have to go. We'll continue our talk later.'

'Is it Rianna?' Vicky asked, anxiously.

'I'll let you know as soon as we find out anything.' Matt said, closing the door and dashing to his car.

*****

Matt tried Alys's mobile and police radio from outside Vicky's flat, where reception was good. He still couldn't raise her.

Images of Hannah's lifeless body lying on the sand seared Matt's mind. Emptiness hollowed him, gutted him.

He raced along the narrow country lanes with blue lights flashing.

Why couldn't he reach Alys? Could the body be hers? That question had been gnawing away at him ever since he'd received the call from Control.

The body had to be Rianna's. Why was he panicking? He never panicked. They didn't have serial killers in Madoc's Haven.

An ambulance, a coastguard Range Rover and a police car had reached the scene before him, and were parked with a handful of private vehicles in the hopelessly inadequate car park that served Petroc Sands.

Matt abandoned his car and set out at a brisk walk, desperate to curb his impatience.

It was a couple of hundred yards down a narrow path by a rushing brook to reach the beach.

As he stepped out onto the sand, he could see two paramedics, the coastguard in his high vis jacket, and a police woman standing by a body that was lying on the sand half-way out towards the sea. A stretcher rested beside the body.

A small group of people with barking dogs stood a respectful distance away from the emergency responders.

The police woman detached herself and walked towards Matt as he strode down the beach towards her.

'Keep away please, sir. There's been an accident.'

Matt noticed from the woman's uniform that she was a PCSO, a Police Community Support Officer.

'DI Matt Vincent,' he told her, holding up his warrant card and keeping on walking.

He felt a flash of relief when he saw that the body's bedraggled hair was blonde, darker at the roots. Then guilt struck. He shouldn't be feeling relief when looking at the body of a young woman lying dead on a beach.

His emotions were in turmoil. He swallowed hard. Knew he was having a panic attack. He should never have come back if he couldn't cope. He wiped cold sweat from his brow.

He forced his policeman's persona to take over as he matched the description of Rianna and the clothes that she'd been wearing to the body at his feet. Her face was battered and swollen, one of her legs was visibly broken, but Matt was certain that it was Rianna Hughes. What he couldn't tell from looking at her was how she'd died.

Had she slipped and fallen off the coast path, or had she been killed? He would have to wait for the post mortem, but he wasn't confident that he'd get a definitive answer even then.

'I'm DI Matt Vincent,' Matt told the assembled group, 'The police pathologist is on his way. Goodness only knows how long it'll take him to arrive.' He turned to the coastguard. 'What's the state of the tide? How long before it reaches the body?'

'I'm Tom, Tom Williams,' the coastguard said. 'Thought I recognised you. Not seen you around for a long time.' He suddenly frowned, concern etching his features.

Matt recognised Tom from a similar scene, ten years before. Tom must have guessed at the emotions that were scrambling his brain.

'Been away. First time I've been back,' Matt said, his throat so tight he could hardly get out the words.

'Tide's on the turn,' Tom said quickly. 'You have a couple of hours before you have to move the body. Not that I can see much point in leaving her here. She probably fell into the sea by accident somewhere else, then washed up here, so it's hardly a crime scene.'

CHAPTER 10

Matt followed the ambulance back up the narrow, twisting lanes from Petroc Sands. He had no doubt that the body was Rianna's, but he needed formal identification. The poor girl was an orphan, so he couldn't ask her parents, and he didn't know if she had any close relatives living. He'd have to ask Dylan to identify her.

As Matt turned to join the main road, his radio and phone emitted a barrage of pings, beeps and warbles. He grimaced. Back into civilisation. Glancing at the dashboard screen, he could see that most of the calls were from Beth and Alys. He uttered a sigh of relief. Whatever made him think that Alys could have come to any harm?

'Call Beth,' he instructed the system.

Within seconds Beth answered. 'It's like the back of beyond down here. You'd never think we're in the twenty-first century. I half expected to see natives daubed with woad.'

'I was born here,' Matt answered sternly, knowing that Beth couldn't see his smile.'

'Sorry, Sir. Didn't mean any disrespect.'

'Where are you?' Matt asked.

'I thought you might need support when I heard a body had been found,' she said. 'I'm in what passes for a police station in Madoc's Haven.'

'Have you met Sergeant Carey, neighbourhood policing team lead?'

'Yes, she's stepped out to talk with someone... No. that's her coming back. Did you want to speak with her?'

'Not on the radio,' Matt said. 'You two both stay put. Get to know each other. I'll join you there in fifteen minutes.'

'Was it Rianna Hughes? The body?' Beth asked.

'Awaiting formal identification,' Matt said, 'but yes, I'm pretty certain.'

Matt hoped that the two women would get on.

'We'll have to wait for the post mortem to know if it was an accident or murder. Even then the evidence might not be clear.' he said.

*****

Two cars made the forecourt of the fire station look crowded. One was a police car doubtless belonging to Alys. The other he guessed was Beth's. Matt had to park a little way down the road to avoid blocking the fire station doors. When Matt had lived in the village, it had its own separate police station, but budget cuts had put an end to that.

The outer door was unlocked, so Matt let himself in. He expected to hear Alys and Beth chatting, but the single room that served as the part-time police station was strangely silent when he opened the door. Both women stood as he entered.

'Afternoon, Sir,' they said in unison.

Matt felt ice in the air, and it wasn't the ambient temperature. He remembered the pressure of Alys's body against his when she'd greeted him. When was it? It could only have been the previous night.

He quickly described the scene at Petroc Sands where Rianna's body had been washed ashore.

'Anything to report?' he asked.

Both women started speaking at once, then stopped, glaring at each other.

'Beth, you go first.' Matt said, a sinking feeling settling in his stomach. This wasn't what he needed.

What had happened to have the two women at each other's throats already?

He watched them both carefully as Beth listed the actions that she'd taken since he'd last spoken to her.

On hearing the discovery of the body at Patroc Sands, Beth had informed the detective chief inspector, alerted the police pathologist and informed the Scenes of Crime team that their expertise might be required.

Beth had followed up on the woman who'd spoken angrily to Ross Keely. She was Wendy Pryce, an archaeology lecturer at the college.

Alys wore the blank expression of a poker player throughout. It was impossible to tell what she was thinking.

'Alys, what do you have?' Matt said. He noticed Beth's body tense, when he called Alys by her first name. What is going on here, he thought wearily.

Alys described her walk along the cliff path, and her meeting with the vicar and his dog.

'I noticed a small gully where the path is right on the edge of the cliff,' Alys said. 'The vegetation in the gully looked trampled. When I looked over the edge, I noticed something fluttering, possibly a fragment of fabric, snagged on a stunted gorse bush.

'I took photos and I've uploaded them to the incident file, along with the coordinates of the location.'

'Good work,' Matt said. 'Anything else?'

'I've just spoken to a friend at the outdoor pursuit centre,' Alys said. 'She's willing to abseil down the cliff and retrieve whatever's snagged on the gorse, assuming it's still there. That's if Scenes of Crime don't have anyone skilled at abseiling. I haven't had time to check.'

'Beth, can you check with them? Matt said. 'If they don't, Alys, can you have your friend retrieve it? You'll need to be there with her.'

'We don't even know if there's been a crime yet,' Beth said.

Matt raised one eyebrow. Was Beth resentful that Alys had used her initiative and found what could prove to be a vital clue? He wasn't going to have professional jealousies hindering his investigation.

'Agreed,' he said. 'But, if there has been, we don't want to lose valuable evidence, do we?'

Beth looked sullen and rebellious. 'No, Sir.'

'Get on to it right away then, please. It'll be dark in a couple of hours. I want that fabric, or whatever it is, retrieved tonight.'

While Beth pulled out her police radio and was calling the Scenes of Crime team, Matt turned to Alys.

'I'm taking Beth with me to see how Dylan reacts to the discovery of the body, and to ask him to identify her.' Matt watched Alys's face as he spoke. She wore her poker player's expression. 'Beth's my detective sergeant and must be involved. I hope that you understand.'

'Of course, sir. I'll remember that when I paint myself with woad in the morning.'

Matt cursed. Alys must have overheard his conversation with Beth over the radio. He hoped that his detective sergeant didn't make a habit of making unguarded comments and upsetting people. He'd need to keep an eye on her.

*****

Matt had Beth drive him to the Black Boar Inn at Brannock's Cross, where Dylan was working as a chef. Scenes of Crime didn't have an abseiler on their team, and the Super would never sanction a full Scenes of Crime investigation without any evidence of a crime, so Alys had been given the go-ahead to retrieve the fluttering fragment of fabric from the cliff face.

The Black Boar Inn was a thatched, grey stone

building with a white L-shaped extension. It was between lunch and dinner service, the landlord told them. They could find Dylan resting in his caravan out round the back.

The caravan was down a track hidden from the inn and its garden by a tall laurel hedge. A narrow mown strip of grass with overgrown weeds on either side led to the caravan. Its weathered cream panels had accumulated patches of grey-green algae. An old Honda motorbike stood propped on its stand nearby.

The air throbbed with the heavy, driving beat of music, not anything that Matt recognised. He rapped on the door.

The music stopped, and Dylan opened the door. 'Oh, it's you,' he said, when he saw Matt. 'You'd better come in.'

The caravan was small, cramped, and smelt musty, but a wall heater at least made it warm.

'You'll have to sit on one of the beds, there isn't anywhere else, and it'll be too crowded if you stand.' Dylan said, unapologetically.

'This is Sergeant Francis,' Matt said, as they squeezed into the caravan and sat on one of the beds, Dylan sat on the other, facing them. The gap between the beds was so narrow that they had to angle their knees so they weren't touching.

'The body at Petroc Sands,' he said. 'It's Ree, isn't it?' Dylan's eyes were red, as if he'd been crying.

'How do you know about the body?' Matt asked.

'Been on the radio, hasn't it?' Dylan said. 'Ree's gone missing. A body turns up. Doesn't take much to put two and two together.'

'I'm sorry you had to hear it on the radio,' Matt said. 'We can't say for certain until there's been a formal identification.' He hesitated. 'Would you be willing to make the identification?'

Dylan sighed, heavily. 'I suppose so.' His breath

caught in his throat, almost a sob. 'I'm sorry for Meg, growing up, not knowing her mum, but I'll look after her.'

This was a conversation that Matt didn't want to get into. He'd told Alys to contact social services before he'd left with Beth.

'You'll have to sort out the court order first,' Matt said. 'Did you get legal advice before your case went before the family court?'

'They have to let me have Meg back now that Ree's gone,' Dylan said, angrily. 'I'm her dad.'

Matt thought it best to say nothing.

'No, I didn't,' Dylan said when he realised that Matt wasn't going to answer. 'I never thought they'd believe Ree's lies.'

'I'd advise you to seek advice, Matt said. 'Contact the Citizen's Advice Bureau. 'They'll be able to help you.'

'I can move back into the flat. Look after Meg there. Vicky can help me.'

Dylan was too young to be a father, Matt thought. He looked pathetically like a child pleading for sweets. He should never have made Rianna pregnant. Matt wondered if Rianna had tricked Dylan into it, for her own motives. That's if Dylan really was Meg's father.

'I'll be in touch when we want you to make the identification,' Matt told him as they left. 'It'll probably be tomorrow morning.'

*****

'What did you think of Dylan Rogers? Could he have killed Rianna?'

Beth drove swiftly and skilfully along the back roads from Brannock's Cross to collect the fragment of cloth that Alys's abseiling friend had retrieved from the cliff face. She pulled into a passing bay sharply to avoid a car that came racing towards them.

'Struck me as naïve. He certainly has the motive,' Beth said. 'He made that clear enough from what he said. We can't use that in evidence though. He wasn't speaking under caution.'

'He has a strong alibi,' Matt said. 'The landlord says he was cooking breakfast for the guests at the relevant time.'

'Assuming we know when she died,' Beth added.

They drove on through the late afternoon gloom.

They met Alys at the Madoc's Haven police station, where she handed over an evidence bag containing the fragment of cloth.

'Take this back to HQ and have the finds' officer log it in,' Matt told Beth. 'Keep it with you at all times until you do.'

'I do know the rules surrounding the chain of evidence,' Beth said huffily, adding a belated, 'Sir.'

Working with these two will be like walking on egg-shells, Matt thought glumly, but he wouldn't allow personal animosities to disrupt the investigation.

'I'm taking Alys with me to break the news to Vicky Morgan and to see if she has anything else to tell us,' Matt said. 'If Rianna's death turns out to be murder, CID and neighbourhood policing will be working together on this.'

CHAPTER 11

Beth was fuming. DI Matt Bloody Vincent had despatched her like an errand girl to take Sergeant 'Flavour of the Month' Carey's scrap of fabric all the way back to HQ while he went swanning off with the woman. Beth heaved a sigh of frustration. It was so bloody unjust. She was his detective sergeant.

She snorted. Little Ms Carey's so-called evidence probably had nothing to do with the missing woman.

Beth's eyes narrowed and a smile twisted her lips as she hatched a plan in her mind. After she'd run her errand to HQ, she'd drive back to Madoc's Haven and see what the two of them were up to while she was safely out of the way.

Matt had told her to follow up on the woman she'd seen arguing with the travel and tourism lecturer Ross Keely, Wendy Pryce. She'd use that as an excuse for going back to the area. Maybe she could earn herself some Brownie points at the same time.

Beth pulled out her phone. A quick look at the online prospectus showed that Wendy Pryce was senior lecturer in archaeology at the college.

Her social media pages filled in the background on Wendy Pryce. She was born in Bangor, was now 31, three years older than Ross Keely and eleven years older than Rianna Hughes. Getting past her sell-by for a man with Ross Keely's tastes. Bloody men.

From her photos, Wendy wasn't as attractive as the much younger Rianna.

Did Ross Keely dump Wendy in favour of Rianna? If he did, Wendy Pryce would have a motive for pushing

Rianna off the cliff.

Beth checked the online timetable and found out when archaeology classes that day were due to finish. Perhaps she'd go and have a chat with Ms Pryce.

*****

Alys was frustrated. She'd desperately wanted to be with Matt when he'd broken the news to Dylan Rogers. She knew she was a better police officer than Beth Francis. She couldn't understand how that woman had made sergeant in the Dyfed-Powys CID.

'How did Dylan take the news, sir?' Alys asked, as she drove Matt the short distance to the affordable housing where Vicky lived.

'He already knew. Local radio was onto it straight away, and it's all over Facebook and Twitter too.'

'Was he upset?'

'Eyes were red. Was wiping his nose. Wanted to know when he could have Meg back. Pretty much spelt out his motives for killing Rianna, but the landlord gave him an alibi, assuming she was killed on her early morning run.'

Alys pulled into a parking space outside Vicky's block of flats and turned off the engine. The car's interior lights came on and she turned to Matt. 'There's something I learned on my cliff top walk that I didn't have time to tell you before. It's in the notes I logged on the incident file, but I doubt if you've had time to read them.'

She studied Matt's face, his eyes. The interior lights dimmed and turned off, leaving the image of his eyes etched in her heart.

She recounted her conversation with the vicar, Cedric Davies, and what he'd told her about Rianna overhearing the conversation between the Welsh Government minister, Aled Ingram, and Rhodri and Griff Llewellyn. She told Matt the background, about the Llewellyns' plans for the Clebaston Manor Resort, and the proposed archaeological dig, and the opposition to it.

'What are you suggesting?' Matt asked.

'There are always rumours of corruption involving major planning applications,' Alys said. 'Rianna was unusually excited afterwards. Perhaps she was blackmailing the Llewellyns.'

'If the sums of money are big enough, that could provide a motive for murder,' Matt said, thoughtfully. 'So who's the county's archaeological advisor?'

Alys shook her head. 'I don't know. I'll ask around and find out.'

*****

The skies darkened as Beth arrived at the college. The lights around the buildings snapped on, illuminating the students pouring from the entrance.

Beth crossed her fingers and hoped that the Pryce woman wouldn't leave by some back entrance.

The flood of students diminished to a trickle, but still there was no sight of Beth's prey. She drummed he fingers on the steering wheel.

The burbling of a high performance engine grabbed Beth's attention. Several students pointed and commented.

A charcoal grey Porsche Carrera glided into the car park, reflections of the college's lights gleaming off its highly polished paintwork.

Beth was impressed. It must have just come from the car wash down the road at the supermarket. Either that or it was fresh from the showroom. A couple of minutes driving on the local roads quickly speckled vehicles with mud.

Stare as she might, Beth could only make out the vague shape of the driver. The reflections from the windscreen made him almost invisible.

The car slowed to a halt in front of the college and sat there, burbling.

Who was the driver, and who had he come to collect? Beth made a mental note of the car's registration. It was this year's reg, so no more than a month old. She settled back to wait, her curiosity piqued.

After a few minutes the entrance door opened, and there she was, Wendy Pryce, looking smartly dressed for a college lecturer. A broad smile transformed her face.

The driver of the Porsche swung himself out of his car. He was a little above average height, late twenties, elegantly styled black hair and designer stubble, wearing a smart jacket over an open-necked shirt and jeans. Beth wasn't close enough to see his eye colour, but she guessed blue-grey. Distinctly dishy, quite a catch for a college lecturer.

He stepped quickly around the car and kissed the woman's cheek. He held the door open for her while she climbed in.

Beth started the engine of her car and followed the Porsche out of the car park. Where were they going, and what was the relationship between them? That kiss didn't look romantic or passionate, but they could hardly stand there snogging in front of the college.

Beth followed the Porsche around the town's one-way system. As she drove, Beth radioed in for details of the vehicle's owner.

The Porsche took the A40 towards Narbeth with Beth following. There was a sudden throaty roar and the Porsche accelerated away. Its tail lights dwindled into the distance. Beth cursed and put her foot down, but she'd have needed one of the force's pursuit vehicles to stand a chance of keeping up with him. She slowed down to a more reasonable speed, not wanting to be pulled over by a local traffic cop.

Her radio beeped into life. The owner of the Porsche was Griff Llewellyn of Clebaston Manor.

Now that was an interesting connection. What was Griff Llewellyn doing cavorting around the countryside with Wendy Pryce?

CHAPTER 12

'I'm sure she wouldn't have slipped and fallen off the cliff edge,' Vicky said. 'Ree's been running along that coast path every day for months, in far worse weather than yesterday.'

Dafi stood in his play pen, gazing round-eyed at Alys, who was crouched down in front of him, holding one of his farm animal toys and asking him what it was called.

'It called a cow,' Alys told Dafi, quietly. 'Mooooo.'

Dafi said mooo, and smiling, took the toy from Alys's hand.

This was a side to Alys that Matt had never seen before. He'd previously regarded her as a bit of a tomboy. That wasn't how he was thinking of her now.

'They said on the telly that Ree was found on the beach at Petroc Sands,' Vicky said, staring at Matt, her face pale and with red-rimmed eyes. 'Did someone...'

'We don't know how Rianna died,' Matt said. 'We're waiting to find out. We'd like you to answer a few more questions, if that's okay with you?'

Vicky collapsed back into her armchair. 'I suppose so.'

'We've checked with the drivers, and she didn't travel by bus into town yesterday,' Matt said. 'One of my team visited the college and interviewed Ross Keely, Rianna's travel and tourism lecturer. She didn't attend her classes there, which is consistent with her having fallen from the coast path during her morning run.'

Vicky kicked off her slippers and sat hugging her

knees.'

'I'd like you to tell us a little more about Rianna's social life than you did last time we spoke,' Matt said. 'It might help us understand what happened to her.'

'You think someone killed her, don't you?' Vicky said, rocking herself backwards and forwards.

'Can you tell us anything else about the relationship between Rianna and Ross Keely?' Matt asked.'

Vicky continued rocking, nibbling her lip.

'Nothing you tell us can hurt Rianna now,' Alys said gently. 'You do want to help us find out how she died, don't you?'

Vicky looked up at Alys. 'It was just a harmless fling. Thought he might help her get through her coursework and exams. Then that lecturer woman interfered, name of Wendy or something.'

'How was that a problem?' Alys prompted her.

'There were complaints about Ross with the girls. He's a bit of a lad, is Ross. This Wendy woman threatened that if he didn't pack it in with Ree, she'd drop him in it. Wanted him for herself. Interfering cow.'

Dafi said, 'Mooo.'

Vicky smiled at him. 'Yeah. Mooo.'

'So what did Rianna do?' Alys asked.

'Told her to butt out. Told her she'd grease the stairs for her.'

Matt suppressed a smile. He assumed that Vicky was talking about Wendy Pryce, the archaeology lecturer from the college. Definitely one for the list of suspects. He took over the questioning from Alys. 'Apart from Ross,' he asked, 'have there been any other men in Rianna's life during the last few weeks?'

Vicky shook her head. 'No one.'

Matt let the silence lengthen.

'Are you sure about that,' he asked.

'Well...,' Vicky said, hesitating.

'Go on,' Matt prompted.

'Ree did have that Griff Llewellyn sniffing around. Don't know if she led him on, but she did fancy him.'

Odd, Matt thought, from what he'd learned about her, he didn't think that Rianna would have held back. 'Has Rianna acted unusually in the last few weeks?'

'How d'you mean?'

'Seemed excited, maybe?'

Vicky shook her head. 'Don't know what you mean.'

Matt decided to leave that line of questioning for the moment. He wanted time to investigate Rhodri Llewellyn's plans for Clebaston Manor, and his opposition to the proposed archaeological dig.

Perhaps he should join Alys at the next meeting of the Historical Society. It would help him understand the opposition to the Llewellyns' plans for the Clebaston Manor Resort and how the Madoc's Haven community had changed since he'd been a part of it ten years before.

*****

Should she call it a day, or should she investigate further? Beth was annoyed to have been shaken off so easily by Griff Llewellyn in his Porsche. She was also curious to find out what was going on between Llewellyn and the Pryce woman.

Beth was like a bloodhound. Once she picked up on a scent, she followed it with dogged determination. Her best bet was Clebaston Manor, home to Rhodri Llewellyn, hotelier, property developer and father to Griff Llewellyn.

There were rumours about Rhodri Llewellyn and his property developments. Beth would love to bring him down, both him and his spoilt playboy son. It wasn't that she was jealous of the wealthy. It was more that her upbringing in a small community in north Wales had taught her that inordinate wealth was a sin.

Griff had shot off in the direction of Clebaston Manor so she was probably right, but she couldn't just walk in and start asking questions. She'd have to play it by ear when she arrived there.

As she drove, Beth reflected on the relationship between Matt Vincent and Ms 'Flavour of the Month' Carey. Her researches had revealed that Matt had left Madoc's Haven shortly after Hannah Andrews' death. The newspaper article stated that the only witness apart from Matt Vincent was fifteen year old Alys Carey. The inquest returned a verdict of accidental death.

Was there more to the story than the inquest revealed? Was Hannah Andrews' death as straightforward as the inquest concluded? Beth would have to dig out the coroner's report.

It was dark by the time Beth reached Clebaston. The turn off was on an unmarked road just beyond the village. She nearly missed it.

The Manor was buried deep in woodland a mile or so from the main road.

Beth had visited the place a year before, following the report of a burglary. She remembered that the manor's entrance gates were close to the buildings themselves. The approach road wasn't private property.

She decided to drive up to the gates and see if Griff's Porsche was parked in front of the Manor. It was a long shot. If Wendy was just another of Griff's sexual conquests, would he have taken her to the family home? If not, why was Griff taking her there?

The woodland was hilly and the approach road tortuous. Beth was a quarter of a mile in when she saw the glare of the approaching headlights weaving through the trees towards her. The road was single lane and there were no obvious passing places. Beth swore, a habit she only acquired since joining the police. This she hadn't anticipated. She stopped.

The oncoming vehicle screeched to a halt just inches from her car.

The driver powered down his window and shouted, 'This is a private road. You've no business being here.'

Technically wrong on the first, but possibly correct on the second count, Beth thought, but didn't say. She was pretty certain that the car was the Porsche, and the driver Griff Llewellyn. She prayed that if she didn't argue, she might not be recognised when they met again next, which they almost certainly would.

'You'll have to back up,' Griff shouted. 'I don't have all night.'

Beth thanked her lucky stars that she taken a police advanced response driver course, but even that didn't include reversing along a twisting, hilly road in the dark without a reversing camera.

Griff was impatient. He followed her closely as she reversed, often leaving just a few feet between the two cars. On the positive side, his headlights illuminated the road behind her, and as she drove with her body partly turned, looking over her shoulder, steering one-handed, the Porsche's headlights didn't dazzle her.

She only blundered twice, nearly driving off the road. Griff had to slam on his brakes to avoid running into her when she stopped. Each time she had to drive forward to straighten up, resulting in a torrent of abuse from Griff as he had to reverse. Serve him right if he reverses off the track, Beth thought.

Eventually she backed out onto the main road. Griff roared out past her without even one word of thanks. Beth could just make out Wendy Pryce in the passenger seat. Why had Griff taken Wendy Pryce to Clebaston Manor? She couldn't have been there for more than half an hour.

Beth would have to record what she'd done on the system. It was bound to come out if she didn't. Was it too much to hope that Matt wouldn't read it? How would he react if he did?

She glanced at the time. Still time to track Matt down and see what he was getting up to with little Ms Carey.

*****

'Do you think Rianna shared what she overheard with Vicky?' Matt asked Alys, as she drove him back to the police station to pick up his car.

'The conversation between Aled Ingram and the Llewellyns?' Alys asked. 'Bound to have done. I thought Vicky looked shifty as if she was concealing something. I was surprised you didn't press her harder.'

Matt shook his head, even though Alys couldn't see him in the darkness. 'Counterproductive. She'd have clammed up.'

'I have the feeling that Vicky and Rianna shared everything,' Alys said.

'Including men?' Matt asked. He remembered the way Vicky had wiped the tear from Dylan's cheek when he was upset. Could Vicky have pushed Rianna off the cliff in a fit of jealousy?

Alys laughed. 'No, I didn't mean men. I meant secrets, details of their love lives. Not that Vicky has much of a love life.'

'What's the story there?' Matt studied Alys's face as they entered Madoc's Haven and came under its street lights. The girlish features he remembered from their youth had matured into a womanly profile, attractive in an understated way. Inspector, sergeant. Not a good idea.

'Where's little Dafi's dad?' Matt asked, smiling at the memory of the toddler saying 'mooo' after Vicky had called Wendy Pryce a cow.

'He's a merchant seaman, away for weeks at a time.'

Alys said. 'I've not picked up on any rumours, so if Vicky has strayed, she's been very discreet.'

'When was he last on shore leave?' Matt asked.

'Weeks ago. He's not due back for another eighteen days,' Alys said, 'I checked. If he was around and he was the jealous type, he'd have been more likely to have killed Vicky than Rianna.'

Alys parked by Matt's car, and they both got out.

The High Street was quiet with few people out and about. Matt thought he saw movement in a car parked a little way down the road. Was there a person sitting in it, watching, waiting for someone?

'So what's the plan for tomorrow?' Alys asked.

'I'll have Beth do some research, have her find out all she can about the connection between Ingram and the Llewellyns. See what's going on there.'

'What do you want me to do?'

Matt suddenly felt uncomfortable. Alys wasn't his to command. She wasn't CID. Standing by her car under the streetlight, it felt more like they were a couple who'd been on a date, about to kiss goodnight. He mentally shook himself. Get a grip.

'Beth's taking Dylan to identify the body first thing in the morning,' he said. 'I'm meeting them there. I'll stay for the post mortem. Until we know the results, there's not much we can do.'

'If Rianna was murdered,' Alys said, 'You'll need a pair of eyes and ears here, someone who knows the local community. You could request my attachment to your team. I'm sure my inspector would approve.'

Matt had already seen Beth and Alys interact, witnessed their rivalry. Could he control it better if Alys was part of his team or was it better to keep the two women apart?

Matt hoped to be senior investigating officer for the case, even though normally a detective chief inspector took that role. It would be his first major investigation.

He didn't want Beth and Alys messing it up.

'I'll wait for the autopsy report before making any decisions,' he said. 'I'll keep you updated. Good night, and thanks for all your help.'

Matt turned rapidly, climbed into his car and drove quickly away. He thought of Alys on the long drive home, the sensation of her body pressed against his.

That night Matt dreamt of Alys, of her body painted with woad.

CHAPTER 13

Alys woke early, snatched a hasty breakfast and drove across the rolling countryside to Madoc's Haven. She loved reaching the brow of the final hill and catching that first sight of the sea.

The mist and drizzle of the last week had cleared and given way to clear blue skies. The wind had dropped. Sparkling wave crests glittered in the sun as a gentle swell lapped on the distant sandy shore.

If she wasn't in a hurry, Alys often pulled into the layby and sat chilling out, watching the gulls wheeling over the sea, or the occasional gannet gliding elegantly further out.

Today she was impatient and annoyed. She drove swiftly down the High Street to the fire station, parked outside and punched the entry code into the door lock.

She'd offered her help and Matt had ignored her. 'I'll keep you updated' indeed! This was her patch. She was the one with the local knowledge. Well, she wasn't going to sit on her backside doing nothing.

She made herself a coffee and decided her action plan as she gulped it down.

The Reverend Cedric Davies, vicar of Madoc's Haven, had already proved himself an interesting source of local news and gossip. Alys wondered what other snippets of information had come his way. She wouldn't be interfering with any potential investigation if she paid Cedric a social call, would she? She felt certain the vicar wouldn't be a suspect.

Cedric lived in one of the few remaining vicarages in the area, and ministered to a far wider area that just the parish of Madoc's Haven.

The vicarage lay in a wooded valley on the outskirts of the village. When Alys knocked on the door, she was greeted by gruff growls and barks. Cedric himself opened the door. His Welsh Collie, Whiskey, pushed past him and sniffed at Alys's uniform trousers. She bent down to pat and stroke him, fondling his ears and making a fuss of him.

'Good morning, Sergeant,' Cedric said. 'Seems you have a way with dogs. Whiskey obviously likes you.'

She straightened up and shook Cedric's outstretched hand.

'Is this a social or a duty call?' he asked. 'I hope we haven't had another missing person or fatality? Or did you want Cassie? She's working at the hotel.'

'Fortunately not,' Alys said. 'No, it was you I came to see, not Cassie. I was interested in what you told me about the proposed dig at Clebaston Manor.'

'Come along in then. Dylan's dad's here. We were discussing renovations to the church roof. Did you know Huw's volunteered to be my new churchwarden?'

That should help him promote his building business to the parishioners, Alys thought cynically.

Cedric ushered Alys into a small, cluttered sitting room. Huw stood up as they entered. Huw was a stocky man, medium height, with dark brown hair and brown eyes. She'd noticed his pickup truck parked nearby in the lane.

'Hello Huw,' Alys said. 'I haven't seen you in a while.'

Huw stood, wiped his hand on his faded denim jeans and held it out. His handshake was firm but, as she smiled, his eyes didn't meet hers.

'I'd best be on my way, get back to work,' he said, making for the door.

Alys studied the room as Cedric let Huw out. It was warm, snug and homely, heated by a wood-burning stove. Whiskey had followed her in and now lay at her feet, gazing up at her with his one brown and one blue eye.

'It's a tragic business, isn't it?' Cedric said, as he came back into the room. 'We heard on the radio that a body's been found over on Petroc Sands. I prayed that she'd be found safe and well. It is Rianna's, I suppose?'

'We're waiting on a formal identification,' Alys said, 'but it's almost certain that it is her. What have the villagers been saying?'

'They're in shock, of course,' he said. 'Some of the less forgiving are saying that it's what she deserved. Most thought the court was wrong, excluding Dylan from his own home and restricting his access to little Megan. Dylan's mother, Gemma, was particularly incensed.'

Cedric looked Alys directly in the eyes. 'Do we know how Rianna died?'

'Too early to say. She may have slipped and fallen off the cliff. There will have to be a post mortem. We'll know more after that.'

Cedric shook his head, and said, 'God rest her soul.'

Alys felt marginally uncomfortable. She hadn't been to a church service since her early teens. 'What did you think of Rianna?' she asked. 'She moved into the village after we left and went to live in Llanbrioc. I only knew her by sight.'

How easy it was to slip into using the past tense. But Alys had assumed that Rianna was dead from the time she first heard that she'd gone missing. Did she have some sixth sense?

Cedric hesitated and rung his hands together. 'Of course, one shouldn't speak ill of the dead, but she did have a reputation.'

Alys waited patiently.

'She was an attractive young woman,' Cedric continued in a disapproving tone, 'as I'm sure you noticed. Men flocked to her like bees to a honey trap. I'm told that she didn't try too hard to resist their advances.'

'Were there any particular men?'

'I don't know anything directly, but there has been gossip about a lecturer at the college in Haverfordwest, and my daughter Cassie told me that, a week or so ago, she saw Rianna accepting a lift after work in Griff Llewellyn's sports car.'

Now that is interesting, Alys thought. Did Dylan know? Jealousy could be a powerful motive for murder.

She moved the conversation on to a discussion of Rhodri Llewellyn's plans for his proposed Clebaston Manor Resort.

'I forgot to ask yesterday, Alys said. 'Who's the county's archaeological advisor? You said it's a woman.'

'Yes. Wendy Pryce, a lecturer at the college in Haverfordwest.'

Alys's heart rate spiked.

Wendy Pryce, the woman Beth Francis had seen arguing with Ross Keely and who he possibly jilted in favour of Rianna. Could the Llewellyns be bribing her to reject objections to the Clebaston Manor Resort development?

Alys remembered seeing a dark-haired woman driving around in the Archaeological Trust's Land Rover. Was that Wendy Pryce?

Alys felt a warm glow of excitement. She couldn't wait to tell Matt.

*****

Alys left several messages for Matt but to no avail. It was almost midday in the hilly uplands when Alys's phone finally rang. She'd just taken details from an angry sheep farmer about the theft of his Land Rover

Defender. It was the fourth to be stolen from her patch in as many months.

Alys glanced at her phone's screen. It was Matt. Her pulse quickened in anticipation.

'Hello, Sergeant Carey?' Matt said, killing her mood stone dead. Surely he wouldn't call her that, unless his bossy detective sergeant was standing beside him?

'Yes, Sir?' Damn the man. Couldn't he have waited until he was alone before calling her back?

'Thought you'd like to know,' Matt said. 'Dylan identified the body as Rianna's. According to the autopsy report, most of her injuries were consistent with falling down a sharply sloping cliff face and landing on rocks at the bottom.'

Alys held her breath. She was sure there was more.

'The body had been immersed in seawater after death,' Matt continued. 'However, the pathologist noted one wound, consistent with a sharp blow to the head with a blunt instrument, possibly a rock.'

'So she was murdered,' Alys said.

'He's prepared to go on the stand and swear to it.'

Alys felt a strange sense of relief that they were no longer in limbo. She felt sympathy for Dylan and Meg, deprived of a partner and a mother respectively. She was angry that there was a killer in the community where she'd grown up. Her mind instantly started lining up suspects in a mental identity parade.

Dylan was the most obvious candidate. It would be a cruel twist of fate if little Meg was deprived of her father too. Alys prayed that her suspicions didn't prove to be true.

'I'll have Scenes of Crime to go over her flat,' Matt continued. 'See if they can find any leads.'

'I found out the name of the county archaeological advisor, as you requested.' Alys said. Damn, that sounded stilted.

Alys heard Beth's voice, faint in the background.

'Must think she's Ms Jane flipping Marple.'

Alys's blood boiled and she cursed Matt's Rottweiler sergeant.

There was silence over the phone for a few seconds. Alys hoped that Matt had muted it while he tore strips off her.

'I'm sorry, Sergeant Carey,' Matt's voice came back on the phone. 'I've more pressing priorities for the moment. Just log the details on the system.'

He rang off, leaving Alys seething with impotent rage.

She replayed the conversation in her mind as she drove down the narrow, twisting byways, back towards Madoc's Haven.

Impetuosity would be her downfall. Her form teacher had written that on one of her school reports. Was it really ten years ago? She was a self-conscious young teenager then, with braces on her teeth and a crush on Matt Vincent.

She shook her head as she drove into the village. She'd lost the braces on her teeth and was no longer a teenager. Not much else had changed.

She resisted the temptation to book the district nurse, Julie Bowen, who'd parked on a double yellow line. She'd doubtless just nipped into the minimarket and delicatessen. It wouldn't be fair for Alys to take out her anger on Julie.

*****

Matt looked at Beth with annoyance. What was it with her?

'If you must make disparaging comments about colleagues, I don't want to hear them,' Matt said, 'and I most certainly don't want them to hear them either.'

'No, Sir. Of course not, Sir,' Beth said. 'Please accept my apology.'

Matt looked at Beth in disbelief. She didn't sound in

the least apologetic. What was it old Dilwyn Probert said when Matt told him she'd been assigned to his team?

'I don't envy you there then, boyo. She's an overinflated sense of her own importance. Looks down on everyone. And her tongue; sharp as a razor. She'll lacerate your soul, given half a chance. Slap her down, soon as she gets uppity. It's the only way.'

Matt hadn't believed Dilwyn initially. Beth had behaved herself, acting efficiently as his deputy, until she'd come face-to-face with Alys.

'If you're going to apologise, I expect your apology to be sincere', Matt told Beth. 'Is that understood?'

'Yes, Sir,' Beth said, standing stiffly to attention, which looked a little odd as she wasn't in uniform.

'How come she's still on the force?' Matt had asked Dilwyn.

'Walks a fine line,' Dilwyn replied, 'on the very edge of insubordination. One day she'll fall over the edge, or someone with guts'll give her a push. You were unlucky. Newest DI always gets her.'

Matt wasn't one to shy away from a challenge. Sergeant Bethan Francis had better watch her step.

CHAPTER 14

Matt wanted to see Dylan's reaction when he learnt that Rianna had been murdered, so he arrived at the Black Boar Inn unannounced.

It was lunch time and the car park held a smattering of cars, not that numerous, but enough custom to keep the inn ticking over until the holiday season began. The Black Boar's customers drove more modest vehicles than the clientele of the Madoc's Bay Hotel.

Matt led the way into the inn with Beth close on his heels. The interior was in stark contrast to the Madoc's Bay Hotel too. The walls were of rough stone, the ceiling white painted beams and the floor flagstones or bare wooden boards. Brown leather armchairs surrounded low solid wooden tables that had weathered the test of time.

Conversation stopped as Matt and Beth entered and walked up to the bar, which also served as a reception desk.

'Back again are you?' the landlord said by way of a greeting. 'Terrible what happened, wasn't it? Shook up Dylan real bad. You're wanting to see him again I suppose?'

'Yes please.'

'Not best timing, middle of lunch service.'

Matt looked at the restaurant area which was only a quarter full.

'Not that we're rushed off your feet,' the landlord said, following Matt's gaze.

Damn, I'm beginning to behave like Beth, Matt thought. 'Do you have somewhere private where we can talk to Dylan?'

'Use my office if you like. Not much room and you'll have to excuse the clutter.'

The landlord's office was in stark contrast to Rhodri Llewellyn's opulent surroundings. Piles of paperwork covered the desk and cardboard boxes were stacked against the walls..

Dylan came in dressed in chef's whites, wiping his hands on a cloth.

'What is it now? I identified her for you, didn't I?'

'Perhaps we could sit down,' Matt said gesturing to one of the two office chairs. Beth stood by the other while Matt stood behind the desk. He waited until they were all seated.

'We came to tell you the results of the post mortem. We believe that Ms Hughes was murdered.'

Dylan's mouth dropped open and he clapped his hands to his face. He shook his head, staring open eyed at Matt. His face turned ashen grey.

'She must have slipped and fallen off the path,' he said. 'Who would have wanted to kill her?'

Matt held Dylan's gaze.

'You can't think I killed her. I loved her.' Dylan said in an agonised voice, shaking his head. Tears sprang from his eyes and trickled down his cheeks. A sob racked his body.

Dylan's raw agony rekindled memories of Matt's own reactions when Hannah had died. He couldn't believe that Dylan was acting. His grief was all too real.

Matt forced himself to be objective. Most murders motivated by jealousy were committed in the heat of the moment. Rianna's killing appeared premeditated and coldly executed. If Dylan had murdered her, it had to have been motivated by outrage at what she had done to him, the court order and his exclusion from the flat and from Meg's life, along with her affairs.

'Can you tell me about the occupation order and the

child arrangements order granted against you,' Matt said. 'What were the court's grounds for granting them?'

'It was all a pack of lies,' Dylan said angrily. 'Ree said I was always shouting and screaming at her, that it scared Meg and made her cry. Said she was scared I'd hit her or the baby.'

'Did you ever hit her?'

'No,' Dylan said, the colour returning to his cheeks. 'I never did.'

Matt wasn't sure he believed him.

'Did you shout and scream at her?'

'No,' Dylan said more quietly, avoiding Matt's eyes. Then, after a long pause, 'Well, maybe once or twice, when she deliberately wound me up.'

'How did she do that?'

'Told me I was useless,' Dylan said so quietly that Matt had to lean forward to hear. 'Said I'd never make anything of my life, not like Griff Llewellyn, or that lecturer of hers at the college, Ross something or other. She said she didn't even know if I was Meg's father.'

Matt was thankful that he hadn't fallen for a woman like Rianna, assuming that what Dylan had told them was true. He didn't have any reason to disbelieve him. He'd just given them the perfect motive for murder.

'If you didn't kill Rianna, can you suggest who might have done it, and why?' Matt asked.

Dylan shook his head sadly. 'Could have been loads of people. I may have loved her, God only knows why, but I wasn't blind to her faults. She was a conniving so-and-so. Perhaps she tried it on with the wrong person. I'd put my money on Griff Llewellyn. He can be a right bastard.'

CHAPTER 15

'I want you to set up a major incident room in Divisional Headquarters in Haverfordwest,' Matt told Beth. 'We can't have one in Madoc's Haven, there isn't enough room, and Force HQ is too far away.'

'Yes, sir.' Beth was on her best behaviour, but inside she was fuming. Not only had DI Matt bloody Vincent walked into the Detective Inspector post that should have been hers, but he'd had the brass-faced nerve to give her a dressing down over that interfering neighbourhood policing sergeant, Alys "Ms Jane flipping Marple" Carey.

Beth needed to do some digging to find out what hold the Carey woman had over DI Vincent. She'd spied on them the previous night, but there was no sign of affection, no goodnight kiss when they'd parted. Perhaps they'd just argued.

'Beth, I was talking to you!'

'Sorry, Sir,' she replied. 'I was just thinking what staffing and resources we'd need for the incident room. What was it you said?'

'I said, I want the incident room fully operational by the time the day shift comes on duty in the morning.'

'Of course, Sir. I'll get onto it right away.' What did he think she was? An incompetent idiot?

'Do we have a match for that fragment of cloth that Sergeant Carey retrieved from the cliff top?'

'Yes Sir. It was torn from Rianna Hughes' hoodie. It was an exact match,' Beth said, much to her annoyance.

'Excellent work by Sergeant Carey,' Matt said.

'Saved us hours of potentially fruitless searching. Perhaps I should have her attached to our team for the duration of the case. I know she wants to move back to CID.'

He's deliberately winding me up, Beth thought.

'Don't you think it would be better if she remained in the neighbourhood policing team, you know, our eyes and ears in the local community?' That sounded lame even to Beth, but she could hardly tell him that Ms Marple would join the team over her dead body. It might be a price he'd be prepared to pay.

'We need to get a Scenes of Crime team to the location where Sergeant Carey found it before it gets dark,' Matt said. 'It's frustrating that we couldn't get one there yesterday.'

If I'd been the DI, we would have done, Beth thought. She couldn't understand why Matt hadn't won the Chief Superintendent's approval. He couldn't have tried hard enough.

'They're already on their way, Sir,' Beth told him. 'I organised it as soon as this was raised to a murder inquiry and forensics came back with the fabric match.'

'Excellent,' Matt said. 'While you're setting up the incident room, I'm going to drive over to Madoc's Haven and take a look at where Rianna met her maker. Message me a progress report on the incident room before end of shift.'

'Yes, Sir.'

I can guess why he's so keen to get over to Madoc's Haven, Beth thought, and it has nothing to do with the crime scene.

Beth waited until Matt was clear of the building before she let out a scream of frustration and rage.

*****

What would Scenes of Crime find on the cliff-tops? The hunt was on!

As Matt drove over the brow of the last hill before Madoc's Haven, the sun blinded him. He yanked down the visor and slowed to take in the view.

The village, the beach and the sea were spread out before him, the sun low in the sky, blazing a shimmering trail across the waves from the horizon to the shore. Not long before sunset and dusk. He'd have to hurry.

Matt parked his car at the beach car park in Madoc's Haven and set out along the coast path. It was ten years since he'd last walked it. Not much had changed, except the parking charges had more than doubled.

The path climbed steeply up towards the cliff tops, a newly tarmacked path at the start, but rapidly changing to rocks and trodden down soil. Matt walked rapidly and soon felt the burn in his leg muscles as he climbed. Did Rianna run this section? If so she must have been fit. He felt the coldness of the air rushing down his throat as his breathing became heavier. He must find a suitable gym. He'd not worked out properly since starting his new job.

Seagulls wheeled in the late afternoon sky, the sea sounds settled to a rhythmic shushing on the rocks, and the wind dropped.

Matt watched a cormorant skimming over the waves as he hurried along. He needed to see the murder scene while there was still enough daylight left.

What had Rianna been thinking as she ran through the early morning murk? Was she thinking of her daughter Meg, or of a possible tryst with her travel and tourism lecturer, Ross Keely? Or was she thinking of the overheard conversation between Ingram and the Llewellyns?

Matt cursed as he stubbed his toe on a rock and nearly sent himself flying.

Was that what Rianna had done? Was her death

just an unfortunate accident? Could the pathologist have been wrong? If not, when they caught the killer and the case came to court, he could already hear the defence lawyer's line of argument.

This could prove a tricky one, his first case as senior investigating officer. He would have to get it right. His future career depended on it.

Even though the weather had cleared, the path was still slick and slippery in places. Some of the gorse bushes were in flower, but it was too early for the spring flowers. The vegetation was still all dull greens and browns.

Matt followed the coast path up and down along its twisting route, sometimes past gentle rocky, turf-covered slopes leading down to the sea, at others on the cliff edge with vertiginous drops above the swirling inlets far below.

He climbed to the top of a rise and there, at the bottom of a dip in the path ahead, he could see Alys and three other figures in white coveralls.

How many ramblers had trodden the path since Rianna was killed? Matt wondered.

He hurried on towards the gully. A short flight of steps descended to the cliff edge before kinking sharply around the end of a fence.

Alys was stripping off her protective clothing. The Scenes of Crime Officers were packing up their equipment, getting ready to leave.

'Good afternoon, sir.'

Why was Alys sounding so cold and formal? Perhaps she had overheard that "Ms Marple" comment from Beth over the phone. Matt was hoping she hadn't.

'I don't know if you've met the Scenes of Crime team?' Alys said. 'Possibly not as you're new to the force?'

She introduced them all.

'Have you found anything significant?' Matt asked

the team leader.

'A few black threads snagged on that wire,' he said, pointing to the three-stranded barbed wire fence separating the coast path from a field full of sheep. 'Could've come from a fleece or a hoody.' He looked at the fence, festooned in strands of sheep's' wool and laughed. 'Not from one of them. Not a black sheep among them.'

Matt smiled before becoming more serious again. 'Is that the way the killer came and made his escape?'

'Most obvious route would be along the coast path,' the team leader said, 'but he'd have to pass close to anyone walking in the opposite direction. Alternatively he could have used the road, hiked across the field and climbed through the fence. That would explain the black threads on the wire, assuming they've come from the killers clothing. If you already have suspects, check if they own a black fleece or a hoody.'

'Any evidence which way he used?'

'We looked for traces of him crossing the field,' he continued. 'Problem is, those sheep trample everywhere. If he did leave footprints, the sheep have obliterated them.'

'If he used the road,' Alys said, 'he'd have had to come by car, motorbike, cycle or walk. I'd vote for him using a push bike. No number plate for anyone to recognise, faster than walking. Relatively easy to hide the bike while he crossed the field, did the deed and then made his escape.'

'Any evidence to support that?' Matt asked, turning back to the SOCO team leader.

He shook his head. 'Sorry sir, none. We checked that out when Alys suggested it earlier. I think we're done here. I'll enter our findings on the system. Best of luck with the investigation.'

*****

'Good work, sergeant,' Matt said, after the Scenes of Crime team had departed. 'If it hadn't been for your sharp eyes, we might never have known where Rianna died.'

Alys nodded an acknowledgement. 'I had a little help from Whiskey, the vicar's dog. He suddenly became very excited and started barking when we came down the steps. He was sniffing round where the vegetation was trampled down. I've no idea what set him off. It's possible that's where the murderer lay in wait for Rianna.'

She hesitated, appeared to soften, 'And please call me Alys. We're not hot on formality here.'

Matt remembered the hug she'd given him when they met in the police station, and the smell of her scent in his nostrils. He felt awkward. It would hardly do for her to call him Matt. If she did in front of Beth, she'd go apoplectic.

'Show me where you found the scrap of fabric,' he said quickly. 'You heard that forensics confirmed that it came from Rianna's running top?'

Alys leant out over the cliff edge and pointed, 'Down there. It was snagged on that sticking out tuft of furze.'

Matt only just stopped himself from grabbing her arm. Fear clutched him. He thought Alys was going to follow Rianna to her death.

Memories came flooding back of another death on this harsh, forbidding coastline. He didn't want to lose anyone else here.

He swallowed hard, and leaned over the edge cautiously. Was Alys fearless or crazy? He'd asked himself that about Hannah too.

It was a hundred foot drop to where the waves swirled and splashed against the rocks below. Sparse tufts of vegetation occupied precarious footholds on the near vertical cliff face.

'The murderer made a mistake,' Alys said. 'She'd

have died even if he hadn't clobbered her. A quick shove would have been enough.'

Matt retreated back from the edge, willing Alys to follow him. 'What makes you think it was a he?'

'Doesn't feel like the way one woman would kill another,' Alys said, stepping back. 'Did the pathologist have any idea what he used?'

Matt relaxed and breathed more easily. 'The ubiquitous blunt instrument. I did press her, and she reluctantly said that it was most likely a rock.'

'Logical,' Alys said. 'Doubtless threw it into the sea afterwards. Untraceable. No forensic evidence. The near perfect crime.'

'He could have got away with it,' Matt said, 'if it hadn't been for you.'

Alys met his gaze, looking deeply into his eyes. Matt suddenly felt breathless and light-headed. He quickly looked away. There was no way this was a good idea.

*****

Matt was in a quandary. Should he request Alys's attachment to his team? She was obviously intelligent, used her brain and would make an excellent detective. But would she be too much of a distraction? He'd already had a foretaste of the potential friction between Alys and Beth. He didn't want to devote his time and energies to getting them working harmoniously together.

Then there were his personal feelings. He could easily fall for Alys. There was chemistry between them. He'd felt it. He was certain she had too. Working with her on a murder case at the same time as falling for her could prove impossible. He and the members of his team, particularly Beth, would be constantly questioning his decisions. He'd be forever treading a fine line between showing favouritism towards Alys and treating her unfairly by verging towards the opposite extreme.

Alys caught Matt's eye. He nodded for her to go ahead.

'I hope I haven't stepped out of line,' she said, with a hint of sarcasm in her voice, 'but as soon as I heard that this was a murder inquiry, I asked the neighbourhood policing team to find out if any of Madoc's Haven residents regularly travel along the road at the time Rianna was murdered, or in the hour or so before and after. They should have a list ready when we get back.'

Matt groaned inwardly, remembering Beth's snide Ms Marple comment. He could see fireworks ahead. 'Excellent, Alys. Very helpful.'

'Also I entered the name of the county's archaeological advisor on the system as you requested.'

'Who is he?'

Alys held his gaze, an unfathomable expression on her face.

'Not a he, a she. Wendy Pryce.'

'Wendy Pryce?' Matt bit his tongue to stop himself from asking why she hadn't told him before. She'd tried to, over the phone, and he'd cut her off short.

His brain went into overdrive as he thought through the implications. Wendy Pryce had an ample motive for killing Rianna, jealousy, if Rianna had stolen Ross Keely away from her.

Then there was the possibility that Wendy Pryce had accepted a bribe from the Llewellyns to reject objections to the proposed dig at the Clebaston Manor site so the proposed development could go ahead without delay. Had Rianna found out? Was Rianna blackmailing Pryce or the Llewellyns to keep quiet?

'But you don't think Rianna was killed by a woman?' he asked.

'No. Just a feeling, a hunch. No proof, nothing to back it up.'

'Let's walk back to Madoc's Haven and talk as we go. There are things we need to discuss.'

They climbed back up the steps in the gathering gloom.

The sun was a bright white sphere surrounded by a halo of yellow. It cast its light across the rippling slate-grey sea. Its reflections looked like a white comet with a pale yellow tail heading out from the land to meet its progenitor.

Wispy white clouds and the vapour trails of aircraft streaked a sky that transitioned from blue-grey through greenish hues to yellow, then orange where it met the low dark line of islands on the horizon.

It was a beautiful sunset.

'It's a good job I have my torch,' Alys said. 'It'll be dark by the time we get back to the car park.'

'Do you have time for a drink?' Matt asked, suddenly realising that he hadn't expressed himself very well. Alys might think he was asking her on a date.

'I need to discuss how our teams should work together', he added quickly. 'We can arrange to meet in the morning, if you prefer.'

There was silence from Alys as they hurried along, sometimes side by side, at others in single file where the path was narrow.

The sun began slipped below the horizon, streaking the sky with horizontal bands of orange and yellow.

'You go in front,' Alys said, switching on her torch. 'That way I can light the path ahead for both of us.'

They continued along the path as darkness descended.

'Okay,' Alys said, finally answering his question. 'I don't suggest we use a pub in the village. Do you know the Armel Arms? It's far enough away to avoid local gossip. I'll have to nip home first and change out of uniform, but that shouldn't take long. Meet you there?'

CHAPTER 16

What did Matt have to say to her, Alys wondered, as she drove out of the beach car park and headed into the hinterland. Apart from saying quietly that he'd see her at the Armel Arms, Matt had been uncommunicative as they made their way back along the coast path to their cars. For a moment she'd thought Matt was inviting her out on a date, but he'd quickly dashed that hope on the rocks.

What had Matt said? 'I need to discuss how our teams should work together.' That wasn't what Alys wanted to hear either. It meant he wasn't going to request her attachment to his team.

She'd been a detective constable before her father had fallen ill. She'd transferred back into uniform to avoid the unpredictable hours. Now she was desperate to get back into the CID, but there were no suitable vacancies. Her inspector wasn't helpful either, told her that she was too valuable in neighbourhood policing to lose. She suspected that a bias against women detectives in some quarters was holding her back too. Men like DCS Stone harked back to a bygone age, positively antediluvian.

Her speed progressively increased, alternately accelerating and braking as she zoomed along the twisting country lanes, relying on the loom of oncoming headlights to warn her of approaching cars. In her growing frustration, she hadn't realised how fast she was travelling. She cursed and slowed down.

Alys had almost fobbed Matt off, told him she was busy, that she'd meet him at the office in the morning.

But it would have been untrue. She sighed with exasperation as she dashed into her house in Llanbrioc.

After checking that her dad was okay, a quick change of clothes and a dab of makeup, Alys was back on the road.

Would Matt already be there? He'd told her that he needed to pick up a few things at the minimarket. Could he remember where the Armel Arms was? It was ten years since he'd lived in the area and the pub wasn't local to Madoc's Haven.

*****

Alys could't see Matt's car as she parked in the Armel Arms car park. Damn, she needn't have rushed.

Silence descended and the diners turned to stare as she walked through the door. The clientele was local and visitors were rare in the winter.

The Armel Arms was hardly a pub any more. It was yet another eatery with just a few tables for those who only wanted to drink.

'Hello, George,' Alys said as she stepped up to the bar. 'Long time no see.'

'Hello Alys and welcome. Nearly didn't recognise you out of uniform. What can I get you?'

The Armel Arms was just inside the territory covered by Alys's team, and she'd help solve a series of break-ins that had caused George a lot of grief. He'd been grateful to Alys ever since.

Alys bought herself a glass of Chablis and took it into a secluded corner where she sat surveying the scene. The diners were mostly older couples, probably celebrating an anniversary, except for two tables which were birthday meals.

It was ten minutes before Matt arrived.

'Sorry, I didn't get you one,' Alys said. 'I didn't know if you'd changed what you drink.'

'No problem. Can I get you a refill?'

'No thanks, I'll nurse this one.'

Matt returned to the table with a pint of speciality beer from the local brewery.

He looked uncomfortable, obviously not knowing quite what to say. Well, Alys wasn't going to help him.

He tasted his beer before carefully putting down the glass and looking into her eyes.

Damn. His gaze straight right to her core. Her chest tightened. She was breathless. She quickly looked down at her drink, not wanting him to see the effect he was having on her.

She looked back up, suddenly angrily defiant. 'You're not going to request my attachment to your team. You didn't have to drag me here to tell me. You could have told me that on the coast path.'

She spoke more loudly than she'd intended. Some of the nearer diners turned to stare.

She closed her eyes and took a long, deep breath. What was she doing? She hadn't seen Matt for ten years. Back then she'd been a silly young schoolgirl. He'd been on the verge of manhood. There was nothing between them, except her ridiculous childhood crush.

Now he was a detective inspector, while she was just a lowly rural sergeant. She must be mad, talking to him like that.

She took a gulp of her wine. 'I'm sorry. I shouldn't have spoken to you like that.'

'No, I'm the one who should apologise,' Matt said. 'I only asked you here because I wanted to explain.

'You don't need to justify your decision. I should never have asked in the first place.'

Matt looked at her, saying nothing. She felt embarrassed, knew she was beginning to blush.

'I care for you,' he said, reaching out and touching her hand. 'I always thought of you as the little sister I never had.'

Was the man mad? Couldn't he see he was twisting the knife in the wound?

'It wouldn't work, having you on my team,' Matt said. 'It would create too many complications.'

Alys was tempted to ask what sort of complications, but thought better of it.

'I think there could be a personality clash between you and Sergeant Francis,' he continued. 'It could get in the way of the investigation. It would be an unnecessary distraction. If that happened, it would damage both our careers.'

Reluctantly, Alys admitted, that could be true.

Matt took a deep swallow of his beer.

'Beth is my sergeant, so you will have to liaise with her. Whatever differences you may have, I'm expecting you both to cooperate with each other for the good of the investigation.'

'You don't need to tell me how to behave,' Alys said angrily, standing up and grabbing her coat. 'Tell that to your pet Rottweiler.'

*****

Matt stood as Alys stormed out of the pub, then sank slowly back into his seat. People at the nearby tables stared at him. He stared back until they looked away and cursed himself for an idiot.

What he'd felt when he'd looked into Alys's eyes was like a lightning strike to his heart. He wasn't even sure he'd experienced that intensity of feeling with Hannah, he certainly hadn't with anyone since, well, not until tonight. And like a fool he'd driven her away.

'That went well, didn't it?' The landlord said as he cleared Alys's glass from the table. 'Nice lass is young Alys. Don't like to see her upset.'

Matt bit his tongue to stop himself from telling the landlord to mind his own business.

'Don't I know you?' the landlord said. Recognition

dawned on his face. 'Didn't I see you on the telly? You were on the local news. Murder of a young woman over in Madoc's Haven, wasn't it?'

Matt drew a deep breath and tried to put the confrontation with Alys to the back of his mind. 'Yes. Rianna Hughes. Did you know her?'

'Can't say I did,' the landlord replied. Then, as he sprayed and wiped the table, 'What are your lot doing about all the things that're going missing?'

What was the man talking about? Why didn't he go away and leave him in peace?

Then Matt remembered the briefing about the theft of agricultural equipment. There was an alert about yet another Land Rover Defender that had gone missing, this time from a farm up near Castlebythe.

'That's not a case I'm working on,' Matt said. 'What are people saying?'

The landlord looked at Matt. 'That it must be the work of a gang. That they're running rings around the police.'

'I can understand the frustration,' Matt said. He downed the remains of his beer in one. As he stood to leave, he said. 'It would make our life easier if farmers put trackers on their Land Rovers and quad bikes.'

'It's money isn't it?' the landlord said. 'Times are hard for farmers right now, and those trackers don't come cheap.'

'Yes they do, and a damned sight cheaper than Land Rovers and quad bikes,' Matt said, and instantly regretted it. Another Beth moment. What was wrong with him?

'Let me know if you hear anything that might help,' Matt said hastily, giving the landlord his business card. 'Even if it's just a rumour or gossip.'

Once outside, Matt paused to gaze up at the sky. His breath condensed in the chill night air.

Damn, damn, damn. Why did he behave like a

pompous buffoon? Why couldn't he just tell Alys how he felt?

He sighed. He'd get rid of Beth Francis and replace her with Alys if he could, but that just wouldn't work. He had no justification for getting rid of her. He'd be putting his personal life before his duty to his colleagues and the force.

He wrenched his thoughts back to the issue of the vehicle thefts, anything to block out his disastrous conversation with Alys.

The gangs were getting more cunning. If they stole a vehicle, they hid it somewhere for a day or two and watched to see if the police came to find it. If they didn't, they assumed that the vehicle wasn't fitted with a tracker. A quick change of registration plates and the vehicle could be spirited away with little or no risk to the gang.

Was the stolen Land Rover Defender from Castlebythe still hidden away in some secluded spot? It hadn't been fitted with a tracker.

As he drove back towards his empty home, his thoughts returned to Alys. Why did she have to be a policewoman? Why couldn't she be a personnel manager or a recruitment consultant? Something totally unrelated to police work that didn't involve long hours.

He'd felt the chemistry when they'd met at the police station in Madoc's Haven and she'd given him that hug. It was even stronger tonight when their eyes met and she'd vaporised his soul. He'd anticipated problems coming back, but he'd never anticipated this.

*****

Alys was furious with herself for losing it with Matt. Okay, she was disappointed that he hadn't requested her attachment to his team, but she could see that his reasons were valid. Working alongside Beth would be impossible, almost as impossible as working alongside Matt.

Was Matt the reason why Alys had never been able to form a long-lasting relationship? Had some hidden part of her always belonged to him?

She suddenly realised that she'd driven the last four miles without noticing them. She was almost home. That glass of Chablis must have gone to her head. She was thinking crazy, irrational thoughts. She hadn't seen Matt in ten years, and now suddenly he was her grand passion, her long lost love. She'd taken leave of her senses.

Her car's headlights picked out the sign for Llanbrioc, and she was home. Hopefully a good night's sleep would restore her sanity.

CHAPTER 17

'It's not set up yet?' Matt said, 'I told you to get it done by first thing this morning. Why didn't you message me?'

'Problem with Estates Management,' Beth responded tersely.

'Meet me there.' Matt barely contained his annoyance. 'You can explain later. We'll interview Wendy Pryce first, then we'll interview the Llewellyns at the Madoc's Bay Hotel.'

Matt terminated the call and kept driving. What was it with Beth Francis? It couldn't be that difficult to organise an incident room.

Matt's eyes were gravelly. Another sleepless night, this time replaying the disastrous meeting with Alys in the Armel Arms.

Half an hour later he turned into the police station car park. Beth stepped out of her car. She didn't look quite like Beth. She'd done something different with her hair and she was wearing dark-rimmed specs. He'd never seen her wearing those before.

'Good morning, sergeant,' he said. 'I almost didn't recognise you.'

'Good morning, sir. Slight change of plan,' she said, ignoring his comment. 'It's Wendy Pryce's half day off from the college. She's visiting a Neolithic site in the north of the county. We'll have to interview the Llewellyns first and catch up with her later.'

*****

Beth turned down the steeply sloping drive to the

Madoc's Bay Hotel. The car park was to the side of the grey stone mansion and its more recent accommodation block.

She parked as far away from Griff's charcoal grey Porsche as she could. She'd hoped that he would be somewhere else. If they met, she certainly didn't want him to recognise her from their confrontation on the track leading to Clebaston Manor.

While Matt was staring across the bay towards the dark mass of the islands far out to sea, she was studying the cars.

'It's a sin, spending that much money on a car,' she said.

'You'll not get much change from a couple of hundred grand for one of those,' Matt said, looking at a latest registration Mercedes AMG saloon. 'Jealous?'

'No!' Beth said vehemently. 'I meant what I said. It's disgusting that people spend that much money on cars while there are millions living in poverty.'

Matt raised an eyebrow. 'We'd better speak to Rhodri Llewellyn first,' he said. 'Thanks for tipping me off about his friendship with the chief constable. I never spoke with Rhodri when I lived here before. I knew his son though, Griff Llewellyn. Don't be surprised by his attitude. We have past history.'

That tweaked Beth's curiosity. She would have to find a local busybody and discover more.

Beth looked around as they entered the hotel's imposing lobby. The dark décor wouldn't be out of place in a gothic horror movie.

'Good morning, inspector.' The hotel receptionist gave Matt a dazzling smile, ignoring Beth.

'Good morning, Penny' Matt said. 'We'd like a word with Mr Rhodri Llewellyn, if he's available.'

Beth inwardly growled. Matt hadn't even introduced her. She might as well be invisible. If he'd been with Ms Marple, he'd have introduced her.

Penny disappeared into the inner recesses of the hotel, returning a few minutes later. 'Mr Llewellyn will see you in ten minutes. May I get you a drink? A tea or a coffee?'

He's making us wait deliberately, Beth thought, to show us how important he is.

Fifteen minutes later the receptionist's phone warbled. 'Mr Llewellyn will see you now,' she told them. 'Please follow me and I'll show you to his office.'

*****

Matt stepped aside to allow Beth through the door first. Rhodri Llewellyn looked up. A flash of puzzlement crossed his face. It disappeared when Matt followed Beth into the room.

'Good morning,' Rhodri Llewellyn stood and held out his hand. 'Inspector Vincent, isn't it? I believe you come from these parts, knew my son.'

Llewellyn's handshake was unnecessarily hard, as if he intended to crush Matt's bones. His gaze was flinty too. Following the fracas in which Matt had split Griff's lip, he'd demanded that Matt be expelled from school. He was disappointed. Matt had already finished his A-levels and left.

Matt kept his face neutral, and held the man's gaze. 'That was many years ago,' he said, determined to draw a line under the past. 'This is Sergeant Francis. We're here investigating the death of Rianna Hughes. I understand she worked here as a waitress?'

Llewellyn nodded at Beth, but he didn't offer to shake her hand. He gestured towards two hard-backed chairs and sat down behind his massive mahogany desk. There were no papers on its surface, nothing to indicate that he'd been working.

'I can only spare you a few minutes. I have to leave for an important meeting at the Welsh Assembly.'

Not a word of sympathy for his murdered waitress,

Matt noted, more concerned that he emphasised his own importance.

'What can you tell me about Ms Hughes?' Matt asked. 'How long did she work for you? Was she a good member of staff? It's helpful to know the background of a murder victim.'

Llewellyn frowned, as if the subject of murder was distasteful. 'You'll need to ask my son. He acts as manager here. He's the one who has the most contact with the staff.'

'So there's nothing you can tell us that will help in our investigation?'

'Nothing, I'm afraid, inspector.'

Was the man being deliberately obstructive? Matt knew from his discussion with Bill Symonds that Llewellyn had disciplined Cassie Davies for taking a phone call from Dylan Rogers about Rianna's disappearance.

Matt was tempted to mention that Rianna had served him and his son when they'd dined with Aled Ingram, the Welsh Government minister, and that she'd overheard their conversation. That might put a dent in his superior attitude, but Matt decided to keep that for later.

There was a sharp tap on the door, and Griff Llewellyn strode into the room. Matt and Beth stood.

'I must leave now,' Rhodri Llewellyn said. 'My son can help you with anything else you need to know.'

'Just one final question,' Matt said. 'Can you tell me where you were last Tuesday morning?'

Llewellyn glared angrily at Matt. For a moment Matt thought he wasn't going to reply. After a pause, he said, 'At Clebaston Manor.'

Matt held his gaze. 'Is there someone we can ask who can confirm that?'

'Downright impertinence,' Llewellyn said, and stormed from the room.

Beth went over and closed the door, which Llewellyn had left open.

Griff went and stood behind the mahogany desk. 'What was it you wanted to know?'

'We're conducting a murder inquiry,' Matt said, disgusted by the Llewellyns' arrogance and lack of compassion. 'We need to interview anyone who knew Rianna Hughes or came into contact with her in the days leading up to her murder. Perhaps we could sit down?'

Griff sat behind the desk and gestured towards the two chairs in front of it.

'How long have you known Ms Hughes?' Matt asked, as he sat back down. Beth moved her chair slightly away from Matt's, before she sat again too.

Griff drummed his finger tips on the desk, as if impatient for the interview to be over. 'About two years. She came to work here the summer before last.'

'Was she a good member of staff? Did she get on well with people?'

'She was attractive, personable. The guests all liked her.'

'What was your relationship with her?'

'What d'you mean, relationship?' Griff said. 'I'm the manager here. She's a waitress. What are you implying?'

'You've said that she was attractive and personable. I thought it was a reasonable question to ask.'

When Griff didn't reply, Matt said, 'So you never spoke to her outside of the hotel?'

Griff remained silent.

'She was seen getting into your car after service finished late one evening last week.'

Griff turned red and banged his fist down on the desk. 'This is ridiculous. What are you trying to prove?'

Beth moved slightly, attracting Griff's attention.

He stared at her for a moment, then said

triumphantly, 'I recognise you! You're that woman who was snooping around Clebaston Manor last night. You were spying on me, weren't you?'

What was Griff talking about? Matt turned to Beth and saw that her face was turning a delicate shade of pink. What had she been up to? Now wasn't the time, but as soon as they left, Sergeant Beth Francis would have some explaining to do, and her explanations had better be good.

'It's your movements I'm interested in,' Matt said.

'Didn't think I'd recognise you? Took your time reversing out of my way, didn't you?' Griff ranted at Beth. 'You were on private property, trespassing. This is police harassment,' he said, turning back to Matt.

Anger bubbled up inside Matt. Beth Francis was a liability, one he could well do without.

Matt eventually quietened Griff down and pulled the interview back to where it should have been all along.

'Was there anyone on the staff who didn't get along with Ms Hughes? Anyone who might bear a grudge against her?'

Griff shrugged. 'Maybe some of the other waitresses. Rianna was very popular with the guests. They gave her the biggest tips.'

'Don't the staff share the tips, divide them up between each other?'

Griff shrugged. 'I don't know. You'd need to ask them.'

'Where were you last Tuesday morning?'

'Here. I'm the manager.'

'Do you live in, or do you travel here every day?'

Griff started drumming his fingers on the desk again. 'I have a room here I can use, but last Tuesday I drove in from home, from Clebaston Manor.'

'What time did you arrive?'

Griff looked uncomfortable. 'I can't remember

precisely. Around half-eight, maybe nine o'clock.'

So, Matt thought, Griff could have intercepted Rianna on the coast path, hit her over the head with a rock, pushed her over the edge into the sea, and then driven on to the hotel. From the look on his face, Griff knew that he didn't have an alibi for the time when Rianna was murdered.

'Can anyone can vouch for the time that you left Clebaston Hall,' Matt asked, 'or for the time that you arrived here, at the hotel?'

'The housekeeper would have seen me leave Clebaston Hall, and the receptionist here would have seen me arrive,' Griff said. 'Ask them, if you must. Now if that's all, I have work to do.'

*****

'What were you doing, following Griff Llewellyn to Clebaston Manor?' Matt demanded, as soon as they were back outside the hotel. You didn't tell me about that.'

'You told me to follow up on the woman I saw arguing with Ross Keely, Rianna's travel and tourism lecturer. Wendy Pryce.'

'That doesn't explain why you went to Clebaston Manor and had a run-in with Griff Llewellyn.'

Matt was furious to have a suspect in a murder case know more about what his sergeant was up to than he did. Beth met his gaze, apparently unrepentant. Matt would soon see about that.

'I went back to the college to find out more about Wendy Pryce.' Beth said. 'She's a senior lecturer in archaeology from Bangor. While I was there, I saw a man pick her up in a Porsche. I didn't know it was Griff Llewellyn. I'd never met the man before. I followed them to Clebaston Manor, but they drove back out as I was driving in. We met on the single track road leading to the manor's entrance gates. It's all logged on the system.'

Matt inhaled and exhaled to calm himself before speaking.

'So, you followed a murder suspect without telling me.'

'He wasn't a murder suspect at the time. Neither was she.'

'What do you mean, they weren't murder suspects at the time?'

Beth avoided his gaze.

'We didn't know the results of the post mortem then.'

Matt stared at Beth in disbelief.

'When did all this this happen?

'The night before last.'

Anger erupted inside him. 'You haven't told me what you've been doing. You've had plenty of opportunity to update me yesterday and today, but you haven't said a word. Instead you adopt a pathetic attempt at a disguise and hope that Griff Llewellyn won't recognise you. In the end I only find out what you've been doing from a suspect.'

'I was acting on my initiative,' Beth said. 'You seemed to like it when little Ms Marple went searching along the coast path by herself.'

'That's impertinence, and you know it,' Matt said. 'I've already warned you about bad mouthing colleagues. I'll not warn you again. Next time, and there had better not be a next time, it'll be a written warning on your record. Understood?'

'Yes, sir.'

'And if you withhold vital information again, it'll be disciplinary action and I'll see that you're kicked out of the force. Understood?'

'Yes, sir.'

'Is there anything else you haven't told me? Any more unexpected surprises?'

'No, Sir.'

Matt didn't think he'd handled that well. How could he have done it better? He thought back to Dilwyn's advice on how to manage Beth. "Slap her down, soon as she gets uppity. It's the only way."

He'd have to find out why Beth acted the way she did. He knew he'd deprived her of the inspector post that she thought was hers, but was that the whole explanation? He shook his head. It shouldn't be necessary, but he'd ask around. Dilwyn's advice didn't address the underlying cause of the problem, whatever that was.

CHAPTER 18

Beth was in a vile mood. Not only had DI Matt Bloody Vincent given her a second dressing down in as many days, but he'd had the gall to threaten her with a written warning and disciplinary action. And now little Ms Marple had risen even higher in the DI's good books. She'd discovered that Wendy Pryce was the county's archaeological advisor. It didn't take a brilliant detective to work that out. Beth mentally kicked herself for not making the link first.

She took a deep breath and exhaled slowly. She'd need to tread carefully and be on her guard. A written warning on her record was the last thing she needed. If it came to disciplinary action, she didn't rate her chances highly. She'd rubbed up too many people the wrong way.

What to do? She'd given up on anger management counselling. Maybe she should give mindfulness a shot. That was all the rage. Hmmm, maybe not the best choice of words.

She drove up the slope into the college car park. Each time she came to the college, the students looked younger. What was she doing with her life, acting as Matt Vincent's chauffeur? The detective inspector job should have been hers, not his.

'I'll lead the questioning,' Matt said, as Beth parked in a visitor parking space at the front of the college.

Of course you will, Beth thought bitterly.

Ten minutes later they were sitting in a small tutorial room with Wendy Pryce. She didn't look as smartly dressed as she had when Griff Llewellyn picked her up in his Porsche and drove her to the family home at Clebaston Manor. Today she was wearing faded jeans and a shapeless grey sweater. She was about the same age as Beth, mid-thirties. Her best attribute was her glossy black hair. Other than that, she looked rather plain.

Now Beth knew more, she guessed the Llewellyns were greasing Ms Pryce's palm, bribing her not to oppose their planning application for the Clebaston Manor Resort.

'We're investigating the murder of Rianna Hughes,' Matt said, after the introductions were over.

'So why do you want to speak with me?' Wendy Pryce asked.

'Because you knew Ms Hughes.'

She glanced at Beth and then back at Matt.

'There is a student here called Rianna, but she's not one of mine.'

'How do you know Rianna, if she isn't one of your students?' Matt asked.

Wendy squirmed uncomfortably on her chair and started fiddling with the ends of her hair.

'If it's the same Rianna, she's friendly with one of the other lecturers, Ross Keely.'

'And what is your relationship with Ross Keely?'

'What business is that of yours?' Wendy said, colouring up.

'We're building up a picture of Ms Hughes's social circle and her movements over her last few days,' Matt said. 'When did you last see or speak to her?'

'I don't think I've ever spoken to her.'

That was a lie, and the DI knew it too. Why was he letting her off the hook? Why didn't he go straight for the jugular? Instead he looked at the Pryce woman, like it was a staring match. Sounds percolated in from outside. Students chattering as they walked past the window; a helicopter clattering by overhead.

Matt broke the silence. 'Can you tell me what you were doing between the hours of six and nine am last Tuesday morning?'

Wendy looked increasingly nervous, alternately tucking her hair behind her ear and pulling at her ear lobe. 'Same as I always do. Got out of bed, showered, grabbed some breakfast, got dressed, came in to work.'

'Can anyone corroborate that?'

'No! What is this? Are you trying to say I killed her?'

'Did you?'

'No!'

'Why did you lie to me just now, when you said you didn't think you'd ever spoken to Rianna Hughes?'

'What d'you mean?'

'I've been told that you and Ms Hughes were fighting over Mr Keely's affections. That you told her to keep off and she threatened to "grease the stairs" for you.'

Wendy sat bolt upright, like a dog poised to attack. 'Ross Keely doesn't do affection,' she snarled. 'All he's interested in is sex. She wanted him to up her grades, make sure she passed. Perhaps he didn't, she threatened him, and he killed her.'

Wendy slumped back in her chair, seemingly exhausted by her outburst. If they needed a motive, she'd spelt it out for them – raging jealousy.

'I'd like you to tell me about the Llewellyns' plans for the Clebaston Manor Resort,' Matt said, changing tack.

'What about them?'

'Is it true that the remains of a monastery are where the Llewellyns plan to construct the resort's accommodation block?'

Wendy straightened up, tucking her hair behind her ears. She looked sharply at Matt, then quickly glanced away. Beth imagined she could see the synapses in Wendy's brain flashing while she decided what to say.

'A few locals came up with an old wives' tale,' Wendy said. 'Nothing credible.'

Beth wondered how much the Llewellyns were paying her.

'So nothing that would delay approval of the planning application?' Matt persisted.

Wendy was back to squirming uncomfortably. She didn't answer.

They must be paying her a lot, Beth thought.

'Tell me, what's your role in the planning process?' Matt asked.

'I'm the county archaeological advisor,' she said, thrusting her chin forward. 'It's a part-time post.'

'So if you recommend a site investigation, geophysics, a dig etc., then the planning application would be put on hold until the results come back?'

'Yes.' Wendy's face was turning decidedly pink, like a little child who's been caught stealing sweets.

Matt stared at her for what seemed like an eternity. Then he said, 'Do you believe that the Vespasian Legendary, written about 1200AD, is an old wives' tale? There's a passage in it recounting the construction of a monastery by Archbishop Egwad. The description of the location matches pretty well with the proposed site of the Clebaston Manor Resort's new accommodation block.'

'That's nonsense,' Wendy said, 'just a half-baked idea an undergraduate came up with in a third year dissertation. Not worth the paper it's written on.'

'That's not what her supervisor thought.'

Wendy banged her fist on the table. 'I'm not answering any more questions, not unless I have my solicitor present.'

'We may ask you to attend a formal interview at the police station. If you wish, you can bring a solicitor with you then,' Matt said. 'Sergeant Francis, can you give Ms Pryce your card? Ms Pryce, please keep

Sergeant Francis informed of your whereabouts if you intend to leave the area, even for the briefest of times?'

Wendy snatched the card from Beth and stormed from the room, slamming the door behind her.

'Why didn't you arrest her?' Beth demanded. 'She couldn't provide an alibi, she had an obvious motive, and she could easily have picked up a rock and whacked Rianna Hughes over the head with it.'

'She's obviously insanely jealous,' Matt said, 'but, apart from that, we don't have any evidence against her. Interesting that she pointed the finger at Ross Keely. What did you make of him?'

'Like Pryce said, all he's interested in is sex. Complaints from parents of young female students. Says it all.'

'Yes, but could he have killed Rianna?'

'Why would he? They were using each other, Ross for sex, Rianna for better grades. If she tried blackmailing him, he might have killed her to keep her quiet, but I don't see why she would have.'

'True,' Matt said. 'Again no alibi but no evidence either. Let's keep him on the list of suspects, interview him again later.'

CHAPTER 19

Cassie couldn't stop thinking about Rianna and what had happened to her. It was horrible, first her body being found on the beach at Petroc Sands. Then, even worse, the news that she'd been murdered. Penny had seen it on Twitter. "Dyfed-Powys police open murder enquiry."

It was a little while before lunch service was due to begin. The few occupied rooms were all made up. Cassie decided to seek out Bill Symonds. She couldn't find him in the scullery. The dishwashers were ready to be unloaded, but Bill was nowhere to be seen. He must have stepped out for a smoke.

Sure enough, there he was behind the bins, puffing on a cigarette, holding a whispered conversation with Huw Rogers, Dylan's dad.

Huw was whispering, '...not a word to anyone. It's our little secret.'

Bill tapped his nose with his finger and gave Huw a wink.

'Okay if I join you?' Cassie asked, curious to know what they were talking about. 'I can't bear it in there. I needed some air.'

'Of course you can,' Bill replied. 'Shocking news, isn't it?'

Huw shook his head. 'The police must have got it wrong. Surely no one would have wanted to murder Ree. She must have just slipped and fallen off the path.'

Cassie shivered but it wasn't just the cold February air. She'd walked the coast path hundreds of times, often taking Whiskey for a walk when her dad was too busy.

'I'm sure Matt Vincent wouldn't have called it murder,' Bill said, 'unless he had the evidence to back it up.'

'It must have been a visitor,' Cassie said. 'No one from the village could have done such a thing.'

Bill took a drag on his cigarette and blew out a long plume of smoke. He sighed and said, 'Not many visitors around, this time of year.'

There was an uncomfortable silence, except for the sounds of the distant sea and the occasional squawk from the gulls. Cassie felt sick at Bill's implication.

'There's always a few twitchers around,' Huw said.

Bill shook his head, frowning. 'I don't like to say it, but I think the answer's closer to home.'

Cassie clutched her shirt at her throat. 'You mean someone we know did it? That's too horrible for words.'

'If she was murdered,' Huw said, 'and I don't believe it for one moment, it must have been an outsider.'

Cassie's throat tightened. She felt empty, hollowed out. 'They could do it again. Kill any one of us.'

She looked anxiously at Bill 'Is that what you think?'

'It's a possibility. You should take care. No more cycling home alone after dark. It's too risky while there's a murderer out there on the loose.'

'But how else can I get to and from work? Griff offered me a lift home in his Porsche last night, but I'm not up for that.'

Huw stared at her. 'You don't think he's the murderer, do you? One of them serial killers?'

Bill laughed. 'Of course she doesn't, you idiot. Cassie's scared of a fate worse than death, aren't you love?'

Huw frowned. 'From the way the girls flock around him, Cassie must be the only one. Most of them would be only too willing to jump into that flash car of his.'

'Well I'm not one of them,' Cassie said. She could feel the heat spreading up her neck and face. 'If he tries it on with me, he'll get my knee where it hurts.'

She jumped with fright as Griff Llewellyn suddenly appeared round the bins shouting, 'Come on, back to work you lot!' '

His face was scowling and red.

'You're not being paid to stand out here gossiping. If I catch you skulking here again, you'll all be fired.'

As they hurried back into the hotel, Bill whispered to Cassie, 'You don't think he overheard what we were saying, do you?'

'He must have,' Cassie said. 'He could have been standing there for ages, listening.' She chuckled quietly. 'At least he knows what to expect if he tries it on with me.'

*****

That evening after dinner service was over, laying up the tables for breakfast lacked the usual giggles and laughter. None of the girls were discussing their latest dates or plans for nights out. All were silent, immersed in their own gloomy thoughts. Rianna was the loudest and liveliest of the waitresses, always entertaining them with tales of her scrapes and conquests. Now they'd never hear her voice again.

Some were jealous of Rianna's good looks and worldly ways, but knowing that she had been murdered cloaked them all in fear. Who was her killer? Would he strike again?

Cassie was dreading the bike ride back to the vicarage along the dark country lanes.

Ellie touched Cassie's arm and said in a low voice, 'Can I give you a lift home?'

Cassie was surprised. Ellie was two years older than her and they had never been good friends. They had very different backgrounds and interests.

'Thanks for the offer,' Cassie said, 'but how would I get to work in the morning? I'd have to leave my bike here.'

'I'll pick you up. You can come in with me.'

Cassie desperately wanted to accept. It was her determination to be independent that stopped her. She didn't want to be reliant on anyone.

'Please,' Ellie pleaded. 'I don't want to drive home alone.'

'I know how you feel,' Cassie said. 'Of course you can give me a lift. I must be off my head to have even hesitated.'

'Goodnight, Bill!' Cassie and Ellie called out as they walked out of the hotel. 'See you in the morning!'

As they stepped beyond the pool of light surrounding the hotel, Cassie could see that the sky was clear. The stars of the Milky Way gave a faint, silvery light, but it was a moonless night, bitingly cold. Cassie shivered, and it wasn't just from the frosty air.

She'd taken the lamp from her bike, and now she shone it around them as they walked towards Ellie's car, a small Toyota that had seen better days.

Apprehension gripped Cassie. The murderer could be crouched between the parked cars. She jumped and let out a yelp as Ellie clasped her hand.

'Sorry,' Ellie said. 'Didn't mean to frighten you. I've never felt scared like this before. I always thought it was safe here.'

Cassie heard the jangle of Ellie's keys. Her car gave a bleep and its headlights came on, blinding them temporarily.

They climbed quickly in and Ellie locked the doors.

Cassie heard Ellie's sigh of relief. Cassie was fearful, but not as scared as Ellie obviously was.

Ellie was a cautious driver, threading her way along the narrow lanes.

'What was that?' Cassie said, as they passed a

narrow track that led away back to the left.

'What?' Ellie asked.

'I thought I saw someone parked down that lane,' Cassie said. 'Unusual. I don't know what they could have been doing there.'

Ellie laughed. 'Lucky someone. Probably making out.'

It wasn't long before Ellie was pulling up outside the vicarage. Its sitting room, study and porch lights were on.

'Thanks for the lift,' Cassie said. 'Send me a message to let me know you've arrived safely home.'

'Will do,' Ellie said.

Cassie's father opened the front door as she walked up the path. She turned and waved. Ellie flashed her lights and drove off into the night.

*****

Bill was worried for the young girls who worked at the hotel. What had happened to Rianna was shocking. He couldn't imagine who could have snuffed out her life. It was a terrible thing to do. Whatever anyone's faults, they didn't deserve to be murdered. He feared that whoever had done it might take another life.

He finished tidying the scullery, putting away the pots and pans, making sure the surfaces were clean and tidy and that the floor was swept and mopped.

He shook his head. What would become of Rianna's daughter, Meg? He felt sorry for Dylan, but perhaps he'd get his home and his daughter back, now that Rianna was gone.

Bill couldn't imagine Rhodri Llewellyn giving Dylan his job back. He was a hard, unforgiving man.

Dylan may have a quick temper, but Bill liked the young man. He was never idle, not like many of his generation, who didn't know the meaning of work.

'You still here?' Griff Llewellyn poked his nose into

the room. 'Thought you'd have finished and gone home by now.'

Bill didn't like young Master Griff. Too many airs and graces. Born with a silver spoon in his mouth, as Bill's grandma used to say. Never done a hard day's work in his life.

'All done now,' Bill said. 'I'll be off and away. Goodnight.'

Unless it was pouring with rain and blowing a gale, Bill enjoyed walking home on a clear starry night. He delighted in watching bats swooping along the lanes catching insects or barn owls drifting silently over the fields and meadows. He'd have to wait for spring before he'd be seeing those, but he might see an occasional fox or badger prowling their territories in search of food.

Bill walked on past the track that led back towards the common. Here, far from any habitation where there wasn't a house for miles, the black velvet sky glittered with swathes of stars. The Plough, Orion, Bill knew all of the major constellations, loved picking them out from the countless multitude of their companions. He searched for Mars and Saturn, but couldn't spot either.

The banks of the lane became higher along the next stretch of the road, restricting Bill's view of the night sky.

The solitude was broken by the distant sound of a vehicle starting up. It was a diesel from the engine note, probably a Land Rover. Odd. With no farm buildings or houses nearby, where could it have been parked? Maybe it was a young couple out courting, but surely it was too cold for that, not without leaving the engine running.

It sounded like it was coming his way. Bill hoped he'd get to the passing bay before it reached him. There was hardly enough room for a vehicle to get past him.

CHAPTER 20

Alys woke with the memory of the Armel Arms still on her mind. How dare Matt Vincent lecture her on behaving professionally? It was his Rottweiler sergeant who'd stepped out of line. Had she deliberately let Alys overhear her disparaging comments?

Alys gulped down a quick breakfast, jumped into her car. She was heading for Madoc's Haven when Ivor Jones called on the radio.

'Yes Ivor, what is it?'

'Hi Sarge. Been a hit-and-run. Bill Symonds. He's in a bad way. Not sure he'll make it.'

'Whereabouts?' Alys asked, alarm bells ringing in her head.

'On the back road from Madoc's Haven to the Madoc's Bay Hotel.'

'Who found him?'

'Penny Evans. She's pretty badly shaken up. She had to drive back to the village to get a signal before she could dial 999. Luckily she spotted Julie Bowen, the district nurse, getting into her car. Julie phoned me.'

'What's the situation now?'

'Julie's with Bill, doing what she can while we wait for the paramedics. Hold on.'

Alys could hear a loud noise in the background before Ivor's voice eventually came back on the line.

'Air ambulance has just flown over. I signalled them where to go. I'm blocking the road at the Madoc's Haven end. We need to get one of the team to block it at the hotel end too.'

'Call one of the PCSOs. Try Fliss first. If she can't, give Holly a call. I'll be there in fifteen minutes myself. And contact Detective Sergeant Beth Francis. Update her on the situation.'

Alys ended the call, turned on her blue lights, and focussed on driving. What was going on? She couldn't believe that Bill being knocked down wasn't connected with Rianna Hughes' death. It was too much of a coincidence. What had he seen, heard or done that made him a danger to the murderer?

*****

Cassie was wide awake when her alarm went off in the morning. It was still dark outside. She shivered as she climbed out of bed and pulled on her dressing gown. She padded across the landing into the bathroom and pulled the cord to turn on the wall heater. It was about time the church shelled out on central heating for the vicarage.

She hadn't slept well. When she was awake, she thought of Rianna and who could have killed her. Her periods of sleep were populated by nightmares. She wouldn't feel safe until the police caught the murderer and he was locked away behind bars.

Washed, but not refreshed, Cassie went down to the kitchen and made herself toast and marmalade and a bowl of muesli. She couldn't face serving breakfast to the hotel guests without something in her stomach.

Her dad wasn't awake so, when she saw Ellie drive up in her car, she let herself out quietly. She wished she had a car of her own, but there was no way she could afford one. She didn't know how Ellie managed.

'Hi Ellie,' Cassie said, as she climbed in. 'Thanks for picking me up.'

The short drive from Ellie's house had been enough to take the chill off the air in the car, for which Cassie was grateful.

Ellie drove out of the village on the main road, but when they reached the turning for the road along the coast towards the hotel, Cassie saw that it was blocked off by a police car with its blue lights flashing. She could just make out Ivor Jones as he got out to stand beside it.

Fear clutched her as she realised that something dreadful must have happened.

Ivor stepped to the side of their car as Ellie powered down the window.

'Morning Ms Jenkins, Ms Davis,' Ivor said. 'There's been an accident. You'll have to go the long way round to the hotel.'

'What's happened?' Cassie demanded. 'Has someone been hurt?'

'I'm afraid so,' Ivor said. 'It's Bill Symonds.'

'Is he badly hurt?' Cassie crossed her fingers, as if that would make any difference.

'He's being taken to the hospital in Haverfordwest. We'll know more later.'

Cassie felt her chest constrict and dizziness overwhelmed her. She sensed Ivor opening her door and unfastening her seat belt.

His muffled voice came to her, as if through a blanket of cotton wool. 'Swing your legs out of the door and put your head between your knees. You stay like that for a minute or two, Ms Davis. You've had a bad shock.'

*****

Matt woke early to prepare for his first case as senior investigating officer. He felt sympathy for Rianna's friends and family, in particular for little baby Meg, but his overwhelming feeling was one of excitement. This was what he'd trained hard to do. Catch murderers.

His most obvious suspect, Dylan Rogers, had an alibi provided by the landlord of the Black Boar Inn.

Either Dylan's alibi was unsound, or Matt would need to look further afield for Rianna's murderer.

He'd only just set out when the call came from Control.

'Thought you'd like to know, sir. We've just had a 999 call from Madoc's Haven. Apparent hit and run accident. Victim's a white male, in his sixties, critical condition. Paramedics in attendance attempting to stabilise his condition. Provisionally identified as Bill Symonds.'

'That's odd. I met him on Wednesday,' Matt said. 'Works as a kitchen porter at the Madoc's Bay Hotel.'

What was going on? Bill Symonds being seriously injured in a hit and run accident within a few days of Rianna dying was too much of a coincidence to be unrelated.

'Thank you Control,' Matt said. 'Who else have you alerted?'

'Ambulance and the neighbourhood policing team sergeant, Alys Carey. She was already on her way to the incident when I called.'

How did Alys get onto the case so quickly? She was obviously plugged into the local grapevine. She wouldn't be effective at her job if she wasn't.

A few minutes after talking to Control, his phone rang and Beth's number came up on the dashboard screen.

'Morning, Sir,' Beth said, when he answered the call. 'You've heard the news about Bill Symonds?'

'Yes. Any news on his condition?'

'None yet. He's in a bad way. Unconscious when he was found.'

'Who found him?'

'Receptionist from the Madoc's Bay Hotel, Penny Evans.'

'What else do we know?'

'Paramedics think he'd been lying there for several

hours before Evans discovered him. Multiple injuries. Said it's a miracle he's still alive.'

'I'm treating this as attempted murder,' Matt told Beth. 'We need a medical report on Symonds' injuries, and we need a forensics team at the site of the incident. If the impact was hard enough to cause multiple injuries, there'll be damage to the vehicle, maybe fragments to help identify it. We'll need Symonds' clothes as well, for trace evidence.'

'Scenes of Crime are on their way, sir,' Beth said. 'As soon as Control called, I assumed you'd be treating it as suspicious.'

'Excellent,' Matt said. 'I'll meet you in Madoc's Haven and we'll decide on next steps there.'

Matt changed down a gear and accelerated past a slow moving lorry. Who would want Bill Symonds dead? There was no shortage of likely motives for Rianna's killing, but none of them applied to Bill. Could it be something he'd seen or overheard?

CHAPTER 21

'What's going on?' Griff Llewellyn demanded, as Alys arrived and stepped out of her car. 'You can't just close a road without any warning. Tell her to get her car out of the way.'

Fliss Abbott, one of Alys's police community support officers, had her car parked blocking the road that led towards Madoc's Haven. She looked pink and flustered.

'My staff can't get through from Madoc's Haven,' Griff said angrily, stepping forward into Alys's personal space. 'I have an hotel full of guests and only half my staff have arrived. It's a disgrace.'

'Please step back sir,' Alys said, keeping her voice neutral and holding his gaze, while her fight-or-flight response started to kick in. 'Officer Abbott is acting under orders. There has been ...'

'Whose orders?' Griff demanded, not moving.

'Mine,' Alys said. 'There's been ...'

'How d'you expect me to run an hotel if my staff can't get through?' Griff demanded, his voice rising. 'Tell her to get that vehicle out of the way,'

Adrenaline flooded Alys's body. She was tempted to tell him that running the hotel wasn't her problem. Instead she placed her hand on his chest and applied gentle pressure. 'I asked you to step back, sir.'

She held Griff's stare, saw his anger mounting. She hoped that her unarmed combat and forcible arrest training were up to the task. She was torn. Her rational self wanted him to back down, but her more primitive side wanted him to go for it.

After a moment's stand-off, he looked down and shuffled back.

'There's been an accident on the road to Madoc's Haven,' Alys told him, her calm voice at odds with her feelings. 'A person has been seriously injured. The air ambulance is in attendance.'

Griff said nothing, but his fists were clenching and unclenching. He was a bully. Alys knew his response would be verbal, not physical.

'I suggest you explain about the accident to your guests,' Alys said. 'The road to Madoc's Haven is likely to remain closed all day, so you should consider making alternative arrangements for staff travelling from the village.'

Alys didn't feel obliged to tell him that he would need a new kitchen porter, and that some of his waitresses were in a state of shock and would be unlikely to be coming to work, whatever their travel arrangements. If he hadn't been so aggressive, she would have been more helpful.

'I'll be making a complaint to the chief constable about your officious behaviour,' Griff blustered. 'You've not heard the last of this.'

'That is your right, sir,' Alys said. 'Would you like to see my warrant card? Write down my name and number?'

Griff glared at her, turned on his heel and marched off down the driveway to the hotel.

Alys let out a long sigh as the tension began to melt away. Turning to Fliss Abbott, she said, 'Are you okay? I'm sorry you had to face him alone.'

Fliss looked drained. 'Just about. Thanks for coming to my rescue, sarge.' She took a deep breath and slowly exhaled, shaking her head sadly. 'What a bastard. He didn't even ask who was injured. Not an ounce of compassion or sympathy.'

CHAPTER 22

'Have forensics arrived yet?' Matt asked, after he'd introduced himself and Beth to PC Ivor Jones, Alys Carey's number two on the Madoc's Haven Neighbourhood Team.

Ivor's police car was parked blocking the turning from the main road towards the Madoc's Bay Hotel. He'd strung blue and white police tape across the side road. A red and white "Road Closed" sign emphasised the point.

Three other cars were parked on the grass verge a little further along. A young woman, obviously a freelance press photographer, took photos and attempted to ask them questions, but Matt shook his head and Beth held up her hand to deter her.

'Not yet, Sir,' Ivor replied. He quickly briefed Matt and Beth, and explained that the air ambulance had already taken the victim, Bill Symonds, to A&E in Haverfordwest.

'Have any other vehicles driven along the road since the incident?' Matt asked.

'Penny Evans, she found Bill lying there when she was driving to work, Julie Bowen, the district nurse. I followed Julie before coming back to block the road at this end.'

'How about from the other direction?'

Ivor shook his head. 'Probably not, or they'd have reported it. I called Sergeant Carey. She and one of the PCSOs are blocking the other end.'

'I don't suppose anyone had the common sense to photograph the scene before the body was moved,'

Beth said.

Matt noticed Ivor's body tense. That's right Beth, he thought, open your mouth and put your foot in it. His sergeant really had no interpersonal skills.

'I took several photos with my phone while Julie was attending to Bill,' Ivor said, speaking to Matt, and pointedly turning away from Beth. 'I photographed some fragments of glass or plastic, possibly a broken headlight lens cover, on the road. Looked like there's blood on them. I avoided treading on them or moving them, and kept Julie and the paramedics clear of them too.'

'Good man,' Matt said.

'Best I could do until the SOCOs arrive,' Ivor said, apologetically.

'Well done,' Beth said, belatedly.

Perhaps she'd noticed the expressions on Ivor and Matt's faces after her initial comment.

'Speaking of SOCOs, here they are now,' Ivor said.

A white police van with its yellow and blue checkerboard markings pulled up at the roadside, and two Scenes of Crime Officers climbed out. Matt recognised them from previously when they'd been searching the clifftop where Rianna had died.

'Keeping us busy,' the team leader said. 'Twice in three days. We'll have to recruit more staff if you keep this up.'

'Best of luck finding the budget for that,' Matt said. 'We'll leave you to it. Witnesses and suspects to interview. Let us know what you find. I'm particularly interested in the fragments of glass or plastic that could come from a headlight lens cover. The make and model of the vehicle they came from would be great.'

*****

'So,' Matt said, as Beth drove him the long way around to the Madoc's Bay Hotel. 'What are your thoughts on the hit-and-run?'

Beth glanced at him sharply before focussing back on the road. Perhaps she wasn't used to a DI picking her brain, but Matt liked to ask his team member's opinions. They might have a different perspective on a crime to his, and it helped him form a judgement of their intelligence and capabilities.

'Not an accident,' she said. 'Too much of a coincidence coming so soon after Rianna's death.'

'Go on,' Matt prompted. 'Motive?'

Beth shrugged. 'Symonds saw, found or overheard something that could incriminate Rianna's killer. Somehow the killer realised, so decided to silence Symonds by running him down.'

'So, if we find Rianna's murderer,' Matt said, 'then we've identified the person who attempted to kill Symonds.'

'It could work the other way round,' Beth said. 'Identify the hit-and-run driver, and you've found Rianna's killer.'

'Where should we look for suspects?'

'Where we're going,' Beth said. 'The Madoc's Bay Hotel.'

'Any favourites?'

Beth was silent for a while. Matt wasn't sure if she was concentrating on driving, or thinking before she answered. Eventually she said, 'I'd like it to be Rhodri or Griff Llewellyn. Affluent, arrogant, stuck up bastards, the pair of them.'

'Personal prejudices aside, do either of them seem likely killers?'

Beth drove on, not answering, so Matt said, 'Can you imagine Rhodri Llewellyn, prominent hotelier and property developer, crouching in a gully on the cliff top, suddenly jumping out and whacking Rianna on the head with a rock, before pushing her over the edge into the sea?'

'I suppose not,' Beth said reluctantly, but then, brightening up, 'He could have paid someone else to do it.'

'Motive?'

'Money, greed, corruption. Didn't I see in the file that Rianna overheard a conversation between the Llewellyns and Aled Ingram, the Welsh Government minister? Maybe she tried to blackmail Rhodri.'

Matt was pleased that Beth had kept up to speed with what was logged in the murder file. It compensated for her failings, notably her lack of tact.

'How about Griff Llewellyn?' Matt asked.

'Younger and more agile than his dad. I can imagine him clobbering Rianna on the cliff top and pushing her off. Same motive as his dad.'

'Rianna was seen leaving the hotel one night with Griff in his Porsche,' Matt said. 'Bill told me that Griff wasn't happy if the girls didn't give him what he wanted. Vicky suggested that Rianna didn't.'

'Bit extreme as a motive,' Beth said. 'If he wanted sex, I'm guessing he had plenty of women queuing up. Stopping Rianna's attempts at blackmail seems a more likely motive.'

CHAPTER 23

Cedric Davies heard a car come to a halt outside the vicarage and looked up from the sermon he was writing for the Sunday service in Llanbrioc. The Church of Saint Aidan in Llanbrioc was one of several churches where Cedric conducted services. There were insufficient funds for each of the small rural churches to have a vicar its own.

Cedric was surprised to see his daughter getting out of Julie Bowen's car and walking up to the front door. Julie had her arm around Cassie's shoulder. What was happening? It wasn't long since Ellie had collected Cassie to drive her to work at the hotel. Why was the district nurse bringing Cassie home?

Cedric opened the front door to let them in. 'What's wrong? Are you ill?' he asked. Cassie looked pale and upset. Nurse Bowen didn't look much better either.

'Bill Symonds has been seriously injured,' Julie Bowen said. 'Cassie's in shock, so I've brought her home. Can you make her a hot drink and look after her? Ellie Jenkins drove herself home, but I need to look in on her to make sure she's okay.'

'What happened?' Cedric asked as he detached Cassie from the district nurse and gave her a hug. 'Did Ellie and Bill have a collision?'

'No,' Julie said. 'It looks like Bill was the victim of a hit-and-run accident last night.' She gave an hysterical laugh. 'Ivor doesn't think he'll make it.'

'You're in shock too,' Cedric said. 'Come in and I'll make you both a hot drink.'

'I must visit Ellie,' Julie said over her shoulder as

she turned and started back towards her car. 'Penny Evans too. She's the one who found Bill.'

Cedric watched Julie drive away, then he took Cassie into the house, all thoughts of his sermon banished from his mind.

'I'll phone the hotel,' Cedric told Cassie. 'I'll tell them you're not coming in to work today.'

*****

Cassie was sleeping fitfully in her bedroom with the curtains drawn when her mobile phone's ringtone jerked her awake. For a moment she was disorientated, unable to distinguish between her dream and reality. Why was she asleep during the day with her curtains closed?

She picked up her phone and glanced at the screen. It was the hotel. Then her memory came flooding back and tears filled her eyes. She pressed the answer icon. 'Yes?'

'Is that Cassie Davies?'

Cassie recognised the voice. It was Griff Llewellyn. Her phone said it was mid-afternoon. She thought her dad had told the hotel she wasn't coming in. What did he want?

'Yes,' she said.

'I need you to come in for evening dinner service,' Griff said. 'The restaurant's fully booked and we can't let the guests down. When can I expect you in?'

'I'm too upset,' Cassie said. 'I thought my father told you. I'm still in shock after Rianna's murder and Bill being knocked down. Nurse Bowen told me I should take the day off work.'

'How do you expect the hotel to serve its guests if you decide to take random days off? It's irresponsible. Do you expect them to wait on themselves?'

Cassie wanted to tell him to wait on them himself, but she was in debt after college and couldn't afford to lose the job.

'If I pay you double-time for this evening, and don't dock you for missing breakfast and lunch service today, will you come in?'

Cassie felt indignant. Accepting twice the rate of pay because someone had tried to kill Bill, and may have succeeded, didn't seem right.

'I can't cycle to the hotel and back home again,' she said, 'not after what's happened. I wouldn't feel safe.'

'Will you come in if I arrange for someone to collect you and drive you home at the end of service? You do want this job, don't you?'

You bastard, Cassie thought. That was a threat. And he hasn't expressed any sympathy for Bill, or for the way I feel.

'I need to talk it over with my dad,' Cassie said. 'Call me back later.' She ended the call without waiting for an answer.

If it wasn't that she needed the money, she'd have stopped working at the hotel ages ago. Griff Llewellyn and Rhodri, his father, didn't give a damn for the staff. They were quick enough to dock the staff's pay if they were a few minutes late, and they treated them like slaves.

Cassie rang Penny and Ellie. They'd both received similar calls from Griff Llewellyn, an unsavoury mixture of bribes and threats.

*****

'It's up to you what you decide,' Cedric told Cassie. 'You're old enough to make up your own mind. Let your conscience guide you.'

I'm not expecting divine intervention, Cassie thought.

'I don't want to be paid overtime,' she said. 'That seems all wrong, profiting from other people's misfortunes.'

'If you decide to stop working for him, in the circumstances he may have to pay a higher wage to get someone else. I can see where you're coming from, but you may be seeing things as a little too black and white.'

Cassie was surprised. She expected her father to take the same moral stance that she did.

'For me, getting to and from work safely is the key issue,' Cedric said. 'I'd never forgive myself if any harm came to you.'

'I don't think I'll ever feel safe going out alone here again,' Cassie said, 'especially not after dark.'

Cedric nodded, but said nothing for a while. Then he suddenly brightened up.

'Is Huw, Dylan's dad, still working at the hotel? Didn't I hear that he was doing up some of the old outbuildings, converting them into holiday apartments?'

'Yes,' Cassie said. 'Cottages actually. He's been at it for weeks. Huw was hoping that Dylan would help him, but Dylan has other plans, and the Llewellyns vetoed it anyway. Dylan's hoping to become a famous chef and open his own restaurant. He was talking about applying for one of those reality TV shows, TopChef or something. Why did you ask?'

'Maybe the hotel would pay for Huw to act as a taxi service for you girls and to stand in for Bill too. You'd feel happy enough having Huw ferrying you to and from the hotel, wouldn't you?'

'Ellie's already agreed to do it.'

'What happens if her car breaks down? It would put my mind at rest knowing that you had Huw to look after you all. He was into martial arts when he was younger, Karate if I remember correctly.'

Cassie thought about it. She didn't really know Huw that well, but he didn't seem to have such a temper as Dylan. He'd always seemed pleasant enough when she'd seen him at work around the hotel. And if he gave a lift to all three of them at the same time, they should be safe enough, shouldn't they?

'I suppose so,' she said, 'but you don't know if the hotel would pay him enough to make it worth his while, and it could delay the conversion of the outbuildings.'

'I'll give Huw a call and speak with Rhodri or Griff.' Cedric said. 'I'll let you know what they say.'

CHAPTER 24

Beth reversed back a hundred yards into a passing bay on the narrow road leading to the Madoc's Bay Hotel. The impatient driver swept past without a word of thanks.

'You should have let me turn on the blue lights and siren,' Beth said. 'Then I could have booked him for obstruction. He'd never have reversed to get out of our way.'

What was it with his sergeant, Matt asked himself. 'We're here to do a job, not to antagonise the public.' Matt told her.

They completed the last mile in silence. As they swept around the final bend, Matt caught sight of Alys. Their eyes met. Matt's inner composure disintegrated. It was the first time they'd seen each other since Alys stormed out of the Armel Arms. He swallowed, his throat suddenly dry. Neither of them smiled.

Alys and a Police Community Support Officer were standing with their cars blocking the road, just beyond the driveway leading down to the hotel.

Beth pulled into the side of the road.

'Good morning, sir' Alys said, as Matt stepped out of the car. Her voice sounded tight. 'This is PCSO Fliss Abbott.' And then, after the introductions were over, 'We've already had a run-in with Griff Llewellyn. He was being his usual obnoxious self. Threatened to report us to the Chief Constable. He was more concerned about staffing the hotel than he was about Bill Symonds.'

'Anything else to report?' Matt asked, eager to

banish their disastrous parting from his mind.

'Three waitresses who live to the north arrived, as well as Huw Rogers, Dylan's dad. Said he'd been told to drive the long way round by Ivor Jones. Several guests left, grumbling. I had to give them directions as they couldn't use the road to Madoc's Haven. I don't think there was anything else.' She turned to her PCSO. 'Fliss?'

Fliss Abbott shook her head.

'We'll drive down to the hotel,' Matt said, 'and start interviewing the Llewellyns, the staff and the guests.'

'You'll not find Penny Evans there. She was the one who found Bill,' Alys said. 'Cassie Davies and Ellie Jenkins won't be there either. Ivor broke the news about Bill when they turned up at his road block. Both in a state of shock, so he sent them home. They may have been the last people to see Bill ...,' Alys hesitated, biting her lip, '... before the accident.'

Except it wasn't an accident. Of that, Matt was sure. He guessed that Alys was going to say "to see Bill alive." Obviously they were both expecting the worst.

'Any update on Bill's condition?' Fliss asked.

'Last I heard, he was in a coma, undergoing surgery,' Matt said. 'You stay here and keep a note of everyone entering or leaving the hotel, or a log of vehicle registration numbers and number of occupants if they won't stop.'

'Already doing that, sir.' Alys said. 'I'll upload it to the murder file, as soon as I get a signal.'

'You'd better follow us down to the hotel, sergeant,' Matt said. 'We need to start taking statements. Officer Abbott, you stay here and record arrivals and departures.'

*****

There was no one behind the reception desk when Matt and Beth walked into the hotel. Three couples were standing at the counter surrounded by luggage. One of the men banged his fist down on the bell.

'I don't know what's gone wrong with this place,' another of the men complained. 'First we have to wait ages for breakfast, now there's no one to check us out.'

'The manager said something about an accident,' one of the women said. 'Then there was that report of a murder on the coast path on Tuesday. I don't think we'll be coming back here again.'

'There's no one to carry our bags out to the car,' the third man said. 'I'm just going to go. They can send the bill on if they want.'

'I'm sorry, but you can't do that, sir,' Matt said, as he pulled out his warrant card. 'I'm Detective Inspector Vincent, and this is Detective Sergeant Francis. We're investigating the attempted murder of one of the hotel staff who was working here last night. We need to take statements from you before you leave.'

'You can't keep us here,' the first man said. 'There's no way we're involved.'

As he was speaking, Alys strode into the entrance lobby in her police uniform. She closed the door behind her, and stood blocking it.

'Please be good enough to wait in the lounge,' Matt said. 'You won't be delayed any longer than is necessary.'

Griff Llewellyn appeared through a door behind the reception desk. 'Sorry to have kept you...' His voice trailed off as he took in the scene.

'Your guests are wishing to pay their bills and check out,' Matt said. 'I need to interview them before they leave. Please send them through to the lounge when they've settled up. I'll need a room for the interviews. Sergeant Carey will show the guests through to me when I'm ready for them.

Griff opened and shut his mouth like a goldfish.

*****

It was mid-morning before the interviews with the guests were over. Two local detective constables arrived to assist in interviewing and taking statements, otherwise it would have taken far longer.

Griff had diverted Huw from his renovation work on the outbuildings, first to help cook and serve breakfast, and then later to take over Bill's duties operating the potato peeling machine in the scullery, and processing the breakfast crockery in the dishwashers.

At mid-morning, Matt sent Huw up the driveway with a thermos of tea for Fliss Abbot, which incensed Griff.

'Aren't you afraid he'll make a break for it?' one of the DCs asked. 'Surely, all of the staff are suspects, aren't they?'

A pall of worry and anxious desperation pervaded the hotel, as the staff attempted to cover the duties of their missing colleagues. Several of the guests checked out early, despite Griff's entreaties for them to stay.

With all of the guests interviewed and their statements taken, Matt and his team moved on to the staff. He assigned the DCs to determine the movements of the waitresses the previous evening. He was keeping Griff Llewellyn and Huw Rogers for himself and Beth.

The two DCs were vying with each other for Alys's attention. Matt felt a twinge of jealousy, then told himself not to be stupid. He'd already decided that Alys was off-limits. He didn't intend to reverse that decision.

'Sergeant,' he said, interrupting one of the DCs in mid-flow. 'Can you rustle up some coffee and biscuits for us, and then find Mr Griff Llewellyn and send him in?'

'Yes, sir,' she replied.

It seemed awkward, Alys calling him sir, after they'd

been in school together, but that was how it had to be.

Griff was full of bluster and resentment when Alys opened the door and showed him into the room. 'It's bad enough being short staffed, without your lot interrupting the work of the hotel.'

'You'll be pleased to know that the hospital has stabilised Mr Symonds' condition,' Matt told him.

Griff looked surprised that Matt had shared that information with him. 'When will he be fit enough to come back to work?'

'He's still in a coma, sir,' Matt said, wondering how the man could have such little care and empathy for someone he knew and employed. 'He may not come out of it.'

Griff said nothing. Did he realise how his uncaring attitude made him appear?

'We're treating the incident in which Mr Symonds was injured as attempted murder,' Matt said. 'We're assuming he knew something that could expose the identity of Rianna Hughes's murderer.'

'That's preposterous,' Griff said. 'Surely these are two unfortunate, unrelated accidents? You're devastating the tourist industry here because you have some hare-brained theory without any evidence to support it.'

Matt decided to ignore Griff's tirade. Was it a diversionary tactic by a man with secrets to hide?

'Can you take us through what you were doing yesterday evening? Where and when you spoke to or saw Mr Symonds?'

'Are you accusing me of something?' Griff said angrily. 'If you are, I'll only speak to you with my solicitor present.'

'I'm not accusing you of anything,' Matt said. 'I'm building up a picture of Mr Symonds' movements in the hours leading up to the discovery of his body this morning. It would save both of us time if you could just answer my questions.'

Griff glared at him with ill-concealed hostility.

'This is harassment. I'll answer your questions, but I'll be complaining to the Chief Constable.'

Matt kept his voice calm and dispassionate, but he felt the heat rising up his neck to his face.

'That's your right,' he said. 'Now please answer my question. Where and when did you speak with Mr Symonds yesterday evening, and when was the last time you saw him?'

'After dinner service was over, I checked that the girls were laying up the dining room for breakfast. Symonds was still tidying up the scullery. When I glanced in later he'd just finished sweeping and mopping the floor. He said goodnight and left. He always walks home. Goodness only knows why.'

'When was the last time that anyone saw you last night?'

Griff hesitated. Matt didn't think he would answer, but eventually he did.

'By the time Symonds and the girls left, most of the guests had turned in for the night. There were a few finishing their drinks in the bar. They'd all disappeared when I came back down to check an hour or so later.'

'So no one saw you from just after Symonds set out on his walk home, and when you came down to supervise breakfast service this morning?'

'What are you suggesting?' Griff said angrily. 'That I jumped into my car and ran Symonds down? Go outside and check. There's not a scratch on it. You'd see damage if I'd used it to try and kill him.'

*****

'Griff told me I mustn't be long,' Huw Rogers said, as Beth showed him into the room and closed the door behind him.

'That's not Mr Llewellyn's decision,' Matt said.

'Naturally, I'll not take any more of your time than is necessary, but I'm conducting an inquiry into the murder of Rianna Hughes and the attempted murder of Bill Symonds.'

Huw's eyebrows shot up. 'I heard Bill'd been knocked down in a hit-and-run accident. Whatever makes you think it wasn't an accident?'

Matt exchanged a swift glance with Beth. Why was everyone so determined to deny that it was a failed murder attempt?

'What makes you think it was an unfortunate accident?' Matt countered.

Huw shrugged. 'It just doesn't seem likely that anyone would wish Bill harm. He's a super guy. Everyone loves him.'

He rubbed at the stubble on his chin. It didn't look like he'd shaved for a couple of days. 'Any news on how he's getting on? Someone said he was in a coma.'

'He's in the operating theatre right now,' Matt said.

The contrast between Griff and Huw's attitudes was marked. Griff hadn't shown the slightest interest in Bill's condition.

'When was the last time you saw Bill Symonds?'

Huw rubbed at his stubble again. 'It must have been yesterday just before lunch. I was taking a break with Bill out behind the bins. Cassie came out and joined us. We were discussing what happened to Rianna. Griff Llewellyn came out and caught us. Threatened us with the sack. Right mood he was in.'

'You're sure that was the last time you saw Bill?' Matt asked. 'You didn't see him again, later in the day?'

Huw shook his head. 'I was hard at it, turning the outbuildings into holiday apartments. After what Griff said, I didn't take another break by the bins, and I didn't go back into the hotel.'

'What time did you pack up and go home?'

'Must have been around five-forty-five. Not much

point working later than that. It was getting too dark to see.'

'What did you do during the evening?'

'Had a swift pint at the Brig,' Huw said, 'then went home for supper and watched a movie with Gemma. That's my wife.'

'What was the movie?' Matt asked.

'The King's Speech. It was on Netflix. Gemma's choice, not mine.'

'Did you go out again later?'

'No. Went to bed sometime around eleven-thirty.'

'Your wife, Gemma, she can confirm this, can she?'

'Sure,' Huw said, 'but I don't see why she'd need to.'

If Huw Rogers was lying, he was good at it.

'I'd like to take you back to last Tuesday, to the morning when Rianna Hughes died.'

Matt sensed Huw's body stiffen, although he hardly moved at all.

'Can you tell me where you were and what you were doing?'

'Same as every weekday morning. Got up, had a shower and breakfast, left the house around seven. Drove here and started work on the conversions.'

'Did you talk to anyone when you arrived or later?

Huw rubbed at his stubble and shook his head.

'Can't say as I did. Not until I joined Bill out by the bins after breakfast service was over and he came out for a smoke.'

'How did you get on with Ms Hughes? It must have been difficult after she took your son to court and he was excluded from their flat.'

The muscles in Huw's face tightened.

'It was Dylan's flat. I put down the deposit on it. He paid most of the rent.'

Huw's voice was almost normal. He seemed in control of his emotions, but what was going on underneath, Matt wondered.

'So what happened when you first met Ms Hughes after the court's decision?'

'I didn't. I steered clear of her. Made sure we didn't come face to face.'

Matt found that hard to believe. With them both working at the hotel there must have been a confrontation. He'd need to ask some of the other staff.

'Thank you, Mr Rogers. That's all for now,' Matt said. 'Thank you for your time.'

Matt waited until Huw had left the room and shut the door before he asked Beth what she thought.

'No real alibi for when Rianna was killed, otherwise sounded plausible,' Beth said. 'We'll need to check with his wife about his alibi for last night. What was she called, Gemma?'

Matt's phone warbled. He looked at the screen and answered. 'DI Vincent. What do you have for me?'

*****

'Sergeant Carey!'

Alys stiffened at the sound of Beth Francis's voice. She turned from the two DCs who were more interested in chatting her up than they were in solving the case. Was the force really recruiting them that young? These two looked more like they were fresh out of school than college.

'Yes Sergeant Francis?' Alys was determined to maintain a polite, neutral front towards Beth Francis after overhearing that "Ms Jane flipping Marple" comment. She'd behave professionally, even if Beth Francis didn't

'DI Vincent wants you in the interview room,' Beth said.

Her precipitous departure from the Armel Arms flashed through Aly's mind.

She was sure that Matt's request would have been phrased more courteously. What was it with Beth? Was she suffering from a massive inferiority complex?

Another thought surfaced. Beth couldn't be jealous could she? Was the Rottweiler hung up on her master? Did she resent the past that Matt and Alys shared?

'Come on in and sit down,' Matt said, waving her towards a chair facing his.

Beth followed her into the room and sat on a chair that was slightly behind Alys and to her right. What was this? Alys didn't feel comfortable. Had she done something wrong?

'Okay if I move my chair?' she said, picking it up and moving it without waiting for an answer. She put it down so she could see both Matt and Beth. 'I'm not being interrogated, am I?'

Matt laughed. 'Of course not.' He became more serious. 'I've just had a call from forensics. The broken headlight cover retrieved from where Bill Symonds was knocked down has been identified as coming from a Land Rover Defender. It's highly likely that it came from the vehicle that knocked him down.'

Alys's heart sank as her brain made the links. What was coming wouldn't make her look good. She could guess what Beth Francis was likely to say.

'Any thoughts?' Matt prompted.

'Yes,' Alys said. 'There's been a spate of thefts from farms in the area. Mainly Land Rover Defenders and quad bikes. I visited a farm up near Castlebythe on Thursday, following up on the theft of a Defender. I don't suppose forensics recovered any paint from the scene of Bill's hit-an-run did they? If they did, you might be able to link the stolen Defender to the hit-and-run. A vehicle's paint's a bit like a fingerprint isn't it?'

'True,' Matt said. 'It could give us a handle on the model and year of the vehicle that ran Bill down, maybe link it to your stolen Defender too. What are your recovery and clear-up rates like?'

Alys was frustrated, but she couldn't hide the truth. 'We've only recovered vehicles that have a functional tracker attached, and that's only a fraction of those stolen. No arrests yet.'

'Why's that?' Beth said, in a challenging tone. Matt frowned at her before turning back to Alys.

'The farmers either won't lay out the cash to buy a tracker or forget to recharge the battery, and the thieves use their common sense,' Alys said. 'When they steal a vehicle, they don't drive it far, they hide it in a disused building or somewhere where it can't easily be found. We think they wait a few days to see if anyone turns up to recover it, meaning that it had a tracker attached. If it's not recovered, they assume it doesn't have a tracker. They change its plates and drive it away with a relatively low risk of getting caught.

'We suspect they know where the automatic number plate recognition cameras are too, so they don't get caught driving it to the hiding place. It's also possible that they use the genuine registration number of a legitimate Defender for their false plates. That reduces their risk when they drive it out of the area.'

'Why recover the stolen vehicles that have the trackers attached?' Beth asked. 'Why not watch one of them covertly to see who's keeping watch on it?'

Alys frowned at Beth. 'I suggested that a year ago, but was refused the resources to do it. I tried watching one unofficially in my own time, but the owner kicked up a fuss and the vehicle was recovered before I could identify anyone checking up on it. I even watched the hideaway for a day or two after it was removed.'

Alys turned back to Matt. 'Allocate the resources the next time a tracked Defender goes missing, then we might find out who's nicking them.'

Matt frowned. 'I'm not sure I'd be any more successful than you were in getting the funding. Mounting a round-the-clock watch over two or three days on the off-chance you might catch the thief would be costly. I'll see what I can do, but don't hold your breath.'

'It could be worth the expense,' Alys told him. 'You might catch the vehicle thieves and Rianna's murderer too.'

'Did the Defender that went missing recently have a tracker attached?' Beth asked, sitting forward.

Alys felt a flash of adrenaline fuelled anger.

'I would have told you if it had,' Alys said, suspecting that Beth was needling her deliberately.

'Enough,' Matt said. 'Here's how we'll proceed. Alys, I'll have a word with your superintendent. If he agrees, I want you and your team to find the Defender that was stolen from Castlebythe. Your team is best placed to do the job as you have the local knowledge. Think where you would hide a stolen vehicle for two or three days where it would be unlikely to be found, but where you could keep an eye on it without being seen to be doing so.'

'We've tried that before,' Alys said, 'but we've never been able to devote ourselves to doing it full time. You'd need to persuade my superintendent to relieve the whole team from all other non-urgent duties for the next few days. Then we might stand a chance of finding it.'

Alys's adrenaline fuelled anger metamorphosed into excitement. If she could locate the missing Defender and it proved to be the one that knocked down and injured Bill, it might lead them to Rianna's killer.

She crossed her fingers and hoped that her super would agree. If she played a major role in bringing a murderer to justice, it would give a boost to her stagnating CV, and might get her that transfer back into CID.

'I'm not promising that I'll be able to persuade your super,' Matt said, 'but I'll do my best.'

He locked his gaze on Alys. 'If I'm successful, we'll need to agree some rules. I don't want you or any of your team putting yourselves in danger. If you think that you might have located the vehicle, you're to report it back to Beth, to Sergeant Francis. Remember, we're dealing with a dangerous killer who has killed once and tried to kill a second time. Don't take any risks. Understood?'

'Understood.' Her fingers were still crossed. She'd do whatever it took, risk or no risk.

'I learned something today that might have a bearing on the case,' she said. She'd been waiting for the best moment to tell him. She'd be gutted if he already knew.

Matt looked at her with eyebrows raised.

'I was chatting to a couple of the waitresses while they were waiting to be interviewed by your DCs.' Alys paused, savouring the moment. 'Ross Keely, Rianna's lecturer from the college in Haverfordwest, was here a couple of weeks ago.'

'Really?' Matt said, intrigued.

'He was carrying out a work-based assessment on Rianna. It counts as part of her coursework mark. When he was leaving there was an altercation in the car park.'

'Who with?' Matt demanded.

'A dark-haired woman in a Land Rover,' Alys said. She couldn't keep the grin from her face. 'It belonged to the Archaeological Trust.'

CHAPTER 25

Dylan's parents lived in a bungalow hidden away in the back roads beyond Solva, a picturesque village on a deep inlet from the sea. Seagulls wheeled and squawked above the yachts and motorboats moored in the harbour. It was ten years since Matt had been there, and it was beautiful.

The sun was low in the sky when Matt and Beth arrived at their destination. To the side of the bungalow, a lean-to sheltered a cement mixer and stacks of building supplies. An aging silver Toyota with a roof rack was parked at the front. Gemma Rogers answered the door when Matt rang the bell. He remembered her by sight from when he'd lived in the area.

'Good afternoon, Mrs Rogers. I'm Detective Inspector Vincent, and this is Detective Sergeant Francis. We'd like to ask you a few questions, if we may?'

Gemma stared at them for a few seconds, then held the door open and invited them in. She glanced outside before closing the door. 'You'd best go into the lounge,' she said, pointing the way. 'I've only just got back from the gift shop. It's terrible what's happened to Bill Symonds. Is there any news how he is? Have you caught who did it yet?'

'He's in a stable condition but still in a coma was the last news I heard,' Matt told her.

'But you haven't caught who did it,' Gemma said, accusingly. 'It shouldn't be that difficult.'

'We're still investigating the incident,' Matt said,

keeping his voice neutral and hoping that Beth wouldn't jump in with one of her insensitive comments.

Gemma shook her head reproachfully and said, 'I'll put the kettle on then. You'll both have tea?'

'Yes please,' Matt replied.

While Gemma left them to rustle up the tea, Matt examined the room. It was cold. A fire had been laid in the fireplace, but it hadn't been lit. The furniture was old, comfortable and lived in.

Photos of Dylan and Meg occupied the mantelpiece above the fireplace and every shelf and table top. Pictures of Rianna were conspicuous by their absence. There were none of her with Dylan or holding Meg. Matt wondered if they'd been binned when Rianna threw Dylan out of his home, or whether there ever had been any.

Gemma bustled in with a teapot, milk jug, cups and saucers and a sugar bowl on a tray.

'Don't stand on ceremony. Sit yourselves down.'

She deftly poured three cups and passed them around.

'What that court did was outrageous,' Gemma said, launching into what sounded like a well-rehearsed refrain, 'kicking my poor Dylan out of his own home. It's so unfair, and I've hardly seen Meg since that Rianna took him to court. When can Dylan have Meg back?'

Matt was amazed. Gemma was behaving as if Rianna hadn't been killed.

He sipped his tea before answering. 'I've advised your son that he'll have to go back to the family court. It's up to them to decide what happens next. I also suggested that he seeks help from the citizen's advice bureau.'

'That's ridiculous. They should cancel the order automatically. It's a scandal that Meg's not with her father. It's... it's uncivilised.'

Matt took another sip of his tea. 'Can you tell me what you were doing last Tuesday morning, the morning that Rianna Hughes died? It's a question I'm asking everyone who knew her.'

'Why? The stupid girl obviously slipped and fell off the path. She had no business to be running along it in that weather. She should have been at home looking after Meg.'

Matt said nothing, but waited patiently, looking at Gemma until she took the hint.

'What I do every morning. Got up, cooked breakfast, did some chores and went to work.'

With patient prompting, Matt elicited approximate times and ascertained that Gemma's husband, Huw, had left the house around seven, while Gemma had remained alone in the house until she left for work at around eight-thirty.

'Is there anyone who can confirm where you were between the time that Huw left, and the time when you arrived at work?'

'Of course there isn't,' Gemma said. 'After Huw left for work I was here by myself. Why do you need to know? You can't think I had anything to do with Rianna Hughes's death.'

'I simply asked a question, Mrs Rogers. I need to know everyone's movements that morning."

Gemma glared at Matt. 'I told you before. The stupid girl probably slipped and fell. Why are you wasting people's time and upsetting folks with all these questions?'

'So there's no-one who can confirm that you were here in the house?'

'No,' Gemma said, with a sigh.

'Thank you,' Matt said. 'Now I'd like you to take us through what you did yesterday evening.'

The sound of a vehicle made Matt glance out of the

window. A mud-splattered pickup truck pulled up outside with "H. Rogers Building Services" in bold letters along its sides.

Frustrating. Matt wanted to confirm Huw's alibi for Bill's hit and run before Huw had a chance to talk to his wife. They should have arrived earlier.

Huw swung out of the driver's seat, stared at Matt and Beth's car for a couple of seconds, then strode into the house.

'You again,' he said, entering the lounge and staring at Matt and Beth. 'What are you doing here? I told you everything I know this morning.'

Matt and Beth stood.

'We needed to ask your wife a few questions,' Matt said, but now that you're here, perhaps you can both help me?'

'Sit yourselves down,' Gemma said. 'I'll fetch Huw a mug and freshen the pot.'

'I'm sure the inspector won't take long,' Huw said. 'I'll wait until they've gone.'

Matt gave Beth's ankle a surreptitious kick to forestall the comment he was sure she was about to make.

'You both come into contact with a wide range of people from the local community,' Matt said. 'What are they saying about the theft of agricultural vehicles, in particular, the Land Rover Defenders?'

'Only that it's about time you police put a stop to it,' Huw replied.

Matt watched Huw's body language carefully as he answered, but could detect nothing that made him suspicious.

'Are there any thoughts or rumours about who's stealing them?'

'Can't be anyone local,' Huw said. 'Must be a gang from outside the area.'

'What makes you say that?'

'Stands to reason. If it was anyone local, they'd stick out like a sore thumb. Someone would see or hear something. Why d'you want to know?'

'The landlord of a local pub was complaining about the spate of thefts,' Matt said. 'I just wondered if you'd heard anything.'

Why was Huw so quick to point the finger of suspicion away from the local community, Matt wondered. Did he know something that he wasn't prepared to share?

CHAPTER 26

Vicky's entry phone buzzed. Who can that be, she wondered. It was almost eleven o'clock and she was getting ready for bed. She was worried that it would wake Dafi. He was teething and she'd only just settled him for the third time that evening.

'Who is it?' she asked.

'It's Dylan. Sorry it's so late. Can you let me in? It's freezing out here.'

Reluctantly Vicky buzzed him into the communal entrance hall. She unlocked her door and took off the chain. Moments later she was ushering him in, closing the door quickly to keep out the cold air.

'What on earth do you want at this time of night?' Vicky demanded. 'You could have phoned, or waited 'til morning.'

'Sorry, I didn't want to ask over the phone, and I couldn't get away until after dinner service was over.'

'Look, you'd better sit down,' Vicky said. 'D'you want a coffee or a tea?

Dylan shook his head. Vicky sat in the armchair and Dylan sat on the settee.

'I'm seeing Meg in the morning,' he said. 'At the family contact centre in Neyland.'

Vicky wondered where this was going. She waited for Dylan to continue. He looked intently at her. His eyes sparkled with moisture. Was it from the cold?

'Would you come with me? Bring Dafi too?'

'Why?' Vicky asked.

Dylan looked down. When he looked back up, Vicky was sure there were tears in his eyes.

'Meg's lost everyone she knows and loves. Ree, me, you, Dafi. She's been stuck with foster parents who she doesn't know and who don't know her. Each time I think about it I want to cry.' He gulped back a sob. 'Look, she's seen more of you and Dafi than she has of me since Ree kicked me out.' He swallowed, then pleaded, 'Please say you'll come, and bring Dafi too.'

Vicky felt tears start from her eyes. She wanted to give Dylan a hug and comfort him, but thought better of it. She had enough complications in her life, without adding another.

The last few days had been empty without Meg and time had dragged. Dafi missed her too. It broke Vicky's heart to hear his plaintive cry, 'Want Meg.' He was restless and wouldn't settle with his toys. It hadn't taken long for his tummy to be upset too.

'I'd love to come, but how do I get there with Dafi?' she asked. 'I can't drive and you've only got your motorbike. It would take ages by bus.'

'I'll phone around, get someone to give you a lift.'

Vicky wasn't sure who she would trust. Some of Dylan's friends weren't the most careful drivers. But then, who else was there?

'Have you heard about Bill Symonds?' she asked. 'Who d'you think did it? It scares me to think that someone we probably know is killing people, first Ree, now Bill?'

'Is Bill dead?' Dylan asked, with horror on his face.

'The latest I heard was that he's at the hospital in a coma, but Julie Bowen doesn't think he'll pull through.'

'I heard it was hit-and-run,' Dylan said. 'Maybe it has nothing to do with Ree's death. And maybe she just slipped on the coast path. That could have been an accident too.'

Was Dylan in denial, or trying to divert attention? She studied Dylan surreptitiously. She didn't believe that he'd killed Ree, although there were many in the village who did. What if she was wrong? She might have a murderer sitting on her settee, with Dafi in the next room, asleep.

'Look, it's getting late and I need to get to bed,' Vicky said. 'Give me a call in the morning if you find someone reliable to give me a lift. Not one of your boy racer friends with some clapped-out jalopy.'

Vicky ushered Dylan out. She carefully locked her door and reattached the chain.

Dylan was right. It must be frightening and confusing for poor little Meg, being taken away from everyone and everything she knew and loved. At least Vicky had been able to pack Meg's favourite teddy and blanket before social services took her away.

But it was frightening for Vicky and the other villagers too, knowing that they had a murderer in their midst. First Ree dead, now Bill fighting for his life. Who would be next?

CHAPTER 27

'Set up an interview with Dylan Rogers,' Matt told Beth. 'Let's see if he has an alibi for the Bill Symonds' hit-and-run.'

'I've already called him,' Beth said. 'As soon as he's finished breakfast service at the Black Boar Inn he has an appointment to visit his daughter at the family contact centre in Neyland. Vicky Morgan's joining him there with her son. I've provisionally arranged for us to interview him at the Milford Haven police station afterwards. If that works for you, I'll message him to confirm.'

Matt was intrigued. Was Beth working to re-establish herself in his good books?

'Excellent. Anything else?'

'Yes, sir. I thought we should follow up on the conversation that Rianna overheard between Rhodri Llewellyn and the Welsh Government minister, Aled Ingram.'

That sounds like a minefield, Matt thought. Beth had told him that Rhodri Llewellyn and the Chief Constable were golfing buddies. Was Beth trying to lure him into a trap?

'I need more information before we confront Rhodri Llewellyn,' Matt said. 'Have one of the team dig deeper into Llewellyn's plans for his proposed Clebaston Manor Resort, the current status of the planning application, if there's proof for the existence of Saint Egwad's monastery other than in the Vespasian manuscript, and whether anyone has lodged an objection.'

*****

Vicky pushed Dafi to the convenience store in his buggy. It was cold and the wind lanced through her clothes. She'd dressed Dafi in his anorak and waterproof trousers. She'd put on his mittens too, but he'd immediately pulled them off and was flapping them around on the ends of their retaining cord.

The locals inside the store were talking in hushed whispers, discussing Bill's condition and the identity of the hit-and-run driver.

Julie Bowen, the district nurse, was in the store grabbing her usual coffee from the deli counter.

'Good morning Vicky!'

The coffee's aroma made Vicky yearn for one too.

'And how's little Dafi doing?' Julie asked, crouching down and touching the toddler's hand. Dafi wriggled and looked shyly away.

She straightened up. 'Terrible business, Bill getting knocked down. We must all pray for him.'

Was this a veiled hint that Vicky didn't go to church? Julie Bowen was regular churchgoer and do-gooder, close to Cedric Davies the vicar.

'Cedric's driving me and Dafi over to Neyland to see Meg this morning,' Vicky told Julie. Vicky was amazed when the vicar had called first thing that morning and arranged to give her and Dafi a lift. However had Dylan persuaded him?

'Dylan wants us to be there with him,' Vicky said. 'Seems odd that he can only see Meg at this contact centre place.'

'I'm surprised they let him see her at all,' one of the local busybodies muttered who'd been listening in on the conversation. 'They still don't know who killed that Rianna Hughes, or who ran Bill Symonds down.'

'Perhaps people should mind their own business,' Vicky said sharply to the woman.

Dafi kicked his legs and said, 'Mooo,' then chuckled.

The woman pointedly turned her back on Vicky.

The bell on the shop door pinged and Gemma Rogers bustled into the shop. 'Vicky, I'm glad I spotted you,' she said. 'I've just heard you're going to see Meg. I wish I was coming with you, but Dylan said there'd be too many of us. Can you give this to Meg? There's one for Dafi too.'

Gemma thrust a bag into Vicky's hands. Vicky peeked inside. There were two small, soft, cuddly toys.

'I would have given it to Meg myself...' Gemma choked back a sob. 'It's so unfair, not being able to see your own granddaughter.' She turned and fled from the shop.

Vicky pushed Dafi back to the flat feeling pleased. Mission accomplished. She wanted people to know that Cedric was taking her and Dafi to visit Meg. It wasn't that she didn't want to be alone with Cedric, specifically, but until the police caught Rianna's murderer, she didn't know who she could trust.

*****

Holly backed into the cramped office that Alys's neighbourhood policing team called home. She carried a tray of hot steaming drinks from the kitchen that they shared with the fire station crew.

Alys smiled at how the choice of drinks reflected her team's characters. Strong sweet tea for PC Ivor Jones, conservative to his core; peppermint tea for artistic Fliss Abbott; and Fairtrade green tea for environmentally conscious Holly Newlyn. Alys always drank strong coffee to keep her senses sharp.

'I know we've done this before when previous vehicles went missing,' Alys said, 'so it should be easier this time. We'll restrict the search area to within a relatively short distance of Madoc's Haven.'

'So,' Ivor Jones said. 'You're assuming that Rianna's murderer comes from Madoc's Haven or nearby. He collects the Defender from its hiding place, uses it to run down Bill Symonds, then drives the Defender back to its hiding place and goes home?'

Alys smiled. 'Basically correct, but you've added a couple of extra assumptions. The murderer isn't necessarily a 'he', and he or she may have taken the Defender to a different hiding place after knocking Bill down.'

Fliss Abbott, one of her two police community support officers looked thoughtful. 'How did the murderer get to the hiding place and back home again? He wouldn't have wanted to be seen. It would ruin his alibi, always supposing he has one.'

Fliss's talents were wasted on being a PCSO, but it helped fund her passion for painting and jewellery making while she struggled to become better known.

'Good question,' Alys said. 'Any suggestions? Holly, you haven't said much.'

Holly Newlyn, Alys's second PCSO and the quieter of the two looked uncomfortable. She didn't like being made the centre of attention which was odd, because her personality changed completely when she was out in the community doing her job.

'If it was me I'd cut across the fields on foot if it wasn't too far,' Holly said. 'Otherwise I'd use a push bike or a maybe a motorbike. A car would be too visible, more memorable.'

'That's logical. Thanks Holly. Let's bear that in mind.' Alys hoped that her superintendent would let her team devote themselves fulltime to finding the missing vehicle.

'Like on the previous occasions, we're looking for places where you could hide the stolen Defender for two or three days, where it would be unlikely to be found, but where you could keep an eye on it without being seen to be doing so.'

'So it's disused or abandoned outbuildings,' Ivor

added, 'maybe old quarry workings or down a little used track, somewhere that isn't visible from the road.'

Alys went to the Ordnance Survey map on the wall and assigned search areas to the team. 'And remember,' she said. 'This time we're on the trail of a murderer. He or she may be watching to see if anyone locates the vehicle. Be alert and don't place yourselves in any danger.'

*****

Vicky felt relieved as she pushed Dafi into the family contact centre in his buggy. Cedric said he'd take them home again after the visit. The vicar seemed harmless enough, but someone local must have killed Ree and tried to kill Bill too.

'Good morning Ms Morgan and it's Dafi, isn't it?'

Vicky recognised Caitlin Gray, the social worker who'd taken Meg away from her. Was it only last Tuesday? It seemed an eternity ago.

'Hello,' Vicky said tersely, as the social worker knelt down and made a fuss of Dafi.

'Thank you for coming,' Caitlin said, looking up and making eye contact with Vicky. 'I'm sure it will help both Meg and Dylan having you here. I'm sorry we had to take Meg away from you, but with her mother's tragic death and the court order against Dylan, we didn't have any alternative.'

Vicky didn't reply. Seeing the social worker again made her angry, made her relive the scene in her flat when they'd taken Meg away.

'What's going to happen to Meg?' she asked. 'When are you going to let Dylan have her back?'

'That's something we need to discuss with Dylan. He arrived ten minutes ago. If you'll follow me, I'll take you and Dafi through now.'

Dylan was sitting cross-legged on the floor with Meg cradled in his arms. He looked up and smiled as he saw

Vicky and Dafi. 'Thanks for coming. Doesn't she look beautiful?'

Meg made a gurgling sound and smiled. Vicky unstrapped Dafi from his buggy and lifted him out. He immediately toddled over to Meg and stroked her head. 'Meg,' he said, smiling. Meg reached out her hand to Dafi who grasped it in his.

The room was light and airy, with brightly coloured walls covered in pictures. There was a low nursery table with small plastic chairs in red, blue and green.

Dafi chuckled and made a bee-line for a box of toys and bricks and started pulling them out onto the carpeted floor.

Vicky glanced quickly at the social worker, unsure what was allowed. The social worker gave her a reassuring smile.

Dafi picked out a set of farmyard animals and stood them in a neat row. He picked up a toy cow and toddled unsteadily over to the social worker, holding the cow out to her.

'Yes, it's a cow,' she said. 'Can you say cow?'

Dafi replied, 'Mooo.'

Vicky sat on the floor beside Dylan and held out her arms. 'Can I hold her? I've really missed her. Dafi has too. He keeps saying 'Want Meg'.

CHAPTER 28

'When can I have Meg back?' Dylan demanded.

'That's a matter for the family court to decide,' Caitlin Gray told Dylan. 'You still have a court order in force against you. You need to apply to the family court to review your case.'

'That's ridiculous,' Dylan said. 'I'm Meg's dad. I should be looking after her, not people she doesn't even know. That court order was based on a pack of lies that Rianna invented, and she isn't around any longer.'

Caitlin Gray looked at Dylan for a long moment before speaking. 'Regardless of the court order, are you really in a position to look after your daughter? You have a full-time job and you don't have a proper home.'

'What about the flat? I can move back in there.'

'Let's suppose the family court cancels the occupation order and you do move back into the flat, who's going to look after Meg while you're at work?'

'Vicky,' Dylan said confidently. 'She was looking after Meg while Rianna was at work. She can look after her again.'

'That's not a situation I'm happy with,' Caitlin said. 'Ms Morgan isn't a registered child minder, and it's a rather different situation now that Meg's mother is no longer with us.'

'What's happened to sexual equality?' Dylan demanded. 'It shouldn't make any difference if it's Meg's mum or her dad who's looking after her. You can't take her away from me. It isn't right.'

'I'm sorry,' Caitlin said. 'Social Services have a duty

of care towards Meg. We have to put her interests first. But we can't do anything until the Family Court reviews the situation. I'd suggest you take advice from a solicitor specialising in family law.'

'And where do I get the money from to do that?'

'You also need to convince the court that you would be in a position to provide a proper home for Meg. It might help if your friend, Ms Morgan, applies to become a registered child minder.'

*****

'Can you tell us where you were last night?' Matt asked.

Dylan sat facing him across the table. Beth sat beside Matt in the interview room, taking notes.

'What do you mean? After dinner service was over and I'd cleaned down the kitchen?'

'Let's start with dinner service,' Matt said. 'Were you there for the whole time? When was that from and to, and when did you finish cleaning the kitchen?'

As Dylan answered and Beth took notes, Matt watched Dylan carefully, looking for any indicators of anxiety or nervousness that might suggest he wasn't telling the truth. He didn't expect Dylan to look comfortable and at ease, but he couldn't detect any tell-tale signs that were out of the ordinary.

'What did you do after you'd finished in the kitchen?'

'Went back to my caravan and watched TV. The boss doesn't like me drinking in the bar with the guests, and I didn't feel like going anywhere else. I'd had a long day.'

. 'So there's no one to vouch for where you were after you went back to your caravan?'

'I didn't have a woman in there if that's what you mean. What is this? Are you trying to fit me up for what happened to Bill Symonds?' Dylan said, angrily, jumping to his feet.

'Please sit down,' Matt said. 'No one's trying to fit you up for anything. But we do need to find out where people were and what they were doing at the time of Mr Symonds' accident.'

Dylan subsided onto his chair and glared at Matt.

'So,' Matt repeated, 'there's no one to vouch for where you were after you went back to your caravan?'

'No,' Dylan said, sullenly.

'Let's go back to the morning of Rianna Hughes' murder.'

'You trying to fit me up for that too? I told you before. I was here at the Black Boar, cooking breakfast.'

Matt took Dylan through the times of the breakfast service, and when he claimed to have walked into the kitchen to start preparing the breakfasts.

'Let me just confirm one point,' Matt said. 'Your first task was to take the side of bacon from the fridge, and slice it on the slicing machine. You were alone in the kitchen doing that until the first of the waitresses arrived?'

'That's right. So what?'

'Just needed to clarify,' Matt said. 'Changing the subject, when we visited you at the Black Boar and spoke with you in your caravan, was that your motorbike that was parked outside?'

'Yeah.' Dylan said suspiciously,

'A Honda ... ?'

'It's taxed and insured and I had it MOT'd last month.'

'And that's how you normally get around?'

'Yeah. Bus services around here are useless. You could stand around waiting all day. Look, when can I move back into the flat?'

'I told you before,' Matt said. 'That's a matter for the family court. Did you seek advice from the citizen's advice bureau like I suggested?'

'Haven't had time, have I?'

'Then I suggest you make time,' Matt said. 'We'll speak with you again, if we have any further questions.'

*****

'We need to interview the landlord and waitresses at the Black Boar,' Matt said. 'Make absolutely sure we know exactly when Dylan was at the inn.

'Then I want you to check out the timings again,' Matt told Beth. 'Is there any way that Dylan could have killed Rianna and got back to the inn before he was first seen there? Could he have sliced that side of bacon the previous evening, not on the morning of her death as he claims? We only have his word for when he did it. I know it can't take that long to slice a side of bacon on a machine, but ten or fifteen minutes could make a difference to whether he has a credible alibi or not.'

Matt noticed the way Beth was looking at him. 'What? Do you think I'm clutching at straws? Don't you think he killed her?'

Beth shrugged her shoulders and slowly shook her head. 'I don't know. He's the person with the most obvious motive. If he caught her by surprise, he could easily have hit her on the head with a rock and pushed her over the edge.'

'What about the hit-and-run? Whoever did that must be linked to the theft of the Land Rover Defender.'

'Or came across it accidentally where it was hidden away, and took the opportunity to use it and confuse the issue.'

Matt looked at Beth appraisingly. She might be inclined to say the wrong thing to people and to act without thinking, but she could provide some useful insights.

'So, if Dylan is our murderer, either he's a member of the gang that's stealing Defenders and quad bikes, or he's a clever opportunist.' Matt said thoughtfully. 'I still can't believe that the two crimes aren't related. That would be too much of a coincidence.'

'It's vital we find out who's stealing the Defenders,' Beth said. 'Do you really think that little Miss...'

Beth faltered as Matt glared at her.

She gulped and started again. 'Meaning no disrespect, Sir, but do you really think that Sergeant Carey and the Madoc's Haven Neighbourhood Team should be trusted with investigating the Defender thefts? They've been going on for years and Sergeant Carey's made no progress in catching the thieves.'

'I've just persuaded Sergeant Carey's superintendent to allow her and her team to devote themselves one-hundred percent to locating the missing Defender,' Matt said. 'I'll not reverse that decision until they've had a chance to find it.'

CHAPTER 29

'Stop!' Alys said, urgently.

Fliss pulled up sharply, throwing Alys forward against her seatbelt.

'I didn't mean that quickly,' Alys said, as her head ricocheted back against the headrest.

Fliss grinned apologetically. 'Sorry. Thought you'd seen a pheasant run out or something.'

Alys massaged her neck. 'Back up to the gateway. I'm not sure what's in that field.'

Fliss put the car into reverse and shot back to the opening in the hedge.

'We're searching for a stolen vehicle,' Alys said, 'not on a blue light call. If you want to do those, become a regular PC. You could still do your painting and jewellery in your spare time.'

'Don't think I'm not tempted,' Fliss said. 'It's difficult making ends meet. The extra pay would be great, but I don't need the added responsibility.'

'If you were a regular PC, I could send you on that emergency response driver course. You'd enjoy that.'

And I wouldn't have to keep bracing to avoid whiplash, Alys added in her mind.

She unstrapped and went to investigate. The banks at the sides of the country lane were high and topped with hedges which made it difficult to see if the Defender was hidden in the field.

What Alys had seen was the back of an old manure spreader that had been left in a corner of the field. She stamped the mud off her boots, sat back in beside Fliss and told her of her find. 'Drive a little slower and we won't need to keep stopping and backing up.'

They'd been criss-crossing the countryside for the last two hours, investigating sheds and disused outbuildings, nosing down rutted tracks, getting out and continuing on foot whenever Alys thought it necessary. 'We should be in a 4x4,' she said wistfully when they returned from a trek down a muddy, pot-holed cart track.

Fliss nodded in agreement. 'What I can't bear thinking about, is that someone we probably know murdered Rianna and then tried to kill Bill too. I've started locking and bolting the house doors, and, if I'm parked, I don't sit in the car without making sure it's locked too.'

'It's the waitresses from the restaurants and hotels I worry about,' Alys said. 'I bet the Llewellyns haven't arranged transport for their staff. They probably expect them to cycle home when they've finished as if nothing has happened.' She shivered at the thought of having to use the same lane where Bill Symonds had been run down. 'We need to check on that.' Alys had been trained in self-defence but, since Rianna's murder, she was still fearful after darkness fell.

She thought back to her meeting with Cedric the vicar, on the cliff top where Rianna had met her fate. For a moment she'd panicked, thinking that he was going to push her over the edge. Suspicion was insidious. You began to think the worst of the most harmless of people, even ones who you'd known for the whole of your life.

The person who Alys disliked the most was Griff Llewellyn, but that was hardly grounds for suspicion. Or was it? He was arrogant, uncaring, self-centred, and Alys knew that he'd tried to force himself on several of the local girls. Fortunately she'd still been too young to interest him when he'd gone off to university. Later, after they'd both returned to the area, she was a trainee police constable and made it clear what would happen if he tried it on.

'Let's call in at the mill for a coffee,' Fliss said.

The old woollen mill stood by a stream where several country lanes met. It had been transformed into a tourist attraction, making goods for sale in its shop and further afield. No disused outbuildings obvious.

Even in winter the mill had a scattering of cars in its car park, their owners attracted to the warmth of its café. Alys worked there the summer that Hannah Andrews had died. She shivered at the memory. She'd been questioned by a sympathetic detective sergeant and forced to relive those terrible moments both then and again later in the coroner's court.

'Are you coming in, or do you want me to get a couple of take-aways?' Fliss asked.

Alys hadn't even noticed that Fliss had parked the car.

Water gurgled in the millstream as they walked over the wooden bridge and on into the café. Customers, alerted by the loud ping of the bell, looked up and did a double take as Alys and Fliss stepped through the door in their uniforms. Alys made a point of smiling reassuringly. People tended to worry when police officers marched in unexpectedly.

Fortified by steaming mugs of coffee and assured by Joyce, who was serving behind the counter, that she'd seen no sign of the missing Defender, they continued on their search, this time with Alys driving.

Up the hill on the left, Alys nosed the car into the entrance of an old disused quarry. She investigated the derelict building that stood near the entrance. It looked large enough to conceal a vehicle, but its interior was dark, dank and empty.

The area was dotted with farms that eked out an existence by letting spruced up farmworkers cottages as holiday rentals and converted barns as bunkhouses during the tourist season. Most of the farms were surrounded by a sprinkling of cottages whose previous inhabitants had long since fled the land.

Alys retreated into her thoughts as they continued their search. Was Matt following up on the conversation that Rianna had overheard about the Clebaston Manor Resort development and Ross Keely visiting the hotel? It was so frustrating that he hadn't requested her attachment to his team. Finding the stolen Land Rover Defender was important, but deadly boring compared to being more actively involved in the investigation.

What really rankled was that Beth Francis was Matt's sergeant. How on earth had that woman landed a job in CID? Her people skills were non-existent. She obviously wasn't a high flyer, or she wouldn't still be a sergeant in her mid-thirties. Not that I'm exactly on track in achieving my ambitions, Alys thought, miserably.

'I'd love to nick the bastard that did that.' Fliss's outraged comment jerked Alys from her reverie. An unsightly heap of worn out armchairs and a settee had been dumped on a patch of grass at the side of the lane. 'I'll report it to the council.'

A mile further on, Alys turned down yet another dead-end track. That could be a metaphor for my life she thought, despondently.

Instead of a farm surrounded by a cluster of buildings, a single thatched cottage stood surrounded by trees in a clearing by a stream. Its name was engraved on a stone slab by the door. 'Ty Nymff'.

'Hmm, Nymph House. A pretty enough name for the cottage.'

Its curtains were all closed. Alys suspected that it wouldn't be let until Easter at the earliest. The grass around the turning circle outside was reasonably short, so obviously someone was maintaining it during the winter months. The window frames gleamed in the fading light.

A spur from the track led around the side of the house. Apart from that, they were at the end of the lane.

Alys climbed out of the car and shivered. It was growing cold in the late afternoon. The sun was already hidden by the trees. It wouldn't be long before it set completely. It would be dark before they were back on the road at the top of the lane.

'I'll take a look around,' Alys said. She shivered again. 'It's getting spooky in the twilight. Best lock the doors until I'm back.'

Her shoes crunched on the gravel as she walked around the house. A robin sang melodiously, but a blackbird flew off uttering its harsh alarm call. A pigeon crashed away through the branches, startled by her presence.

Alys came to an abrupt halt as she rounded the back of the house. There was a large, cuboid shape, covered by a tarpaulin. It looked like a vehicle laid up for the winter. But why leave it here, hidden away from sight behind an unoccupied house?

Alys looked all around, on the alert, senses heightened. Could this be what she was looking for?

As she stepped forward to raise the edge of the tarpaulin and discover what was beneath it, Alys heard a vehicle approaching down the lane. Her breath caught in her throat and her heart pounded.

She heard their patrol car's engine start and jumped aside as Fliss slewed their car around the back of the house and cut the engine. Fliss climbed out and stood beside Alys.

The single track lane was the only way in or out. Was this the murderer, come to check up on the stolen Defender? If it was, would he be armed, and would he try resisting arrest? Alys wondered how capable Fliss would be in a fight. She wasn't hopeful. At least she had an incapacitant spray on her belt although she'd never used one outside of training.

She heard a car stop at the front of the house where, only seconds ago, theirs had been parked. Its engine stopped and silence descended.

The birds stopped singing; dusk was deepening. In the gloom, Alys could hear the crunch of the gravel as someone walked around the side of the house towards them.

CHAPTER 30

Vicky felt lonely and frightened. She hadn't realised how much she relied on her friend for company. It was five days since Ree had left a sleepy Meg in her arms and dashed off for her morning run, excited at the thought of her lunchtime tryst with Ross Keely. That was when the nightmare began.

Vicky took out her phone and messaged her husband, Nick. She wondered if his ship was docked or at sea. Would he have an internet connection? She hoped he did and was somewhere quiet. It would be evening in Qatar. Had she been mad to marry him, knowing that he'd be away for extended voyages abroad?

Her phone pinged. 'Call me,' was his terse reply.

'We can talk to daddy,' she told Dafi, excitedly.

'Talk daddy,' he responded, perking up and climbing onto her knee.

She pulled up the video call app and waited and prayed it would connect.

Then suddenly Nick's face was there on the screen, smiling.

'Hello, love. I'm missing you, more than you can ever know,' Vicky said, blowing him a kiss.

'Daddy, daddy!' Dafi waved his arms in the air, then poking his finger at the phone, said, 'Want Meg.'

Nick waved back, told Vicky that he missed her too, and chatted briefly with his son.

'You play with your toys,' Vicky told Dafi. 'You can say goodnight to daddy later.'

She was relieved when Dafi climbed off her knee

and settled with his farmyard animals on the floor.

'Have they found out who killed Rianna yet?' Nick asked. He wasn't a great fan of Rianna, disapproving of what she had done to Dylan. 'How's Bill? Has he come out of his coma?'

'They don't have a clue, and no one expects Bill to live. I'm frightened. I don't know who I can trust.' Vicky swallowed a sob. 'Most of the village think it was Dylan who killed Ree, but I don't know why he'd try to kill Bill.'

'Who d'you think did it?' Nick asked.

Suddenly Dafi was at her side, holding up a toy cow. 'Moo,' he said proudly.

'What have you got there?' Nick asked. 'Moo isn't its name. That's the noise it makes.'

Dafi became bashful, half turning away. Then his face lit up. 'Cow,' he said coyly.

'Clever boy,' Vicky said proudly, before sending him back to his toys.

Vicky dropped her voice to a confidential whisper. 'Did I tell you what Ree overheard at the hotel?'

Nick shook his head.

'Rhodri and Griff Llewellyn were dining with some guy. They were discussing bribing Wendy Pryce, which made Ree prick up her ears. Cassie Davies, the vicar's daughter, recognised the man from the telly. It was Aled Ingram, the Welsh Government minister who deals with planning appeals.'

'Who's Wendy Pryce?'

'Don't you remember? She fancies Ross Keely, that lecturer Ree's been having a fling with.'

'So?'

'You remember that big development that was on the telly, the one the Llewellyns are planning to do over at Clebaston Hall?'

'Vaguely.'

'Well, Wendy Pryce advises on planning

applications. She's into history and that kind of thing. Seems she could put a spanner in the works and stop the development. The Llewellyns are looking to buy her off. That's what Ree overheard.'

'So Ree thought the Llewellyns might make it worth her while to forget what she heard?' Nick said. 'Blackmail? Would they really kill her for that?'

'That development's worth a shedload of money. They say it'll bring work for hundreds of folks in the area.'

'I can see Griff Llewellyn doing it. Stuck up, arrogant bastard,' Nick said.

'He tried it on with Ree last week. Gave her a lift in his Porsche. She pushed him away. Said it would make him more eager.'

The video link started to fail, interference fragmenting the image.

'Quick Dafi! Come and say goodnight to daddy,' Vicky said, but it was too late. The connection had died.

Dafi stood unsteadily and toddled over to her. 'Where's daddy?' he said, poking his finger at the screen. 'Want daddy.'

Dafi wasn't as upset at his daddy disappearing as he was at the loss of Meg from his daily routine.

Vicky sighed. He should have a full-time father, not one he didn't see for a month at a time. She'd hoped Nick would give up being a merchant seaman and find a shore job, but that hadn't happened. There weren't many shore-based jobs around for marine engineers. She might as well be single for all the time she and Dafi spent with Nick. If it wasn't for the fact that she loved him, she'd be looking for someone else.

Her thoughts turned to Meg and her dad, Dylan. Poor little Meg didn't have a mother and, until Dyl got himself sorted out, she didn't have a daddy either. She thought back to the social worker's suggestion that she should apply to be a registered child minder. It might help Dyl to get his daughter back, and Dafi his lost playmate. She desperately hoped that it wasn't Dylan who'd killed Ree. That would be cruel, if Meg lost both her mum and her dad. Had Ree done or said something that had finally tipped Dylan over the edge? She tried to push the thought from her mind.

She realised with a jolt that it was past Dafi's bedtime. She smothered him with hugs and kisses and settled him in his cot before reading him his favourite bedtime story, "Beep, Beep, Beep, Time for Sleep!" His favourite machine was the mechanical digger.

Dafi snuggled down with his comfort blanket and thankfully was soon fast asleep.

She wished that she could sleep as soundly as Dafi, but now he'd caught some of her nervousness and had started waking in the middle of the night.

Vicky treated herself to a mug of hot chocolate and sat down to think.

Should she tell the police what Ree had overheard and what she was planning to do? Like Matt Vincent said, nothing she told them about Ree could hurt her now.

She took a sip of her hot chocolate, not too hot, soothing and sweet.

Why couldn't she have married someone like Matt Vincent? He might work long hours but he wasn't away for weeks at a time. Why was he still single? He was definitely a catch for someone. Maybe for that police woman, Alys Carey? Vicky had noticed the way she looked at him.

Vicky jumped up, suddenly scared. Had Ree put her blackmail plan into motion? If the Llewellyns had killed Ree because she'd overheard them planning to bribe Wendy Pryce, would they guess that Ree had passed on the information to her? They might come after her too.

She checked that the front door was locked with the security chain in place, then she made sure that all the windows were locked tightly shut.

A car pulled up outside. The engine noise died, and a car door slammed. Vicky's heart raced. She turned off the lights, pulled aside the curtain and peered out into the street.

CHAPTER 31

Behind Ty Nymff, darkness smothered the scene. Alys held her breath and transferred her torch to her left hand. Her heart pounded and adrenalin flooded her body. She was pumped, her nerves tingling.

Someone was coming around the side of the house towards where Alys and Fliss stood frozen by their car. A blackbird flew past, squawking its alarm call. Gravel crunched underfoot.

Alys pulled her incapacitant spray from her belt and flipped back the cover. She'd never had to use it for real, just knew that it was most effective if squirted at the forehead between the eyebrows. Would her aim be accurate? Would she get the distance and timing right?

The footsteps stopped.

Alys didn't dare breathe, worried that her breath might condense in the cold evening air and warn the person that she was waiting just around the corner.

'Hello! Are you there?'

It was a man's voice.

She clasped the can more tightly and pressed her finger on the trigger button almost, but not quite, hard enough to release the spray.

Alys had suspected, but had never really believed it could be him. She flicked on her torch as he stepped around the corner.

'Police. Hold it right there. Don't come any closer,' she said.

Fliss gasped as Alys's torch beam illuminated Cedric's face.

'Cedric! What are you doing here?' Fliss said.

'It's me, Cedric,' the vicar said at the same moment. 'I know you're the police, I followed your car down here. Can you turn off that torch? It's blinding me. It's Alys, isn't it?'

Alys lowered the torch beam marginally, but not so much that she couldn't still see Cedric's eyes and the expression on his face.

'What are you doing here?' she demanded.

'I told you. I followed you down here.'

'Why?'

'The house belongs to one of my parishioners, a couple actually. They asked me to keep an eye on it while they were away. When I saw a police car turn down here, I was curious. I thought there might be something amiss.'

Alys stared at him. It sounded too glib. 'What are their names?'

Could Cedric be Rianna's murderer? The person who'd knocked Bill Symonds down in a brutal hit and run? Had he really seen them drive down the lane, or had he chosen the wrong moment to come back and move the stolen vehicle.

'James and Liz Wheeler,' Cedric said. 'They're on a cruise in the Caribbean.'

'What's under the tarpaulin?' Alys asked. She'd not had time to look. She'd feel pretty stupid if it wasn't the stolen Defender.

'What tarpaulin?' Cedric asked. 'I can't see anything with your torch shining in my eyes.'

Alys stepped two paces back, still keeping her torch beam on Cedric. 'Fliss. Shine your torch on the tarpaulin.'

Cedric shielded his eyes from Alys's torch and stared as Fliss ran her torch beam over the shrouded vehicle.

'That wasn't there last time I checked on the house,' Cedric said. 'You tell me.'

Either Cedric was quick-witted, a convincing liar and murderer, or what he'd told them was true. Alys was torn. Should she believe him, or not?

'When was that?' Alys asked. 'When did you last check the house?'

'It must have been last Tuesday. I remember, because I'd only just had time before getting ready for the Historical Society meeting.'

If there was a stolen Defender under the tarp, it could be the one used in the hit-and-run, the same one that was stolen from the farm near Castlebythe. That had been stolen on Tuesday night.

Was Cedric the thief? Could he have stolen it after the Historical Society meeting? Or could he have chanced upon it after it had been stashed by the thief, and then used it to run down Bill Symonds on Friday night?

'Fliss,' Alys said, 'lift up the tarp and see if the nearside headlight cover's broken.'

Fliss stepped swiftly over and raised the tarpaulin. There was a sharp intake of breath.

Alys kept her eyes on Cedric. 'Well?'

'It's a Defender,' Fliss said. 'The nearside headlight cover's smashed. There's what looks like dried blood on what's left of it. Damage to the bodywork too.'

'You can't think I had anything to do with running down Bill Symonds?' Cedric's voice came out higher than normal. He sounded panicked, alarmed.

Alys's grip on the incapacitant spray can tightened. She pulled her finger off the trigger in case she sprayed Cedric accidentally, but she was ready to jab it back down if necessary. Her heart thumped in her chest. Would Cedric attack her or turn and run?

'You must admit it looks suspicious,' she said, as calmly as she could. 'You need to come down to the station and answer a few questions.'

'Are you arresting me?' he asked, incredulously.

'No,' she said. 'I'm not arresting you, but Detective Inspector Vincent will probably want to interview you. Please wait by your car while I check.'

'I've a meeting of the Diocesan Advisory Committee this evening in St David's. It had better not take too long,' Cedric said, before turning and striding back around the house.

'Aren't you afraid he'll make a run for it?' Fliss whispered, putting her hand on Alys's sleeve. 'Why didn't you arrest him?'

'I'd need reasonable grounds to believe he was driving the Defender when it knocked Bill Symonds down,' Alys said. 'I've no evidence that he's even seen it before. But keep your ears open. If you hear him drive off, we'll chase him down. And take some photos of the damage to the Defender and its registration plates. It's the one stolen from the farm up near Castlebythe.'

While Fliss photographed the damage to the Defender with her mobile phone, Alys gritted her teeth and radioed Beth Francis. That's what Matt had told her to do at the end of their disastrous meeting at the Armel Arms. She gave a terse update on finding the Defender and the vicar's unexpected appearance.

'The DI will want to interview the vicar,' Beth told Alys. 'Escort him here to the station in Madoc's Haven.'

'That'll mean leaving the Defender unguarded. I can't leave PCSO Abbott here by herself. The DI told me not to expose any of the team to unnecessary danger.'

'Then get your PC to hold her hand.'

Beth terminated the call. Alys seethed with instant anger. She turned to Fliss, 'I'm sorry, you'll ...'

At that moment they both heard the sound of an engine starting.

'It's Cedric,' Fliss shouted. 'He's making a run for it.'

Alys and Fliss sprinted for their car.

'You'll have to stay here with the Defender,' Alys

shouted at Fliss.

'No way, I only do ASBOs and parking tickets.'

'You'll have to. Get on the radio to Ivor. If anyone turns up before he does, hide somewhere.'

Alys jumped in, buckled up and reversed out from the back of the house, leaving Fliss standing there.

There was no sign of Cedric or his car.

Alys turned on her blue lights and siren as she jolted and bounced up the track and turned out onto the road. Cedric was nowhere in sight.

CHAPTER 32

Cassie was angry and upset. Griff said the restaurant was fully booked, but that blatantly wasn't true. Half the tables were unoccupied and a pall of uneasiness dampened conversation, except for one group of diners, whose raucous chatter jarred her nerves.

Cassie, Ellie and the other girls waiting at table were used to being rushed off their feet. With little to do, time dragged, allowing them to brood on the disasters of the last few days. Rianna's carefree banter would normally have lifted their spirits, but her absence was a festering sore, eating away at their mood.

Popping into the scullery to seek Bill's sympathetic ear wasn't an option either. Even if she knew Huw Rogers well enough, his presence loading the dishwashers would be a painful reminder that Bill was lying in a coma in a hospital bed, if he was even still alive.

Griff Llewellyn dragging her in to work unnecessarily was a cruel form of torture. The man had no humanity, and she suspected that he'd try to wriggle out of paying them what he'd promised.

Griff and his father, Rhodri, were seated at a secluded table where they could survey the whole dining room, as they frequently did. Cassie felt that they were watching her every move, checking her waitressing skills. To make matters worse, tonight she was assigned to wait on the pair, a task that she hated. She was always conscious of Griff's eyes devouring her body, stripping her bare. It made her flesh crawl.

Normally careful of others' privacy, tonight Cassie

listened for snatches of the Llewellyns' conversation, wondering if Ree had attempted to blackmail them and had paid the price. She could believe that Griff was capable of forcing himself on a woman, but was he capable of murder? And if he wasn't, who was? She shivered even though the dining room was warm.

The dark décor that Griff had introduced when he'd transformed the building into a boutique hotel reminded Cassie of a gothic horror movie. Perhaps she was living in one.

'...not enough. She wants more.'

Griff frowned as Cassie approached to clear their plates. Who were they talking about? Not Ree, or Griff would have said 'wanted', not 'wants'. Who then? One of the other waitresses? She'd love to plant a listening device on their table. She could set the camera on her phone to record, and conceal it in the basket of bread rolls...

'We're not paying you to day-dream.' Griff's voice cut through her thoughts. 'Hurry up and get the plates cleared.'

'Yes sir,' Cassie said, thinking that it should have been Griff who'd been pushed off the cliff and not Ree.

She was serving Griff his dessert when his phone warbled. As he pulled it out to answer it, Cassie spotted the caller's name on the screen. Wendy Pryce. Cassie quickly averted her gaze, pretending not to notice.

Griff rejected the call, saying to his father, 'I'll answer that later.'

Rhodri Llewellyn's gaze was fixed on her. Had he seen her glance at the phone's screen? Did it matter if he had? Was she growing paranoid? Cassie hurried back into the kitchen to serve her other tables their desserts.

Why was the name Wendy Pryce familiar? She'd definitely heard it before. She'd ask her father when she got home.

*****

'Cassie!'

Cassie stopped at the sound of Griff's voice behind her. She erased the dislike from her face as she turned to him in the narrow corridor, and replaced it with what she hoped was a neutral smile.

'I spoke to you too harshly in the dining room,' Griff said. 'It's a difficult time for us all. Let me make it up to you. Let me run you home in my car. That way you don't have to wait for Huw and the others to finish before you get home.'

Not unless I'm wearing a cast iron chastity belt, Cassie thought, repulsed by the idea of Griff's hands on her body. His eyes were bad enough.

'That's kind of you,' she said, 'but I promised dad that I'd let Huw drive me home with Ellie and Penny. I can't break my promise.'

She turned quickly and stepped into the dining room, where the other girls were laying up the tables for tomorrow's breakfast and waiting for Huw to finish loading the dishwashers in the scullery.

*****

Their duties finally finished, the three girls climbed into Huw's Toyota pickup truck. It was fortunate that he had the four door version with seats for them all. Not so fortunate that it was several years old, smelt musty, and rattled as if it was falling apart.

Penny, the receptionist, climbed in the front with Huw, leaving Cassie and Ellie to sit in the back. 'We've had loads of cancellations,' she said, 'not just for dinner tonight, but from people who've booked to stay.'

'It's not exactly great PR,' Ellie said, 'having people murdered and knocked down on the hotel's doorstep. Griff said he wants us back in the morning, but I can't see that lasting long. We'll be sitting around twiddling our thumbs.'

'He offered to give me a lift home tonight.' Cassie shivered. 'That man gives me the creeps.'

Wendy Pryce! Cassie suddenly remembered where she'd heard that name. Cassie's dad had been to a talk that she'd given about ancient Welsh saints, and the ruins of the abbeys and monasteries in the area. She was an archaeology lecturer at the local college. Why was she phoning Griff Llewellyn? Could Wendy Pryce be the she who 'wants more'? She'd ask her dad what more he knew about the woman.

Huw drove up the hotel driveway and turned right at the top. The headlight beams illuminated the narrow lane, the high hedge-topped banks closing in on either side.

How often had Cassie cycled along this lane after evening service? Would she ever feel safe enough to do it again? Her thoughts turned to Bill.

'It's horrible to think it was only two nights ago that Bill was walking home along here,' Cassie said. The thought of what had happened made her feel ill. 'Who could have run him down and just left him for dead?'

Ellie caught hold of her hand and gave it a squeeze.

'We still don't know if it was deliberate,' Huw said. 'It could have been an accident.'

They drove on in silence, each immersed in their own thoughts, wondering where exactly it was that Bill had been knocked down and left for dead. Cassie felt certain it wasn't an accident. The same person who'd murdered Ree had tried to kill Bill too. But why?

Soon Huw was pulling up outside Cassie's home. The front door opened and she saw her father silhouetted against the hall light.

'Both promise you'll phone when you get safely home,' Cassie said to Ellie and Penny.'

'What! Don't you trust me?' Huw demanded.

'It's not that I don't trust you,' Cassie said. 'It's just that if they phone it'll set my mind at rest.'

CHAPTER 33

Fliss ran to the front of Ty Nymff and watched as Alys disappeared up the track. Seconds later, the pulsating howl of the patrol car's siren reverberated around the valley. Fliss caught occasional glimpses of blue flashing light sparkling off dew-decked trees.

The siren sound suddenly stopped. Fliss's heart hammering in her chest.

What was she thinking, just standing there? She must be losing her senses. She should be radioing Ivor.

Relief blossomed when Ivor answered her call.

'How soon can you get here?' she asked, after a hasty explanation.

'Satnav says twenty-three minutes. I shouldn't meet any delays.'

Fliss's confidence level plummeted. Would that be soon enough? She terminated the call.

Silence returned to the valley. As her ears adapted, they picked up the sounds of the night: the trickle of water in the brook as it eddied around rocks; the whisper of the wind through the trees; the distant hoot of an owl.

Fliss shivered but only partly because of the cold. She was scared.

If Cedric wasn't the murderer, who could it be? Was it someone she knew?

She guessed that the murderer wouldn't come alone. He'd need someone to bring him, unless he lived within walking distance of Ty Nymff.

Something crashed through the undergrowth. Fliss jerked around, fear flashing through her senses. She flicked on her torch but could see nothing. Maybe a badger? It sounded heavy and determined. Get a grip, Fliss, she told herself and clicked off her torch.

She prayed that Ivor wouldn't be delayed, that he'd arrive before anyone came to collect the Defender. She knew her own limitations. She was happy issuing fixed penalty notices for minor offences or demanding someone's address if they were committing anti-social behaviour. But could she go up against a criminal who'd killed and attempted to kill a second time? She'd be stupid to try. She'd probably end up a victim herself.

She looked around. Where would be the best place to hide? She'd need to see any vehicle coming down the track as well as watching the front and the side of the house.

Some of her colleagues would be able to recognise the headlight configurations of different vehicles; distinguish between Ivor's patrol car and one that wasn't his. That wasn't in her skill set, more's the pity.

She couldn't be directly in line with the track, or she'd be caught in its headlight beam like a startled rabbit.

Damn. Her hi-vis jacket would be disastrous give-away. What could she do with it? She couldn't just take it off. The night was too cold. She'd end up with hypothermia. And ideally she'd need a getaway route, in case she was spotted.

The other side of the stream might be her best bet. She flicked her torch back on and searched for a way across, hoping that the batteries would last. Her hand shook and she moved jerkily, like a puppet on a string.

It was madness to stay here alone, she thought. Why did I let Alys leave me? Who would get to Ty Nymff first? Ivor, or the murderer come back to collect the Defender?

She breathed a sigh of relief when she spotted four stepping stones across the brook. It led to a faint path that meandered up through the trees on the far side of the valley. Fliss quickly crossed and looked for what she hoped would be a suitable vantage point from which she could see but couldn't easily be seen.

The trees on the hillside were deciduous, bare, offering few hiding places. She spotted what looked like a tangle of blackthorn or maybe hawthorn, totally leafless, but sufficiently dense that she hoped it would give her some cover.

Ouch! A sharp pain jabbed as something scratched the back of her hand. There must be brambles too. She put her hand to her mouth and tasted blood.

What was that sound? Was it a vehicle starting up in the distance? It couldn't have been parked far away. She wasn't expecting Ivor for at least twenty minutes. Was it the murderer and his accomplice, coming to collect the Defender?

Her muscles tensed. Panic struck.

*****

Alys stopped at the top of the track and looked both ways along the road. She killed the siren but left the blue lights flashing.

Which way had Cedric gone? Had he given her the slip?

Hoping that he'd headed back towards Madoc's Haven, Alys turned left and accelerated hard.

The road was narrow and twisting, alternately bounded by barbed wire fences or hemmed in by banks topped by wind warped hedges.

Alys heard Fliss's call on the radio and Ivor's reply. He'd be with her in twenty to twenty-five minutes.

Would that be soon enough? Fliss had looked aghast when Alys abandoned her outside the cottage. She was slightly built with no experience of violent confrontations. Would she have the good sense to hide? Surely she wouldn't attempt to play the hero?

Alys chased on through the dark, her car's flashing blue lights bouncing off the banks and hedgerows on either side.

Still no sign of Cedric up ahead. Where was he? Had he tricked her, turned off or hidden down a side turning?

The road plunged downhill into a wooded valley, where a bridge crossed an unseen stream cloaked in darkness. She swooped up onto the exposed plateau on the other side.

Alys caught a glimpse of a glimmer up ahead, then the flash of red brake lights. Please let it be Cedric.

The road was as sinuous as a snake as it wound through the undulating countryside.

Then, there he was up ahead, disappearing around a bend. Alys switched off her blue lights and closed the distance.

Alys decided to give him the benefit of the doubt, assume that he'd either misheard her instruction or grown too impatient and had gone on ahead, eager not to be late for his diocesan meeting.

*****

Fliss wasn't sure if she'd heard a vehicle engine starting. It couldn't have been that far away. Where could it have been hidden? Ty Nymff was an isolated rural cottage. There was no other habitation within miles.

Fliss held her breath, strained her ears. Was it moving? She peered across the valley. Yes, she could hear the noise of an engine; see the loom of headlights through the trees. It was driving down the track to Ty Nymff.

If it was the murderer coming back for the Defender, she couldn't risk being spotted. She'd have to run for her life and might not get away.

Panic struck as she struggled to get her hi-vis jacket

off.

She yanked the poppers apart, but her frozen fingers refused to grip the zip-pull. Finally she tugged the zip down and yanked the jacket off. Its sleeve snagged on a bramble, but she ripped the jacket free and threw it to the ground. She dropped to her knees behind the tangled mass of leafless bushes. Fliss shivered as the cold bit into her skin, raising goose bumps.

The engine noise grew louder; the headlights were getting closer. The vehicle was almost at the cottage.

Fliss's heart pounded. Her blood pulsed in her ears.

The vehicle swooped into sight and swung around in front of the cottage, sending a shower of gravel ripping through the undergrowth and raining into the brook as it skidded to a halt.

She couldn't make out the vehicle's registration number and besides, the angle was all wrong. She couldn't even identify the make. It looked like a medium sized panel van, a Ford or a Renault? It could be anything.

The driver left the engine running, both doors opened and two people jumped out with torches. Did they know she'd remained at the cottage?

Fliss threw herself down on her hi-vis jacket, flattening herself to the ground as the torch beams probed the wooded hillside and all around. She stopped breathing, desperate not to let them see her breath condensing in the cold night air.

She almost screamed. Things were crawling over her hands, but she daren't move or try to brush them off. What were they?

After what seemed an eternity, the torch beams stopped combing the cottage's surroundings.

Fliss could hear voices speaking quietly, urgently, but she couldn't make out what they said. The noise of the engine partly drowned them out. She risked raising her head, then her body off the ground and tried to silently brush the creepy-crawlies off her hands. One of them bit her. A sharp prick of pain. Damn, they must be ants, probably wood ants. She stopped trying to rid herself of them, and risked standing up to see better.

She clicked on the body camera attached to her equipment vest in the vain hope that it would capture something worthwhile.

The way the vehicle was parked in front of the cottage, it was silhouetted against the light reflected from its surroundings. She could make out its shape but not much more. She couldn't see its registration plates.

A figure opened one of the van's rear doors. Fliss was hopeful for a moment, but the registration plate must have been on the other door.

Whoever it was took something from the back of the van and slammed its door shut. Both of them walked around to the back of the cottage, the gravel crunching under their feet.

Should she change her position? Try to read the registration? She could hear sounds from the back of the cottage, guessed they were pulling the tarpaulin off the Defender. Were they changing its plates too?

She moved cautiously forward. She didn't want to let Alys down, but if she was unlucky, she could end up getting herself killed.

Someone was coming back! Fliss knelt quickly, hoping the person wouldn't glance across the brook at the hillside, hoping there was insufficient light for her to be visible. She still couldn't make out any distinguishing features, although from the way he walked, she was convinced it was a man.

Her heart skipped a beat. She'd remembered her radio, but she'd forgotten to mute her phone. If anyone called her, it would alert the murderer and his accomplice to her presence. If she turned it on to mute it, the glow of its screen might give the game away anyway. She was in an agony of indecision.

Then she heard the engine of the Defender start. At the same moment the engine of the van that brought the two men revved up.

Fliss jumped to her feet, desperate to see its registration.

The Defender drove out from behind the cottage, its headlight beams bathing the hillside with light and blinding Fliss. All she could see as it followed the other vehicle up the track was the after-image of its headlights burnt onto her retinas.

Had they spotted her? Would they stop and come back? She scrabbled on her equipment vest for her radio.

Could she alert Ivor in time for him to catch up and follow them? Then she'd have to alert the team, force control centre too, broadcast to the world that she'd failed to glean a single worthwhile piece of evidence.

CHAPTER 34

Alys followed Cedric into Madoc's Haven and down the High Street. He pulled in beside Matt's car at the fire station. There wasn't room for Alys without blocking the fire station doors, so she parked a little way down the street.

The evening air was cold, condensing her breath as Alys walked back to the building. No Cedric. Someone must have already let him in.

She punched the entry code into the keypad and, opening the door, was immediately confronted by Beth Francis, glaring at her.

'What are you doing here?' she demanded. 'Why did you leave your PCSO guarding the stolen Defender all by herself?'

Alys's emotional temperature rocketed through the ceiling. How did Beth Francis know that?

'I was making sure that the Reverend Davies arrived here and didn't just disappear.'

The office door opened and Matt stepped out into the corridor.

'Good work, discovering the stolen vehicle,' he told Alys. 'Sergeant Francis, keep the vicar company while I have a word with Sergeant Carey.'

Beth scowled at him before doing as she was told.

Matt glanced at her retreating back and waited for her to shut the door before turning back to Alys. 'I meant it. Finding the Defender was just the break we needed.'

'Only doing my job, sir,' Alys said stiffly, inwardly seething, wondering how Matt could bear working with the woman. She was a liability. He should put her on a disciplinary charge.

'But do I gather that you left PCSO Abbott guarding the Defender by herself?' Matt said, locking onto her gaze. That vehicle's vital evidence.'

How did they both know? Had Fliss or Ivor called them? Or had Beth Francis been listening in on their radio conversations and dripping poison into Matt's ears, turning him against her?

'Give me a brief summary of everything that happened,' Matt said, 'from finding the Defender until you sent the vicar here to be interviewed.'

'I didn't send him here to be interviewed,' she said tersely, and described finding the vehicle hidden under the tarpaulin and Cedric's unexpected appearance.

'What were your impressions? Do you think he could have stolen it, or used it to knock Bill Symonds down?'

Alys bit her lip, recalling her questions and Cedric's reactions. 'If he did, he's quick-witted and a convincing liar. I believed him when he said he had nothing to do with either stealing the Defender or running Bill down.'

'Then I don't understand why you brought him here to be interviewed instead of staying with PCSO Abbott until your PC arrived to relieve you.'

'I didn't bring him here. I told him to wait by his car. When he suddenly drove off, I thought he was making a break for it. As he drove straight here, I'm guessing he was just being impatient.'

Alys hated having to explain her actions, particularly when she realised that she'd made a serious error of judgement.

'But you just said that you thought he had nothing to do with the Defender theft or running Bill down. Why take off after him?'

'I didn't have time to think,' Alys said, trying to keep her rising frustration from her voice. 'I heard him driving off. I thought he was trying to escape.'

Alys's radio bleeped. It was Fliss.

'They're taking the Defender. Over.'

Darkness washed through Alys's thoughts. What a nightmare. Guarding the Defender should have been her number one priority. Like an idiot, she'd chased off after the vicar instead, leaving Fliss alone without backup.

Alys turned and dashed for the door, shouting, 'I'll try to cut them off.'

*****

'I can't understand why Sergeant Carey left her PCSO to guard the vehicle by herself,' Beth said. 'If it's the one used in the Bill Symonds hit-and-run, and that seems likely, it was inexcusable.'

And you should have torn strips off her instead of giving her a pat on the back, Beth thought. She only just managed to stop herself from saying it. Whatever made the incompetent idiots appoint Matt Vincent as DI when the job should have been hers, she couldn't understand.

The interview with the vicar, Cedric Davies, had been routine and inconclusive. He didn't have a solid alibi for the theft of the Defender, Rianna Hughes's murder or for the Bill Symonds hit-and-run, but neither did their other main suspects.

His explanation of why he was visiting the cottage where it was found was plausible. They'd still need to confirm with the owners that he was keeping an eye on the property for them.

Beth would have questioned the vicar more aggressively. She thought Matt Vincent was a wimp.

And unless they could prove that the two men who'd taken the Defender were the vicar's accomplices, they had no evidence against him.

'We need to meet the Scenes of Crime team when

they arrive at the cottage,' Matt said. 'When do they expect to get there?'

Beth checked her watch. 'In about half an hour, maybe less. We should get over there now. I phoned the vehicle recovery crew, told them to turn around and go home.'

Another waste of time and resources.

They locked up the Madoc's Haven office and climbed into the car. Beth keyed the postcode of the cottage into the satnav and started off. She drove up the hill from the village, leaving its street lights behind them. The cloud cover was complete and the darkness closed in. No moon or stars relieved the blackness.

'Let's hope forensics get some evidence from where the Defender was parked,' Matt said. 'Maybe they left prints on the tarpaulin.'

If you were more dynamic, we'd have solved the case by now, Beth thought.

She drove swiftly and decisively around the narrow, twisty country lanes. There were few other cars on the roads. A slight mist meant that the headlights of those that were showed above the hedgerows ahead.

The satnav counted down the distance to their destination. Beth slowed as it warned her of the impending final turn. Ty Nymff was down a track off a longish straight. Its name was painted in white on a slab of grey slate set in the bank at the entrance.

As Beth turned down it, the headlights picked out two parallel stony strips with a ridge of grass running down the middle. It was bumpy but with no major potholes, and the vegetation on the banks was neatly trimmed.

At the bottom of the track, a white police van with its yellow and blue checkerboard markings was parked blocking access to the area in the front of the cottage.

Brilliant white light bounced off the cottage and off the slopes that defined the valley. A generator hummed, powering the SOCOs floodlights.

*****

Fliss jumped out of the SOCOs' van as Beth parked behind it. She looked cold, anxious and on edge.

'I'm sorry, sir' she said, miserably. 'I couldn't get the registration numbers of either vehicle or even tell for certain the make of the van the men arrived in. I only have the vaguest impression of them too.'

'So you learnt nothing of value?' Beth chipped in.

Fliss looked dejected. 'No, sergeant. Not unless I caught something on my body camera.'

'No chance of that out here in the dark,' Beth said.

'I want you to take a look where the Defender was parked,' Matt said to Fliss, ignoring Beth's comments. 'Tell me if anything else has been moved, apart from the Defender and the tarpaulin. Then take me through everything you saw, said and did, from the moment you first drove down the track, to the SOCOs arriving.'

'You can use coveralls and overshoes from our van, sir,' one of the SOCOs said, as he appeared from around the back of the cottage and collected some items of equipment.

A few minutes later, when they were all suitably garbed, Matt led the way to the rear of the cottage. Matt followed as closely as he could the path taken by the SOCO.

The Scenes of Crime Officers were examining the tarpaulin and combing the ground around it in the dazzling glare of the floodlights.

'Need a bucketful of fingerprint powder to do the whole tarpaulin,' one of them said.

'Do you need to check the vicar's mobile phone record?' Fliss asked. 'If he's the murderer, he could have called his accomplices to remove the Defender while he was driving to Madoc's Haven.'

'Good thinking,' Matt said. 'Beth, can you get onto

that first thing in the morning?'

Beth looked fit to explode. 'Already on my list, sir.'

'Sir,' one of the SOCOs called out. 'This could be useful.' He was holding something small and whitish in a pair of tweezers. 'It's a roll-up fag end. From its state it can't have been here more than an hour or two. Probably dropped by the person who took the Defender. Should be saliva, DNA on it.'

Matt reviewed his mental list of suspects. As far as he was aware, none of those he'd met smoked, certainly not roll-ups. The only person he'd interviewed whose clothes reeked of stale tobacco smoke was Bill Symonds, and he was still lying in hospital in a coma.

'Beth. You interviewed Ross Keely. Do you think he's a smoker?'

Beth shook her head. 'Hard to say. Couldn't smell it on him, but he was doused in cologne.'

*****

Alys was frustrated. She'd driven back and forth frantically, covering the likely back roads the driver of the Defender would have taken to get clear of the area. Ivor had been doing the same. They'd been in constant communication over the radio. Control had alerted other response teams to join the hunt, but none of them had seen anything.

They had no way of knowing if the Defender was being driven out of the area or stashed again locally in a new hiding place. It was almost certain that its registration plates would have been switched, so the automatic number plate recognition cameras couldn't help.

Finally abandoning the hunt, Alys drove back to Ty Nymff to collect Fliss and drive her home.

When she arrived, Fliss was standing with Matt and Beth by the SOCOs' van. They were stripping off their white coveralls and overshoes.

'Your team will have to search the local area for the Defender all over again,' Matt told Alys. 'Losing the Defender so soon after you found it is a setback, but it's one we'll have to work through.'

Alys was gutted, seeing Matt putting on a brave face to cover her incompetence.

'Get some sleep and start looking again first thing in the morning,' he continued. 'My suspicion is that they'll have sneaked the Defender out of the area, but we can't risk making assumptions.'

'Yes, sir,' Alys said with a heavy heart. 'Come along Fliss. I'll drive you home. Goodnight sir, sergeant.'

*****

'Sorry Fliss, I should never have chased off after Cedric,' Alys said, as she turned out of Ty Nymff's track for the second time that evening. 'I put you in an impossible situation. I should have radioed control and waited for Ivor to come.'

'Don't worry,' Fliss said, touching Alys's arm. 'We both thought Cedric was bolting. You did what you thought was best at the time.'

Alys glanced at Fliss, glad to have her as a friend as well as a colleague.

'How are you feeling? Are you okay?'

'Still got the adrenalin shakes. It was a bit like going on that roller coaster ride over by Canaston Bridge. The one that drops you a hundred feet and leaves your stomach behind. They must have seen me when they drove the Defender out. I was scared they'd come back and come after me.'

'I didn't know you were a thrill seeker,' Alys said.

'I'm not. An ex-boyfriend took me, with the emphasis on ex. The things a girl does for love.'

Alys drove on in silence for a while, reliving the events of the evening.

'Whoever's stealing the Defenders has to know where to steal them from,' she said. 'It might be a bit obvious just driving around on the lookout for vehicles to nick. Someone might notice and start asking questions, particularly if it's a local.'

'Unless it's someone who has business driving around the area,' Fliss said. 'Like a vicar who covers several parishes.'

Alys glanced sideways and caught an ironic smile on Fliss's face.

'Exactly,' she said, 'but I still don't think it's Cedric. So, who else apart from him?'

'The most obvious candidates are the postman and the parcel delivery drivers.'

'Anyone else?' Alys prompted.

Fliss ran her fingers through her hair as she thought. 'Someone who has business visiting farms,' she said. 'Salesmen selling agricultural products? Fertilisers? Farm equipment? They'd have to drive around, making calls. It would be easy for them to note which farms had Land Rovers or quad bikes worth stealing.'

'We'll go back to the farms that have lost vehicles and find out who visited them in the days or weeks before the thefts took place.'

Postmen would be such frequent visitors that they wouldn't stand out, unless they behaved strangely. Agricultural product salesmen would be far more memorable. Parcel delivery drivers fell in between, unless one of the farm residents was an online shopaholic.

Something niggled at the back of Alys's brain, but what it was eluded her. Perhaps if she drove home and soaked in a hot bath with a chilled glass of Chablis, it would come to her. Even if it didn't, she needed to unwind.

Matt would never support her move to CID now.

CHAPTER 35

Strong coffee and a shower helped dispel the after-effects of Alys's sleepless night. She was determined to make sense of what had happened the previous evening at Ty Nymff and then to move on.

She'd assembled her team in their Madoc's Haven office. The mood was subdued with little of the usual banter and chat. Alys quickly summarised the events of the previous evening, mainly for PCSO Holly Newlyn's benefit.

'What I don't understand,' Alys said, 'is how our villains turned up so quickly after I drove away from Ty Nymff.'

'Maybe the two guys are the ones who steal the Defenders and sell them on. Perhaps they'd already planned to collect it last night,' Holly said. 'It was just a coincidence that they arrived when they did.'

'They must have been parked pretty close,' Fliss said, turning to Alys. 'I'm sure I heard their engine start just after you left. Did you see anyone as you drove away?'

Alys shook her head, reliving the moment she turned out of the track and accelerated away. 'It was pitch black and I was too focused on catching up with Cedric.'

'They were sitting there watching,' Ivor Jones said. 'When they saw you and Cedric drive away, they just grabbed their chance and collected it.'

Fliss shook her head. 'They watch the stolen vehicles to see if we turn up, meaning the vehicle's fitted with a tracker. If we do, they don't touch it. It's too risky.'

'What if word got out that we were combing the countryside looking for it?' Ivor said. 'That would mean it didn't have a tracker. Did any of us say what we were doing, buzzing around the countryside like bluebottles?'

Holly blushed salmon pink. 'I mentioned it to Edwin up at Crugdu. He caught me nosing around his cowshed.'

'Edwin's an old woman,' Ivor said. 'Probably straight on the phone to his mates. You might as well have told the whole countryside.'

'Enough!' Alys said firmly as both Fliss and Holly objected vociferously. She'd speak with Holly later. She was still young and naïve.

'Any other ideas?' Alys said.

'I know you don't think he's involved in Rianna's Murder and Bill Symonds' hit-and-run,' Ivor said, 'but the vicar could have phoned an accomplice while he was driving back to Madoc's Haven.'

'I still can't believe that Cedric had anything to do with it,' Fliss protested. 'Besides, the timing's all wrong.'

Something niggled at the back of Alys's mind to do with the timing, just out of reach. Then it came to her.

'Cedric said he saw us turn down the track and followed us,' Alys said. 'He could have phoned his accomplices before he drove down the track to the cottage. That would have given them time to get in place. Then he lured me into chasing after him. I'll request approval to access his mobile phone records.'

'I still don't believe Cedric had anything to do with it,' Fliss repeated. 'Even if he had time to call an accomplice, it doesn't mean to say that he did.'

While Ivor, Fliss and Holly debated whether Cedric was the murderer, Alys relived the terrible moment when Fliss radioed to say that the Defender had been taken. She could only imagine the recriminations that were flowing down from senior management. Matt would be getting it in the neck for her incompetence. She'd already had a dressing down over the phone from her boss. She trembled to think what Beth was saying behind their backs.

'I've just remembered.' Fliss's voice was suddenly broke through Alys's thoughts. 'Just before we turned down the track to Ty Nymff, there was a layby screened by trees. I bet that's where they were sitting, waiting until it was dark.'

'I know it's a long shot, but can you take a look at the car's dash cam footage?' Alys said. 'See if you can make anything out.'

Ivor snorted with derision. 'Fat chance of that.'

Fliss darted him a frown before turning her attention back to Alys. 'Beth Francis rubbished the idea, but I did turn on my body cam last night. I'll take a look at that too. Can we get digital forensics to work their image enhancement magic on it?'

Ivor slowly shook his head. Alys despaired at her PC's perpetual pessimism.

'It's worth a try but don't get your hopes up.' Alys was grateful that she had Fliss to counter Ivor's negativity.

'I spoke with Beth Francis this morning,' she continued. It was an experience she'd rather forget. 'The Defender wasn't picked up by any of the automatic number plate recognition cameras, so either it's still in the area, they spirited it away along the back roads, or they changed its plates before driving it off. The bottom line is, we need to get back out there and find it.'

'Again,' Ivor added, sotto voce.

*****

Matt was smarting from the angry tirade that he'd

received from the Detective Chief Superintendent. All the man cared about was his budget. He was furious that Scenes of Crime had been called out to investigate a vehicle that wasn't there.

The super ignored the fact that the SOCOs had retrieved the cigarette end with its potential DNA evidence, together with fingerprints from the tarpaulin.

Matt's desk phone rang.

There was a moment's hesitation before a woman's voice said, 'It's Vicky Morgan. It's about Rianna, Rianna Hughes.'

Matt's pulse quickened. 'Yes, how can I help?'

'Have you found out who killed her yet?'

'Not yet. Do you have something to tell me?' Matt held his breath and hoped. He needed a breakthrough. He'd guessed that Vicky had been holding something back.

There was another pause. Matt could imagine Vicky summoning up the courage to tell him what she knew. He kept quiet, hoping that was the best way to make her continue.

'It's about what Ree overheard at the hotel,' Vicky finally said.

'And what was that?' Matt asked gently. With some people you needed the patience of a saint.

'The Llewellyns were discussing their plans for that new resort they're planning to build over at Clebaston Manor. With that Welsh Government minister who's always on the telly, I think his name's Ingrams.'

'Aled Ingram?' Matt prompted.

'Yeah, that's right. They were talking about paying him and that Wendy woman to block any objections to their planning application, to make sure it goes through quickly.'

'What was Rianna intending to do with the information?' Matt asked.

Vicky hesitated for several seconds before saying,

'She wanted them to pay her too.'

At last. Confirmation that Rianna was planning to blackmail the Llewellyns. Definitely a motive for murder.

'Why didn't you tell me this before?'

'I'm scared, scared for both Dafi and me. If they killed Ree to keep her quiet, they could come after us too. They might have guessed that Ree told me. It's no secret that Ree and me were friends. We worked together at the hotel before Dafi came along.'

'Do you know if she asked the Llewellyns for money?'

'I'm not sure. I think she might have done.'

Damn. Matt was hoping for something more definite.

'I'll need you to make a formal statement, confirming what you've just told me,' he said. 'Are you prepared to do that?'

'Will that stop the Llewellyns from coming after me and Dafi?' Vicky asked. 'Can you put us in one of them witness protection programmes, like they do on TV?'

On most TV movies that Matt had watched, being on a witness protection programme usually guaranteed the witness's speedy demise.

'I'm sure you aren't in danger' he said. 'There's no evidence that Rianna's death is connected to what she may have overheard at the hotel, but I'll ask Sergeant Carey to call around and speak with you, if that'll put your mind at rest.'

CHAPTER 36

'Take a look,' Fliss said smiling, her voice tinged with excitement. 'It's my body cam footage from when they drove the Defender away last night. Ivor was right, there's no way you can make out the licence plate, but what do you think?' She passed her iPad to Alys.

Alys stared at the screen, holding her breath, willing it to reveal the identities of the two men.

The image was in grayscale. Headlights appeared from behind the cottage. Then the screen whited out as they shone straight at Fliss's body cam.

'Weren't you scared they'd stop and come after you?' Alys asked. Her heartrate spiked. She hated to think how Fliss must have felt.

The white out resolved as the Defender swung around the front of the cottage, its headlights picking out the other van as it was turning back up the track.

'Of course I was,' Fliss said, pausing the video. 'That's why I had the shakes afterwards. I was all set to beat the Olympic record for 10k or whatever it took. Fortunately they didn't.' She stabbed her finger at the screen. 'There! Look!'

Alys looked, but all she could see was a grainy grayscale image of the disappearing van with few, if any, distinguishing features.

'There's no way you can read its registration plate or what's written on its panels,' Alys said, shaking her head, bitterly disappointed. 'I don't know why you're so excited,' She passed the iPad back to Fliss.

'No,' her PCSO said. 'Take a closer look. Can't you make out anything at all?'

Alys took back the iPad, unconvinced. 'I don't know. Maybe an old Ford Transit panel van?'

'What else?' Fliss asked, frustration creeping into her voice. 'What about its side and back doors?'

Alys shook her head and shrugged. 'Maybe some advertising. It would help if you could see it in colour.'

'I know who it belongs to,' Fliss said triumphantly. 'Do you remember that dodgy farmer from Brynfawr, Sam Scruton? Was taken to court by Trading Standards? Went around the farmers' markets, flogging what he claimed was grass fed mountain lamb and naturally reared grass fed beef? All cheap imported rubbish from goodness only knows where. That's his van. You can't make out any detail, but that pattern of shapes is unique.'

Alys barely remembered the Scrutons' van, let alone the graphics and sign writing on it.

'This is why you have an artist on the team,' Fliss said smugly.

'Just don't get poached by the fraud squad,' Alys said, although she wasn't convinced. 'I've heard they're recruiting experts in the fine arts. We'd miss you.'

'I bet Scruton was the person who drove the Defender away. Question is, was the other driver his son?'

Fliss's detective work placed Alys in a quandary. Fliss seemed convinced. Should she tell Matt and Beth what Fliss had deduced, or should she check it out before letting them know? The temptation to follow it up herself was intense.

If it hadn't been for Beth, she'd never have hesitated for an instant.

'Get the address, postcode and map coordinates of their small holding,' she told Fliss, 'and look up the registration number of his van. Upload that together with your body cam footage and deductions and details of Scruton's criminal record to the murder file. When you've done all that let me know, and I'll phone DI Vincent.'

Fliss smiled. 'She's really got under your skin, hasn't she?'

'What do you mean?' Alys said, sharply.

Fliss's smile widened into a grin. 'Not what, who? Detective Sergeant Beth Francis, of course.'

Alys groaned. 'It's not that obvious is it?'

'Well, I did hear you muttering 'poisonous witch' under your breath.'

'Don't you dare repeat that to anyone.'

Fliss looked wounded.

'Sorry, I shouldn't have said that.' Alys rested her hand on Fliss's arm. 'I know you better than that.'

*****

The sun was rising higher in the sky when Alys pulled up outside the vicarage. An aging silver Toyota was parked in the lane in the shadow of the sheltering trees. Daffodils in the vicarage borders gave a vibrant splash of colour to the garden. An early bumble bee hovered over them and then flew on.

Alys's knock on the door triggered Whiskey's gruff growls and Cedric's voice telling him to hush.

'Ah,' Cedric said when he opened the door and saw them. 'Our intrepid guardians of the law.' His normal welcoming smile was missing from his face. 'What can I do for you this morning?'

Alys guessed they weren't flavour of the month after their confrontation the previous meeting outside Ty Nymff.

Whiskey pushed past the vicar and sniffed at both Alys and Fliss. Fliss knelt down and made a fuss of him. 'Aren't you the handsomest dog in the world?'

'You'd better come in,' Cedric said. 'Gemma Rogers is with me, Dylan's mum. We were just discussing little Meg. Such a shame her being separated from everyone she loves.'

Cedric held open the door and Whiskey led them all into the sitting room.

'Fliss, excellent timing,' Gemma said after they'd exchanged pleasantries. 'I need some more of your pilgrim brooches and bracelets ready for the tourist season. Can you drop some by when you have a moment?'

Alys was amused at the web of interactions that bonded the Madoc's Haven community together. Fliss the PCSO was also Fliss the jewellery maker. She'd doubtless been hard at work making and stockpiling her creations during the long winter evenings. Last time Alys called on Cedric, it was Huw the builder and new church warden who was visiting the vicarage.

Gemma picked up her handbag and coat and said to Cedric, 'I must be getting back. Let me know if you have any more thoughts that will help Dylan get Meg back. What with the gift shop and keeping the books for Huw, I can't take on looking after Meg full-time.'

'What can I do for you ladies?' Cedric asked after he'd shown Gemma out. 'I told Matt Vincent and his sergeant everything that I know last night.'

'We just wanted to check if you told anyone that we'd found the stolen Land Rover Defender yesterday evening,' Alys said. 'Did you message or phone anyone?'

'Why would I do that?' Cedric asked with a perplexed frown. 'Oh. I did tell Cassie after Huw delivered her home from work. Is that a problem?'

'When would that have been?'

'About ten o'clock, I think, maybe half-past. Why are you asking?'

Alys was reluctant to tell him that the Defender had been magicked away, that they'd lost it. As it was driven away before ten when the forensic team arrived at Ty Nymff, Cedric telling Cassie didn't matter.

As Alys and Fliss made their excuses to leave, Alys received a message from Holly asking if they could meet up at the police station.

'I still can't see Cedric as a criminal,' Fliss said as they drove down Madoc's Haven High Street. 'If he is, he'd use an anonymous pay as you go phone to communicate with his accomplices.'

*****

'I went back to see Edwin this morning,' Holly blurted out when Alys stepped into the office. The young police community support officer looked upset and embarrassed.

'What did he say?'

'He was only trying to help us find the Defender,' Holly said. 'I'm sorry I'm so stupid.'

'So who did he call?' Alys asked.

'Several of the local farmers,' Holly said, not meeting her eyes, 'people he thought might have disused outbuildings where a stolen vehicle could be hidden.'

'And they called their friends who called their friends,' Alys said. Ivor was right. It was like the bush telegraph, making it impossible to keep secrets in a close-knit community like theirs. 'Did you get a list of who they were?'

'Some of them,' Holly said. 'Edwin was a little vague, said he couldn't remember exactly.'

Holly reeled off the names from her notes, but there were none that excited Alys's interest. She'd have to confess to Matt and Beth that one of her team had alerted the thieves to the police search, and probably alerted the murderer too.

That let Cedric off the hook, or at least substantially lowered the odds that he'd had anything to do with the Defender's second disappearance, unless he was the murderer.

CHAPTER 37

Matt was frustrated. The blurred images from Fliss Abbott's body cam would never persuade a magistrate to grant him a search warrant for Sam Scruton's farm.

Even if Scruton had snatched the Defender from under their noses the previous evening, he'd hardly be stupid enough to hide it away on his own land. However, Matt wanted to meet the man for himself, to see how he reacted to a visit from the police. That might tell him if he was worth following up.

As Beth drove, Matt's attention was distracted by the countryside and its hedgerows. Where the road dipped into wooded valleys, clumps of primroses were waking to the spring sunshine on the grassy banks. Although it was several years since Hannah's death and Matt leaving the area, he felt more at home in Pembrokeshire's country lanes than he ever had working the Avon and Somerset Police's territory.

He hastily thrust all thoughts of his teenage years into the compartment where they belonged.

Scruton's farm was a dispirited collection of dilapidated buildings surrounding a manure strewn yard. Weeds grew unchecked around the base of a telegraph pole to which a sign was attached bearing the name of the farm. The sign was so streaked with grime and algae that it was hard to make out the name, 'Scruton's Farm'.

A van was parked at the roadside, an aging white Ford Transit. "Scruton's Farm Produce" was sign-written on the vehicle's rear doors and sides. Painted rectangles showed pictures of contented cows and woolly sheep with promises for the freshness of the meat.

'Take some pictures of the van,' Matt told Beth. 'Similar angles to the ones captured by PCSO Abbott's body cam.' Now that he'd seen the vehicle, he felt more hopeful that Fliss Abbott was correct.

As there were no signs of activity or noises from the farm buildings, Matt and Beth knocked on the farmhouse door. It was opened by a man in his twenties, dark hair, scruffily dressed and unshaven. He looked at them suspiciously. They were too smartly dressed to want farm produce, too official.

'What d'you want?' he said, unwelcomingly.

Matt held up his warrant card. 'I'm Detective Inspector Vincent and this is Detective Sergeant Francis. Who are you?'

'Rob Scruton.'

His jaw set and a sullen expression made his already unpleasant face even less pleasing. Matt had seen many of his type answering charges in court.

'We'd like to speak with your father,' Matt said.

'Then you're out of luck. He's not here.' He started to close the door.

Matt stopped him by putting his foot in the way. 'Can you tell me where he is and when he'll be back?'

'No to both. Is that all?'

'Who is it?' a man's voice came from inside the house. The door was yanked open and an older version of Rob Scruton, equally unprepossessing, appeared behind him.'

'Police,' Rob Scruton told him. 'Didn't know you was here.'

Matt didn't believe that for one moment. 'Samuel Scruton?' he asked.

'What if it is?' After a quick glance, he didn't meet Matt's eye.

'We're investigating a series of crimes, including

murder, vehicle theft and failing to stop after an accident,' Matt said. 'We'd like to ask you some questions.'

'Nothing to do with me,' Scruton said quickly.

'What were you doing yesterday evening?'

'Same as every evening. Looking after the animals, feeding them, usual stuff.'

'So you didn't go out in the van? You were here all evening?

Scruton moved his weight from one foot to the other and avoided meeting Matt's eye. 'Might have gone into Madoc's Haven to pick up some stuff from the minimarket.'

The man gave off the vibes of an habitual liar, a petty criminal. 'What time was that?'

'Don't remember. After dark. Didn't bother to look at the clock.'

He was covering himself, being vague so that he could adapt his story as circumstances required. Matt had encountered too many of his type before.

Matt went through the motions of asking what Scruton had been doing at the times of Rianna's murder and Bill's hit and run. Scruton was evasive, not really answering Matt's questions. Matt turned his attention to Scruton's son, but he was cast from the same mould.

'Not a wasted journey,' Matt said to Beth as she drove them back towards their HQ in Carmarthen. 'I wasn't convinced when I saw Fliss Abbott's pictures, but now I've met the pair of them, father and son, I'm sure they're both involved. We need more evidence, something more concrete.'

Beth was suspiciously silent. Matt wondered what she was thinking. He needed to know more of her background, what made her tick. When he had time, he'd do some discreet digging.

*****

Sergeant Beth Francis had not slept well and was in a vile mood.

Why did the DI give Ms Marple all the cushy tasks? Surely it couldn't be that hard to find the stolen Defender? Again. It would probably lead her straight to the villain, then she'd get all the credit for solving the case.

Beth grabbed her car keys and shot out of the door.

It was a short drive to Dyfed-Powys Police HQ and soon Beth was sitting at her desk. She quickly powered up her computer and viewed the incident file on the stolen Defender. From its vehicle registration number and a few swift searches, she ascertained its year of manufacture, date of first registration, paint colour and a host of other details.

Beth then searched the automatic number plate recognition camera database, and determined that the stolen vehicle hadn't driven past any of the cameras located in West Wales since its theft.

So, either the thieves knew the locations of the cameras and skilfully avoided them, they'd given it false plates, or it was still within a short drive of Madoc's Haven.

Damn. Ms Marple might yet succeed in her quest.

Then inspiration struck. Beth's fingers flashed over her keyboard and a cherubic smile lit her face. She'd show Ms Alys flipping Marple.

*****

Matt was worried. In the limited time he'd known his detective sergeant, he'd never seen her look so radiantly happy. Her features were transformed, but was that good news or bad?

'Yes, Beth? What do you have for me?' he asked, gesturing for her to sit down.

'You remember the Scruton's van,' Beth said, 'the Ford Transit we saw outside their farm?'

I'd have to be an idiot not to, Matt thought, as he nodded for her to continue. Damn, I'm beginning to think like her.

'I checked it out on the automatic number plate recognition database.'

'And?' Matt prompted.

'Not long after the Defender disappeared from Ty Nymff, the Scruton's Transit was picked up travelling to Port Talbot. It was registered by cameras on the A40, the M4 and in Port Talbot itself.'

'Really?' Matt said, sitting up straighter. 'Now that is interesting. Why on earth would they drive to Port Talbot at that time of night?'

'That's not all,' Beth said. 'From the timings, it looks like when they got there they turned round and drove straight back home.'

'Curious and curiouser.'

'About 160 mile round trip, a bit over three hours.'

'Excellent work,' Matt said. From the look on Beth's face, that wasn't all. 'What else do you have?' he asked.

'I searched the database to see if the cameras had picked up the movements of any Land Rover Defenders at around the same time.'

Matt nodded encouragingly. He was growing impatient. Beth looked as pleased as a cat that had just caught next door's pet gerbil.

'Strangely enough,' Beth said, 'there was a Defender that drove to Port Talbot at almost exactly the same time as the Scruton's Transit. They could have been glued together.'

'But it didn't make the return journey,' Matt guessed, 'and it didn't have the same registration as the stolen vehicle.'

That deflated Beth's mood for a second or two. Matt almost felt guilty. Almost, but not quite.

Beth bounced back fast.

'The same Defender was picked up by a camera on

the Manchester ring road at about the same time as it was driving past Carmarthen. Two hundred miles away.'

'So they cloned the Manchester Defender's registration plates,' Matt said, 'and thought they'd get away with it.'

He'd obviously misjudged his detective sergeant. She had hidden talents.

'Well done, Beth,' Matt said. 'Get onto Port Talbot police. We need them to find that Defender and have their forensic team go over it for Bill Symonds' blood and the Scrutons' prints.'

Matt felt happier than he had since the start of the case. 'And get a search warrant for the Scrutons' farm. We're looking for their plate cloning gear.'

'Get onto Sergeant Carey,' he added as an afterthought, 'Tell her to call off her team's search for the Defender.'

If possible, the grin on Beth's face grew even broader. Too late Matt realised that Beth wasn't the best choice of person to relay the message to Alys.

Matt mentally shrugged. He didn't have time to act as referee between the two women.

It was clear that the Scrutons were members of the gang stealing the Land Rovers, but how did that relate to Bill Symond's hit-and-run, and to Rianna Hughes's murder? What motive could they have had for either?

The three crimes had to be connected. There was no way it was a coincidence.

CHAPTER 38

'It's time we had a break,' Alys told Fliss. 'Let's grab a quick coffee at the mill.'

They'd spent all the previous day and the first part of the morning revisiting the possible hide-aways that they'd searched the first time around, and still no sign of the Land Rover Defender.

'This is a waste of time. I can't believe it's still anywhere near,' Fliss said.

'Maybe they decided not to risk driving it out of the area,' Alys said, determined not to agree that the task they'd been set was a pointless exercise.

'If I was them, I'd clean it up to remove every last trace of forensic evidence, fit false plates and drive it far away,' Fliss said,

'I'm not sure the Scrutons are that bright,' Alys said, although secretly she agreed with Fliss. 'The question is, are they working alone, or as part of a gang?'

Alys pulled into the woollen mill car park. Knowing Fliss's rally driving aspirations, she'd made sure that she was in the driver's seat.

'Isn't that Julie Bowen's car?' Fliss said. 'She must have had the same idea.'

Sure enough, Julie was inside the mill's café, drinking coffee and chatting to Joyce.

'Hello Alys, Fliss,' Julie said. 'Have you found out who ran Bill down? I've been onto the hospital. He's still in a coma.'

Alys remembered that Julie was Bill's first, or was it second cousin? She felt guilty. She didn't like to admit that they'd found the vehicle used and then had it stolen from under their noses.

'We're still working on it,' she said. 'What are the local folks saying?'

Julie put her hand on Alys's arm, and said in a confidential tone, 'Can we go over and sit at that table in the corner? There's something I'd like to discuss.'

'Of course,' Alys said, her curiosity tweaked. Then to Joyce, 'Can you bring us over the usual please?'

The three of them settled in the corner. 'What's this all about?' Alys asked.

'I'm worried at what's happening and the way it's affecting the community,' Julie said. 'It isn't healthy. A lot of people think Dylan killed Rianna, but I can't see it.'

'What makes you say that?'

'He wouldn't do that to Meg. He adores his little baby. He wouldn't deprive Meg of her mother, it's not in his character.'

'Not even in a fit of rage?' Fliss asked.

'No,' Julie said, emphatically. She hesitated, looking conflicted. 'I wanted to say that, before I told you what I saw.'

'Go on,' Alys said.

'The night before last, quite late, I was delivering some dressings to one of my elderly patients. What with everything going on, it slipped clean from my mind.'

Alys waited, with growing impatience.

'She lives close to Vicky Morgan,' Julie continued, lowering her voice. 'Dylan Rogers rode up on his motorbike and went into Vicky's block of flats.'

'What are you saying? Do you think Dylan and Vicky are lovers?'

'Well, it's possible, isn't it? Vicky's husband is away for weeks at a time, and Rianna did kick Dylan out of his home. Young people that age have urges and precious little self-control.' Julie suddenly looked aghast. 'Present company excepted, of course.'

'Which are you talking about,' Fliss said laughing, 'the urges or the self-control?'

Julie blushed and looked offended. 'I'm not trying to stir up trouble. I just thought you should know,' she said, ignoring Fliss's comment and looking at Alys.

'Thanks for sharing that,' Alys said.

'It's a shame Vicky's married,' Julie said. 'If she and Dylan were a couple, Meg and Dafi could grow up together. That would solve a lot of problems.'

*****

'What did you make of what Julie Bowen was saying?' Alys asked Fliss as they walked back to their car.

'Well, you definitely need to keep your urges under control,' Fliss said. 'You positively glowed when Matt Vincent turned up outside the Madoc's Bay Hotel. You were practically swooning.'

She dodged as Alys took a playful swipe at her.

'Shut up, idiot,' Alys said, blushing. 'I meant about Vicky and Dylan.'

'Julie's a gossip, but I don't doubt what she saw. Might give Dylan an even stronger motive for getting rid of Rianna, but he's always been in the frame for killing her.'

At that moment, both their radios beeped. It was a message from Control to all Madoc's Haven neighbourhood policing team officers, telling them to meet DI Matt Vincent at the Madoc's Haven station for an important briefing in one hour's time.

Alys and Fliss looked at each other.

'What do you think,' Alys said, 'have they found the Defender, or has somebody else been killed?'

*****

The road outside the fire station was awash with police vehicles, including an unmarked car that Alys recognised. It was the one Matt had driven on the night of Rianna's murder.

Her team's office inside was bursting. Matt and Beth were with the two detective constables who'd tried chatting her up at the Madoc's Bay Hotel and another pair she didn't recognise.

Alys and Fliss squeezed in beside Ivor and Holly. The room was hot and stuffy, and Alys could smell Ivor's damp uniform. She wanted to throw the window open wide, but she couldn't get near it.

Matt looked eager and alert. Beth Francis looked smug, far different from her expression when Alys had last seen her in the aftermath of the Defender's disappearance. Was that only the night before last?

'Welcome everyone,' Matt said, and made brief introductions. 'Here's a quick update on our latest findings. A search of the ANPR database shows that a Land Rover Defender using false number plates and a Transit van belonging to Sam Scruton travelled from somewhere in this area to Port Talbot the night before last.'

'Just after the Defender was stolen from under the noses of the neighbourhood policing team,' Beth Francis muttered audibly.

Anger flashed through Alys's body. She forced herself to relax. Now wasn't the time to respond.

Matt glanced sternly around to suppress the outbreak of whispered asides.

'As you all know,' he continued, 'a stolen Defender is implicated in what we assume was the attempted murder of Bill Symonds.

'Port Talbot police suspect a local breakers' yard is handling stolen vehicles. They believe some are broken down for the lucrative trade in replacement vehicle parts.

'At the same time as they execute a search warrant at the breakers' yard, we'll raid the Scrutons' farm looking for number plate making equipment.'

'About time we pinned something on the Scrutons,' Ivor Jones said, as Beth passed around photocopied sheets.

'As you can see from the handouts,' Matt continued, 'most number plate printers look just like an office laser printer. They print onto self-adhesive transparent sheets that are then stuck onto metal number plate blanks. So you're looking for number plate blanks, something that looks like an office printer, and transparent sheets with the same dimensions as vehicle registration plates. Any questions?'

When there were none, he said, 'You have a rough sketch of the farm and its buildings. You'll work in pairs. I've allocated each pair a building or set of buildings to search. Sergeant Francis and I will go in first and serve the search warrant on the Scrutons. You'll follow and carry out the search. Assuming the search is successful, we'll take the Scrutons in for questioning. Let's make this work!'

As they all picked up their gear, Beth said to one of her DCs, 'Let's hope none of the local team go shooting off their mouths like last time. We need this one to be a surprise.'

Holly blushed and Alys clenched her teeth. 'If it wasn't for my team,' she said quietly, 'you'd never have suspected the Scrutons.'

'Who d'you think searched the ANPR database?' Beth responded.

'Cool it the pair of you,' Matt told them. 'Team rivalry's good, but not if it gets out of hand.'

Alys was furious with herself for letting Beth get under her skin. She was determined not to let it happen again.

'What I don't understand,' she said, 'is why the Scrutons would have wanted to kill Bill Symonds. What would be their motive?'

'Obvious,' Beth said. 'He must have stumbled on evidence that they were stealing the Defenders.'

'So what's the link with Rianna's murder?' Alys said, holding Beth's gaze, challenging her.

'Perhaps she did too,' Beth said with a shrug.

'I don't buy it,' Alys said. 'It's more complex than that.'

'Enough!' Matt said, cutting across their argument. 'There'll be time to speculate later. Let's get on with it.'

CHAPTER 39

Julie Bowen parked and hurried up the path to the vicarage's front door. Whiskey's barks and gruff growls announced her arrival.

Cedric opened the door before she had time to ring the bell.

'Why in such a rush?' he asked as Whiskey sniffed at Julie and wagged his tail. 'You shot up the path as if the devil's at your heels. We're only discussing the agenda for the next Historical Society meeting.'

'I've no idea what's going on,' Julie said, forgetting to bend down to pat Whiskey in her excitement. 'A whole procession of police vehicles went shooting down the High Street. Matt Vincent was in the leading car. Alys and Fliss were following and there were at least three other cars hot on their heels.' Julie finally stopped for air and patted Whiskey and fondled his ears.

'I didn't hear any sirens,' Cedric said, frowning. 'Which direction were they headed in?'

'No sirens. They all had their blue lights flashing. They were off up towards the Preselis,' Julie said, her heart pounding. 'Do you think there's been another tragedy, someone else killed or injured? After Rianna and Bill, that would be too much to bear.'

Cedric shook his head and held the door open. 'Sounds more like they were on their way to arrest someone. I wonder who,' he said thoughtfully. 'Come along in and let me make us a coffee.'

When they were settled in the lounge with their drinks, Cedric said, 'The agenda for next month's meeting. There's a lot of interest and concern over the Llewellyns' plans for the Clebaston Manor Resort. The community's split down the middle. Half the people want it for the jobs and tourists it'll bring to the area, the other half are opposed because of the potential destruction of an archaeological site, the disruption, and the influx of tourists. What do you think? Should we devote the whole meeting to it?'

'Isn't that a little insensitive, so soon after Rianna's murder and Bill's accident?' Julie said. She was surprised that Cedric had even suggested it.

Cedric raised his eyebrows. 'I can't see Rhodri Llewellyn being worried about that. From what I hear, he's intent on bulldozing his plans through, regardless of what else is going on.'

'True, but we are in the middle of a murder enquiry,' Julie said. 'Shouldn't we at least run the idea past Alys to see what she thinks?'

'Okay, can you do that?' Cedric said, dismissively. 'Assuming we go ahead, we should ask Wendy Pryce to give the introduction. She's the county archaeological advisor and she'll know what's happening with the planning application and the proposed dig. I can't imagine Rhodri being willing to speak, but you could always give him a try too. Maybe he'll think he can win over the opposition.'

What was Cedric up to, Julie wondered. Surely he'd heard the rumours that the Llewellyns were bribing Wendy to say that the evidence requiring the dig was unfounded? Hadn't his own daughter Cassie been the source of some of them? Weren't they a possible motive for Rianna's murder?

Julie stared at Cedric over the rim of her cup as she took another sip of her coffee. Odd, very odd. Perhaps it was an oblique attempt by Cedric to scuttle the Llewellyns' opposition to a dig? Or was there more to it than that?

'So,' Julie said. 'Minutes; matter arising – we should give an update on the Rediscovering Ancient Connections project; the Clebaston Manor Resort development proposal; and any other business.'

Cedric nodded his agreement.

'Do you have a few minutes to discuss Dylan Rogers and Meg?' Julie asked. 'I'm worried for Meg. It must be terrible for her, no longer seeing her mother, being taken away from Dylan and from Vicky and Dafi too. She's surrounded by people she doesn't know.'

'I took Vicky and Dafi to meet Dylan and Meg at the supervised contact centre in Neyland on Monday,' Cedric said. 'Vicky said it went well.'

'That was kind of you,' Julie said. She decided to run her new idea past Cedric.

'What do you think of Vicky and Nick applying to become foster parents? They could foster Meg and they'd all be reunited.'

Cedric at first looked surprised and then pensive. 'Isn't Nick being away for such long periods of time a problem?'

'I checked that out. Even single people can foster children in the right circumstances, and Vicky's not single.'

'Why wouldn't they just adopt Meg?'

Julie smiled. 'Dylan might find himself a new partner and want Meg back. Besides, if Vicky and Nick fostered Meg, they'd be paid...'

'... and it needn't be permanent,' Cedric said, completing the sentence for her.

A glow of satisfaction permeated Julie's mind.

'What if the police find that Dylan killed Rianna and tried to kill Bill?'

'They could still adopt Meg,' Julie said, feeling crushed, wishing she'd never shared her idea. What was wrong with the vicar? Couldn't he have faith in his flock?

CHAPTER 40

Beth led the cavalcade of police vehicles around the narrow country lanes at breakneck speed as if she was in the RAC rally.

'Slow down a little,' Matt told her. 'Make sure the others can keep up.'

Beth's "little" was infinitesimally small, but fortunately they didn't run into any oncoming traffic.

Ten nerve frazzling minutes later, Beth swung the car into the Scrutons' farmyard and slid to a halt amidst a shower of muck and squawking chickens.

As Matt jumped out, Alys's police car pulled in behind them, leaving the rest of the cavalcade to park out on the road, all still with their blue lights flashing.

'What are you lot doing here?' Sam Scruton shouted as he ran out of his house with his son just behind him.

'Samuel Scruton?' Matt said, striding up to him. 'This is a warrant to search your farm and all of its buildings, premises and vehicles for items related to the theft of vehicles and the production of false number plates.'

'You can't do this,' Scruton shouted. 'It isn't legal.'

'This document says it is,' Matt replied, thrusting a copy of the warrant into Sam Scruton's hand. 'You'll remain in the house with two of my officers while the rest of my team conduct the search. I'll let you know when we've finished.' He detailed Ivor and Holly to take the Scrutons into the farmhouse and gestured for the search team to get started.

Matt leaned back against his car and watched as they went to work. The farm and its buildings were in a shambolic state. Paint was peeling off doors and window frames, the once white-washed walls were grey and streaked with years of water cascading down them from leaky gutters, and rusting equipment and litter lay discarded in unsightly heaps around the farmyard.

He studied the sign writing on the panels of the Scrutons' Transit van proclaiming grass fed mountain lamb and naturally reared grass fed beef. No one in their right mind would buy meat from the Scrutons if they could see the place. Maybe vehicle theft and petty crime was their main source of income. It didn't appear that farming could be.

One of Alys's PCSOs, Fliss Abbott, came jogging from a lean-to shed towards him. He pushed himself upright. 'Found something?' he asked.

'We think it's the number plate printer, sir. There are some blank number plates too.'

'Well found! Go tell Scenes of Crime to get to work. They'll know what to do.'

As she turned to jog away, he said, 'And Officer Abbott ...'

She turned back to him expectantly.

'Good work identifying their Transit from your fuzzy body cam footage. That was the breakthrough we needed.'

Fliss smiled happily and jogged off towards the SOCO's van.

Beth scowled.

Twenty minutes later Matt's radio beeped. It was Port Talbot police.

'We've found a land Rover Defender at the breakers yard. It has a broken nearside headlight cover with what looks like dried blood on what remains of it. We've checked the VIN number and it doesn't match the plates. It's definitely your stolen Defender. Our SOCOs are working on it now. What news your end?'

'We've just found the plate cloning printer and

number plate blanks. We're taking in the suspects for questioning.'

'We've made three arrests. More to follow. Thank your sergeant from us. Neat piece of work. Any time she's in Port Talbot, we'll stand her a drink.'

'Great teamwork all round,' Matt said. 'We'll fingerprint our suspects and upload the prints to the database. We'll be in touch.'

'Well done Beth,' Matt said, as he ended the call. 'You heard that? You're flavour of the month in Port Talbot.'

Maybe you could apply for a transfer there, Matt thought. Do us both a favour.

CHAPTER 41

Sam Scruton sat sweating in the interview room at divisional HQ in Haverfordwest. The air conditioning was so fierce that Matt had goose bumps on his arms. He thought of putting his jacket back on.

'Last night your Transit van was picked up on camera driving to Port Talbot and back,' Matt said. 'At almost exactly the same time, a stolen Land Rover Defender was picked up driving along the same route to Port Talbot. They could have been glued together. The Defender didn't come back.'

'So what? Lots of vehicles on the road at night. Chance, I reckon,' Scruton said. 'What's that got to do with me?'

'We found the Defender's original number plates in the back of your Transit van,' Matt said. 'Would you like to explain that?'

Scruton slumped back on his chair.

'Not saying that I did it, but what if someone drove the Defender to Port Talbot,' Scruton said, defiantly. 'They can't hang you for it, can they?'

'Funny you should say that,' Matt said. 'The vehicle was used in a murder attempt three nights ago.'

'You can't pin that on me!' Scruton shouted, jumping up. 'First time I saw the Defender was last night!'

'So you admit to driving a stolen vehicle?'

Scruton collapsed back onto his chair. 'I'm admitting nothing.'

Matt stared at Scruton.

'You'd never seen the stolen Defender before last

night? Then explain why you went to a lonely cottage late yesterday evening, fitted false number plates to a stolen vehicle, and drove it to Port Talbot.'

Scruton squirmed, then finally muttered, 'I was told to.'

'Who told you to?'

'I dunno.'

Matt laughed. 'You expect me to believe that?'

'It's true,' Scruton said, sullenly. 'Got a text message, didn't I? Told me where to go, what to do.'

'Who sent it?'

'Dunno. Got the message, did what I was told.'

'Just supposing I believe you, why would you do that? For someone you don't know?'

Another long pause. 'Two hundred quid.'

'How were you paid?'

Scruton sighed. 'A hundred in the glove box of the Defender, the other hundred when I delivered it.'

'Not much, when you're looking at a charge of attempted murder and the theft of five vehicles.'

'I told you I didn't do that. And what d'you mean five vehicles?' Scruton said, angrily.

'Oh,' Matt said, 'I forgot to tell you. We found the number plates of another four stolen vehicles tucked away in your outhouse. Silly keeping them, wasn't it.'

Matt banged his fist down on the table, making everyone jump. 'Now stop messing me around. Tell me what you know about this mythical sender of text messages, or I'll charge you with attempted murder right here and now.'

'I told you,' Scruton said, looking worried. 'I don't know who sends the texts. Never met him, never spoke to him on the phone.'

'How do you know it's a he?' Matt demanded, locking Scruton's gaze.

Scruton stared back, but his eyes looked unfocussed. Matt could almost see the cogs in the man's brain turning.

'Dunno. Just thought it would be,' Scruton finally replied.

'How did this person get in touch, back at the beginning?'

'Messaged me.'

'And you went along with it, did what you were told? Why?'

Scruton looked uneasy, shrugged. 'Easy money, wasn't it? Watch a vehicle for a few days. If no one comes looking, drive it to Port Talbot.'

'Why you? Why did you agree when you'd never even met this person?'

Matt waited patiently. 'You'd better tell me the rest. From the evidence we've found and what you've already said, there's no point holding back now.'

'He knew something,' Scruton said. 'Threatened to tell you lot.'

'What was it?'

Scruton laughed. 'I'm not that bloody stupid.'

'Verdict's already in and sentence passed on that one,' Beth muttered.

Scruton glared at her.

'What was special about last night?' Matt said, ignoring Beth's comment. 'From what you've said, if you saw someone looking, you'd have left the vehicle alone.'

Scruton sighed. 'Said he'd give me another couple of hundred. I'm still waiting for it.'

'How do you know you'll be paid?'

Scruton shrugged. 'Dunno. Always came through in the past.'

'Your sender of text messages might have something else in mind. If I was you and you suspect this person's identity, I'd be worried.'

Scruton looked startled. 'What d'you mean?'

'Your stolen Defender was used in an attempt to kill

Bill Symonds, probably because he'd guessed the identity of Rianna Hughes' murderer. Supposing you're let out on bail, it might be wise if you and your son took it in turns to sleep at night.'

CHAPTER 42

'Well done everyone,' Alys said, eager to sustain her team's exhilaration following the raid. 'Sam Scruton's admitted to driving the stolen Defender to Port Talbot, but claims he didn't steal it. He said last night was the first time he'd seen it.'

'Hogwash.' Ivor Jones radiated disbelief. 'He ran Bill Symonds down, now he's trying to wriggle out of it.'

'Sam Scruton says he was just the delivery driver,' Alys said. 'After each theft he received a text message telling him where the stolen vehicle was hidden. He watched it from a distance to make sure it wasn't fitted with a tracker. If it was, someone would come looking. If it wasn't, he drove it to the breakers' yard in Port Talbot. They sold it on abroad or broke it down for parts.'

'Who sent him the texts?' Holly asked.

'Scruton claims he doesn't know,' Alys said. 'They're sent from an anonymous pay-as-you-go phone. If Scruton's telling the truth, we need to identify the mysterious sender.'

'Is the sender the thief or the mastermind behind the thefts?' Fliss asked.

'Good question,' Alys said. Fliss's talents were wasted as a PCSO. 'Let's assume for the moment it's one and the same person. Matt and I discussed this on a call earlier when he updated me on Sam Scruton's interview. Whoever's stealing the Defenders has to know where to steal them from. It could be someone who has business driving around the area.'

'Or someone working at the Land Rover service centre in H'west?' Holly said, tentatively.

'Only the posh folks use them,' Ivor chipped in, then added, 'Loads of parcel delivery vans drive around the area, postmen too.'

Alys held up her hands. 'Okay. Lots of ideas then. Let's focus on locals who knew Rianna and Bill.'

'Know Bill,' Fliss said, 'He's not dead yet.'

'Might as well be,' Ivor muttered.

Guilt flooded Alys's mind. It was all too easy to write Bill Symonds off as dead.

'Thanks Fliss. You suggested Cedric Davies knew both victims well and drives around the area visiting parishioners. Who else?'

Suddenly everyone was talking at once.

'Julie Bowen, the district nurse, visiting patients.'

'Dylan Rogers' dad, Huw. Seen him out and about touting for business.'

'That's right. I've seen his builder/handyman flyers all over the place.'

'You can't suspect Cedric.'

'Wendy Pryce. Seen her in the Archaeological Trust's Land Rover. Last time was over by Whitesands Bay. Loads of prehistoric stuff on St David's Head.'

'Didn't I hear Dylan Rogers goes foraging for nettles and seaweed?'

'One of us,' Holly said.

That stopped the babel of voices.

Everyone looked at Holly. She blushed. 'Well, it's true, isn't it? Being seen out in the community is part of our job. The last few days we've been buzzing around like angry hornets.'

Ivor shook his head. 'Ridiculous saying that. I'd put my money on Griff Llewellyn. He's always going on about sourcing the best local produce for his hotel's kitchens.'

'All great ideas,' Alys said. 'I'll pass them on to the

DI. Well, maybe not Holly's last one.' She grimaced. 'Tomorrow we'll review the previous Land Rover thefts and see if there's anything we might have missed, anything we thought was too insignificant to be included in the case notes. Get your thinking caps on and we'll meet again in the morning.'

This was what Alys loved. Investigative work. It made her more determined than ever to get a transfer back into CID.

CHAPTER 43

Before Matt had time to grab a coffee and sit down, his phone rang. He was summoned to Detective Chief Superintendent Norman Stone's office.

Either reception had alerted Stone or the man had nothing better to do than slash his department's budgets and watch the CCTV for Matt's arrival.

'Any progress on the Rianna Hughes murder?' DCS Stone demanded as Matt stepped into his office. 'I'm getting hassle from the Chief Constable and the Police Commissioner. They want to know what's going on. They don't appreciate comments in the press about the damage this is doing to the tourist industry, having unsolved murders on the coast path.'

Matt gave a brief summary of the investigation to date. He concluded by saying, 'We're holding Samuel Scruton and his son, Robert Scruton, on charges of theft and driving without insurance. I'm opposing bail while we investigate the further charges of causing grievous bodily harm while driving a stolen vehicle, the attempted murder of Bill Symonds and the murder of Rianna Hughes.'

'But you don't think the Scrutons killed the Hughes woman or were driving the van when Symonds was knocked down?'

'They claim not, sir,' Matt said, dodging the question.

'Not much to tell the Chief Constable and the Commissioner, is it?'

'It's good progress for a case that's less than a week old,' Matt said. He refrained from saying that they

248

might have made better progress if Stone had granted permission to launch a full scale search when he'd requested it.

Matt suspected that the eagerness to solve the case might be related to the upcoming election for the post of Police Commissioner. The current Commissioner was up for re-election and rumour had it that he, the Chief Constable, Rhodri Llewellyn and Aled Ingram were all members of the same exclusive club.

'You're young and ambitious,' DCS Stone said, 'and I'm sure you're determined to get an early result. A lot of responsibility when it's your first case as senior investigating officer.'

'I won't disappoint,' Matt said, wondering where this was leading.

'Focus on the Scrutons and the dead woman's partner,' DCS Stone told him. 'You'll most likely find he's behind the vehicle thefts and knocking down this Symonds character.' He paused before continuing. 'Don't allow yourself to be distracted by irrelevant issues. It's unlikely that this case has anything to do with ancient monuments.'

So that was it. He was being warned off. Well, he wasn't going to accept that, but he'd have to tread carefully. He didn't want Stone taking him off the case for some spurious reason.

'I'm not sure I understand, sir. Are you talking about Wendy Pryce, the archaeology lecturer? Matt said. 'She's on our list of suspects because she's known to have been jealous of Rianna Hughes over another lecturer, Ross Keely, who was Rianna Hughes' lover. They were overheard by several people having a violent argument not long before Rianna's murder.'

Matt smiled inwardly. That should take the wind out of the DCS's sails. Just to make sure, Matt added, 'Our questioning of Wendy Pryce has nothing to do with her interest in ancient monuments.'

Matt guessed that Wendy Pryce had told Griff that Matt was asking too many awkward questions. The Llewellyns were then using their influence with the Chief Constable to rein Matt in. To hell with them. He wasn't going to bow to their pressure. He'd just have to investigate the bribery allegations so subtly that they wouldn't find out until it was too late.

CHAPTER 44

The Madoc's Haven Neighbourhood Policing Team reconvened in their office the following day. Alys's nose twitched at the smell of Fliss's peppermint tea, and took a sip of her coffee. Bliss.

'All the stolen Defenders were from before they made the keyless entry system more secure,' Fliss said.

Alys was impressed. Fliss had been doing her homework.

'It's not only Land Rover,' Fliss continued. 'All the manufacturers jumped on the keyless entry bandwagon without a thought for security. If it's an older model, a smart thief with the right electronic gadgets can steal anything from a Ford Focus to a Lamborghini in under thirty seconds. The fastest on record is eight.'

'Two thieves,' Holly corrected. 'Typically it takes a pair of thieves, which makes me still think it could be the Scrutons stealing the vehicles.'

'Technology,' Ivor muttered. 'You can't beat a good old-fashioned crook lock.'

Alys smiled at the contrast between her PC and her two PCSOs. Different ages, different backgrounds, different outlooks. She'd met Ivor's dad. He reminded her of Sam Scruton.

'Don't know what you're smiling at,' Ivor said. 'It's what the insurance companies are telling the owners.'

'I'm not saying you're wrong,' Alys said, 'but back to the matter in hand. What else has anyone found?'

'They're getting better at it.' Ivor said. 'I answered one of the first calls. Nearly caught one of them. They made a noise, alerted the owner. The vehicle was fitted with a tracker. I caught up with it near Wolf's Castle. Chased it around the back roads near Spittal but he lost me when I got blocked by an oncoming car. We found it abandoned close to Treffgarne. His mate must have picked him up.'

'I remember that,' Alys said. 'I was away on a course at the time. Heard about it when I came back.'

It was when Alys was taking her sergeant's exams. She was just a PC then like Ivor, but more ambitious. 'Didn't they find fingerprints on the controls?'

'Yes, a bit smudged. He'd tried to wipe the vehicle clean but was in too much of a hurry. No match found on the database. We could try looking again, now we have the Scrutons' prints.'

'Good idea. You said the thief was a "he". Is that supposition, or do you know it for sure?'

Ivor shrugged and shook his head. 'Supposition, I guess.'

'Ivor's right about them getting better,' Holly said. 'The first case I was involved with they caught one of them on CCTV, not that you could make out much. Dark clothes, balaclava, medium height, medium build, probably male, but even that's not certain. That was the assistant, the one that went right up close to the house. Didn't capture the actual thief on camera.'

'Anything else anyone?' Alys asked.

Holly, Fliss and Ivor all shook their heads.

'So it's likely that two people are involved,' Alys said, summing up. 'That makes sense. The assistant takes the thief to the location and assists with the crime, and probably later collects the thief from where the stolen vehicle is quarantined.'

'The assistant could use a motorbike,' Holly said, with a sudden burst of excitement. 'Less memorable than a car. Witnesses tend to remember the colours and makes of cars. Motorbikes, not so much.'

'Interesting,' Alys said, thoughtfully. 'Both Dylan Rogers and Rob Scruton own motorbikes. You'd need to be a biker to recognise the makes. I certainly couldn't, not in the dark.'

Ivor was slowly shaking his head, looking lost in thought.

'What is it, Ivor,' Alys asked.

'Talking about all those early cases reminded me,' he said. 'I was visiting neighbouring farms, asking if anyone had seen or heard anything. Huw Rogers was re-roofing an outhouse on one of them. It didn't seem important at the time.'

Ivor paused, looking pleased with himself.

'Go on,' Alys prompted, impatiently.'

'He had a young lad helping him. Surly little sod. Didn't know him or think it was important at the time.'

'So?'

'I knew there was something niggling at the back of my mind when we raided the Scruton's farm yesterday. The connection's just popped into my mind. I'm pretty certain the young lad was Rob Scruton.'

Hope flared in Alys's mind. 'How certain are you?'

Ivor gestured doubt with his hand.

'Eighty, maybe ninety percent. Wouldn't like to swear to it in court.'

'Now that's an interesting connection. If Huw Rogers and Rob Scruton are stealing the Defenders, Sam Scruton was just spinning a yarn with his mythical texter. He must have known it was Huw Rogers all along.'

'The DI needs to check Huw's fingerprints against the ones lifted from that Defender I chased around Treffgarne,' Ivor said. 'If they match, Bingo! We've got him.'

'Let's not get ahead of ourselves,' Alys said. 'You're only eighty or ninety percent sure. It's an interesting hypothesis, but that's all it is. I'll pass it on to the DI, along with the rest of our findings. We have the smudged prints and a video of the thief's assistant from two of the earlier cases. I'll suggest that DI Vincent checks those against the Scrutons to see if it either excludes or incriminates them and suggests that he obtains Huw Rogers' fingerprints to check them too. Is that a fair summary?'

'Sounds good to me,' Fliss said.

Ivor and Holly both nodded their agreement.

Alys was fiercely excited. Progress at last! It was her team that was generating the leads. The smudged fingerprints and the CCTV footage were promising lines of enquiry, as was Holly's suggestion that they should be looking for a pair of thieves, possibly one of them with a motorbike. Even the fiasco of the vanishing Defender had resulted in the Scrutons' arrest. That was down to Fliss's powers of observation.

What Alys was struggling with was the thought that Huw Rogers could be a murderer and a thief, or was that just a wild fantasy? Had the Scrutons progressed from being petty criminals to murderers? Had Rianna discovered that they were stealing the Defenders and tried blackmailing them? Or were the Defender thefts a distraction? Did the Llewellyns kill Rianna in their determination to push through their plans for the proposed Clebaston Manor Resort?

Alys was frustrated. She was supposed to report to CID through Matt's Rottweiler sergeant. She was prepared to bet that Beth would present all her team's best ideas to Matt as her own. Well, sod protocol. She'd bypass Beth and speak directly with Matt.

CHAPTER 45

Gemma shuddered at the sight of the caravan with its weathered cream paint blotched with grime. She'd hated it when Dylan's music blasted through her house, but now she'd put up with it, if only he'd come home and bring Meg with him.

She banged on the caravan's door. The heavy, driving beat stopped abruptly to be replaced by the swish of the wind through the hedge and the twitter of sparrows.

'Mum, what are you doing here?' Dylan said.

'What sort of greeting is that? I've not seen you since...' Her voice tailed off. 'Why haven't you been to see us? How was Meg?'

He jumped down and gave her a hug.

'Get along inside,' Dylan said. 'It's chilly out here in the wind.'

He ushered her into the caravan. It was the first time Gemma had visited him at Brannock's Cross. She wrinkled her nose in disgust at the smell of mildew and neglect that pervaded Dylan's temporary home. It was a disgrace that he'd been kicked out of the flat that she and Huw had helped to finance.

'It was great seeing Meg. She seemed fine. Really happy to see Dafi.'

'I'd have loved to see her too,' Gemma said. She couldn't keep the resentment out of her voice.

'They're not letting me have her back,' Dylan said, with a catch in his voice. 'Matt Vincent should get on with it and catch the bastard who killed Ree.'

Gemma bit her tongue. She'd almost said Rianna

got what she deserved. It was what she thought. The things that girl had done, the way she'd behaved ...

'I visited Citizens' Advice yesterday,' Dylan continued. 'They said the court's unlikely to let me have Meg back if the police suspect me of killing Ree.' He gulped back a sob and wiped a tear from the corner of his eye. 'And I need to come up with a plan for Meg's future. It's all so unfair.'

Gemma tried to give him a hug but it was difficult in the cramped confines of the caravan.

'Will they let you back into the flat?'

Dylan shook his head miserably. 'The court has to decide that too.'

'Let me make you a tea,' Gemma said.

'I'll make it,' Dylan said. 'I've only got herbal. Is that okay?'

Gemma grimaced. 'It'll be fine.'

'Mum,' Dylan said tentatively as he filled the kettle. 'When they clear my name and this is all sorted, will you look after Meg for me?'

He looked at her with a mixture of hope and desperation. It broke Gemma's heart.

'You know I'd love to, but I can't. I have to keep working at the gift shop. I can't afford not to.'

His look changed to one of disappointment and annoyance.

'Surely you don't have to?' he said. 'You and dad must be pretty well set up, what with all the building work he's doing and that cottage he did up and sold a couple of years back.'

Gemma wished she'd never heard of that damned cottage. She sighed. She didn't want to burden Dylan with her problems. She'd never do that.

'Sorry love, it's out of the question,' she said.

She tried to stand up and give him a hug but he pushed her away and thrust a cup of herbal tea into her hands.

'I don't see why you can't,' he said, truculently. Then his mood shifted. 'You could foster her.'

'What?' Gemma said, putting the herbal tea down untouched and collapsing back on the bed.

'You could foster Meg. They pay foster parents good money. Then you wouldn't have to work at the shop.'

Gemma laughed. 'I can't see them paying me to look after my own granddaughter. They'd have to be mad to do that. If they did, they'd have every mum in the land demanding to be paid to look after their grandchildren.'

'It was just an idea,' Dylan said with a frown.

'What you need to do,' Gemma said, 'is find yourself a nice young woman and get married. Then she could look after Meg. It was never right, you and Rianna living in sin.'

'You shouldn't listen to that old busybody, Cedric Davies. Living in sin,' Dylan said contemptuously. 'What century do you think you're living in?'

'Cedric's daughter, Cassie, she's a pretty young thing. She'd make you a good wife. Or how about Alys Carey? Neither of them would do what that Rianna did to you.'

'You don't get it, do you?' Dylan shouted, his face flushing bright red. 'I loved Rianna. You always hated her. You're probably glad that she's dead.'

Suddenly Gemma was frightened. Dylan was trembling with rage.

'You'd better get out,' he shouted. 'I've got work to do. Thanks for your help.'

Gemma fled away from the caravan back to her car, Dylan's sarcasm echoing in her ears. She'd thought that her son had learnt to control his childhood tantrums. She was evidently wrong.

CHAPTER 46

Matt answered his phone on the second ring.

'Good morning, sir. Sergeant Carey here. Are you free to talk?'

She crossed her fingers and hoped Matt would interpret that as meaning could his Rottweiler sergeant overhear their conversation.

'Good morning, sergeant. What can I do for you?'

Did that mean Beth was lurking nearby, or was Matt giving her the cold shoulder because she'd ignored protocol and called him and not Beth?

'I met with my team this morning. We reviewed all the recent Defender thefts. We came up with some information that you might find helpful.'

'Yes?'

Damn the man. Was he being deliberately disinterested or was the Rottweiler straining at her leash beside him? Alys swallowed her annoyance and continued.

'About four years ago when the Defender thefts in the area were just kicking off, PC Jones was reacting to the theft of a vehicle in progress. The thieves made too much noise and alerted the owner. It was a Defender with a tracker fitted. Ivor chased it around the countryside but they got way. The vehicle was later found abandoned. Forensics recovered some smudged fingerprints from the vehicle's gear lever.'

'They didn't match any on the database, I suppose?'

He could at least try sounding enthusiastic.

'No. But we've made a list of possible suspects for the person behind the thefts, based on our local knowledge.'

Alys ploughed on, describing the team's thinking.

Matt sounded marginally more interested when she told him of Holly's suggestion that the thief and the accomplice used the accomplice's motorbike to travel to the scene of the theft, and then to take the thief back home from the stolen vehicle's temporary hiding place.

'There are two locals who own motorbikes and who could be acting as the thief's accomplice,' Alys said. 'Rob Scruton and Dylan Rogers.'

'That is interesting.'

'There's more. When Ivor was interviewing neighbours concerning another Defender theft, Huw Rogers was repairing the roof of a nearby farmhouse. He had a surly young lad working for him. Ivor's pretty certain it was Rob Scruton.'

'Are you suggesting that Huw Rogers is stealing the Defenders, with Rob Scruton acting as his assistant?'

'Either that or it could be Huw and Dylan. Huw does building work and maintenance all around the area. He could easily spy out suitable vehicles to steal. Dylan or Rob could take Huw on the back of their motorbike to steal the Defender and then return him home again after they'd stashed the stolen vehicle away. Older motorbikes are pretty anonymous, especially after dark.'

'All highly speculative. It could be someone else entirely,' Matt said thoughtfully, 'but Dylan does have a motive for killing Rianna.'

'So does Huw. But it still doesn't explain Bill's attempted murder, unless he saw, heard or guessed at something that could incriminate Rianna's killer.'

'Bill's still not regained consciousness, so we can't ask him.' Matt said.

Alys brightened up. 'No, but I could ask Cassie Davies if she remembers anything. She was friendly with Bill. He was like an uncle to her. It's worth a try.'

*****

It seemed that little Ms Marple could do no wrong in the DI's books. She'd come up with some hare-brained ideas that she thought would crack the case wide open. Why couldn't she get her wellies back on and stick to her rural policing duties?

'Have the results come back from the Scrutons' fingerprints yet?' Matt asked.

'Just come in. Their prints are all over the number plate cloning printer and the plates from the stolen vehicles we recovered from the farm,' Beth said. 'They must have kept the plates to prove what idiots they are.'

Matt smiled. 'Have you heard back from the Port Talbot police?'

'They couldn't find Sam Scruton's prints on the Defender. He was either wearing gloves or wiped it clean. They found Rob Scruton's on its false plates. He must have done the swap at Ty Nymff before they drove it away.' From under the nose of your green wellie squeeze, Beth added in her thoughts.

'How about the smudged print from the previous Defender theft?'

'No luck there, but we don't have comparison prints from Dylan Rogers, Huw Rogers, Griff Llewellyn, Wendy Pryce or from any of the other potential suspects.'

'Did you view the CCTV footage from the older theft?'

Of course I did. What do you think I do? Wander the countryside all day whistling a happy tune like the green wellie brigade?

'Yes. All I could make out was the height, build and maybe the gender of the accomplice. It could have been Rob Scruton, but it's impossible to say.'

'Okay, here's what we'll do. We'll need to interview the Scrutons again now we have the fingerprint evidence; I want you to apply for an extension so we can hold the Scrutons for a further twelve hours; and get a progress report on Bill Symonds. See if there's any chance he'll come out of his coma.'

'Yes, sir.'

'And do an ANPR search on Dylan Rogers' and Rob Scruton's motorbikes and on Huw Rogers' pickup for the night that Bill Symonds was knocked down. If any of them were out and about late it would blow a hole in their alibis.'

Doesn't he know that ANPR cameras are a rare as hens' teeth out there in the sticks?

'Of course, sir, I'll get onto it right away.'

We should be pulling the Llewellyns and Wendy Pryce in for questioning, Beth thought. The Clebaston Manor Resort application stinks of bribery and corruption. She'd even heard rumours that the Super was leaning on Matt Vincent to pull back from investigating them. Not if she had her way, but she wouldn't get caught like she had the last time.

*****

'When shall we three meet again?' Alys said, as she walked into the woollen mill café with Fliss close on her heels.

'In thunder, lightning, or in rain?' Julie Bowen completed the quotation for her. 'Not sure I like the allusion though.'

Alys and Fliss ordered themselves drinks and sat down with her.

'I'm glad I bumped into you,' Julie said. 'I wanted to correct something I told you last time we met in here.'

'What's that,' Fliss jumped in quickly, 'about the urges and the self-control?'

She dodged the intended jab in the ribs from Alys's elbow.

Julie blushed. 'You'll never let me live that down,

will you?' She took a sip of her coffee. 'No, what I said about Dylan and Vicky. I was wrong'

'In what way?'

'When I saw Dylan parking his motorbike late in the evening outside Vicky's flat, he went to ask if she'd go with him to see Meg at the contact centre in Neyland and take Dafi with her. It was all perfectly innocent.' Julie looked contrite. 'I shouldn't go spreading rumours.'

'Best not,' Alys said, 'particularly if they're untrue.'

'I had an update from the hospital this morning,' Julie said, more cheerfully. 'They think there could be early signs that Bill might come out of his coma. Too soon to be certain. We just need to have faith that he will.'

'Excellent news,' Alys said, hoping that Julie was more accurate with this than she was with her suggestion of an affair between Dylan and Vicky.

'Any progress on who knocked him down?' Julie asked.

Alys shook her head. 'We need to discover everything we can about what Bill did, saw and heard that might have made him a threat to Rianna's murderer.'

'You think the two are linked?'

'Too much of a coincidence to think otherwise.'

Joyce arrived with Alys's coffee, Fliss's peppermint tea, and a fresh coffee for Julie.

Julie took a sip of her drink, then said, 'I don't know if it's important, but I've just remembered something Cassie Davies told me. I'd popped into the vicarage to see if she was okay. I'd driven her home earlier, the day Penny Evans found Bill ...'

Julie gulped back a sob. Alys remembered that Julie was one of the first on the scene, had given first aid, and that she was Bill's second cousin. Alys put her hand on Julie's forearm and gave it a gentle squeeze.

Julie gave a weak smile and took another sip of her coffee. Her hand was trembling. 'Sorry. We were discussing whether it was safe for Cassie to ride her bike to work.'

Alys's interest was immediately aroused. 'What did she tell you?'

'She thought someone had borrowed her bike. When she went to ride it back home one evening, it wasn't where she left it. She mentioned it to Bill, and he said he might have seen someone riding it that wasn't her.'

'What exactly did Bill tell her?' Alys asked, now fully alert.

'Apparently Bill glanced out of the window while he was loading the potato peeling machine first thing one morning. Just caught a brief glimpse. The window wasn't very clean. He thinks he saw someone ride into the hotel on a pushbike. He couldn't see who it was. They were almost completely obscured by the bins.'

'Why was that odd?'

'Well, Cassie's the only one who rides in on a bike, but he knew that Cassie had already arrived. She was doing early-bird room service. The rest of the staff drive in by car, except Bill, who always walks. That was the same day that Cassie had to grope around in the dark to find her bike. It wasn't where she usually left it.'

'Which day was that?'

'I don't know. I didn't think to ask.'

'But it could have been the morning that Rianna was murdered,' Alys said. 'Excuse me. I need to make a call.'

*****

'So you think someone from the hotel used Cassie's bike to get to where Rianna was murdered and back again?' Matt asked.

'It ties in with what we speculated when we met the SOCOs on the cliff path,' Alys said. 'We thought the murderer might have hiked across the field after getting there by bike. As long as he or she wore a hoody and averted their face, in the unlikely event that they met anyone on the road at that time in the morning, they'd probably escape recognition.'

'If that's true, and it's pure conjecture, it means that the killer is someone who works at the hotel.'

'Or lives there.'

'So the most likely suspects based on what we already know or suspect are Huw Rogers, Griff Llewellyn or possibly the receptionist, Penny Evans.' Matt said.

'When I was at a meeting of the Madoc's Haven Historical Society the night that Rianna died,' Alys said, 'Huw's wife Gemma was furious with Rianna for having Dylan kicked out of his own flat and that she could no longer see Meg. She also said, and I quote, "Huw was tamping mad".

'His alibis for both murders are that he was at home watching movies, with only his wife to corroborate.'

'And there's the connection with Rob Scruton. I had Ivor revisit the farm where Huw was doing the roofing, and they confirmed that Rob Scruton was Huw's assistant.

'Right,' Matt said decisively. 'It's time we brought Huw Rogers in for questioning. Let's hope his prints match the smudged one from that earlier Defender theft.'

CHAPTER 47

Alys felt excited, exhilarated and scared. The three police cars were so close on each other's tails it was like a miniature road train. She uttered a silent prayer. If Beth stopped suddenly, there was no way that Ivor or Fliss could stop in time.

'What's got into you?' Alys demanded. 'He doesn't even know we're coming.'

A smile twitched Fliss's lips. She eased off on the accelerator for a few seconds, dropping back a little from the back of Ivor's car.

'Beth threw down the gauntlet. The way she took off was a challenge. I'm just annoyed that Ivor was on her tail faster than me. I've never seen this side of him before.'

'We're on our way to arrest a suspect, not compete in a race.' Alys shook her head sadly. 'You've been watching too many cop movies. This is Pembrokeshire, not Chicago or LA.'

Several heart-stopping minutes later, Matt's car, with Beth driving, slowed to a leisurely pace at the Hotel's entrance gate, as if they had all the time in the world.

As arranged at the briefing, Beth drove between the stone pillars guarding the entrance to the hotel and stopped a few yards down the sloping drive. The gateway was only wide enough for a delivery truck or a bin lorry to get through.

Ivor stopped his car between the stone pillars, blocking it and preventing any vehicles from leaving. He and Holly got out looking tense and alert.

Fliss parked their vehicle in the lane. Alys jumped out and stretched, easing the tension in her limbs, but not in her being. Her heart pounded and she was on edge, but the drive from Madoc's Haven wasn't the main cause.

The scene below was idyllic. Waves rolled in gently from the west with glistening crests tracing their progress as they approached the cliffs beyond the hotel. Gulls drifted lazily on the breeze and a lone gannet skimmed effortlessly along the horizon.

Alys was in no mood to appreciate it.

She'd arrested plenty of suspects, usually on drug charges or for public order offences. She'd never assisted in the arrest of a murder suspect before.

She joined Ivor and together they climbed in behind Matt and Beth in their car, leaving Alys's two PCSOs guarding the entrance.

'Let's do this,' Matt said. 'Nice slow approach. Don't want to frighten anyone.'

'All strapped in?' Beth asked, with a saccharin smile. She started on down the drive at a sedate pace towards the hotel buildings.

'Do you think he'll admit to anything?' Alys said. 'What do you think he'll do?'

*****

Matt's heart was beating fast as he approached the reception desk. You could never predict how an arrest would go down. Some suspects, realising the futility of their position, would meekly submit. Others, often the ones you least expected to, would respond with violent fury.

Penny Evans gave Matt a wide welcoming smile. Her fingers flew to the neck of her blouse. She straightened its collar which was already perfectly straight.

'Welcome, Detective Inspector,' she said, her eyes

shining brightly.

Matt sensed Beth's silent snarl as Penny ignored her completely.

Penny's smile froze as Alys and Ivor, both in uniform, stepped into reception behind Matt and Beth. 'There's nothing wrong is there?' she asked anxiously. 'There hasn't been another killing, has there?'

'Good afternoon, Penny,' Matt said, ignoring her question. 'We're here to see Huw Rogers. Can you tell me where we'll find him?'

She glanced at the watch on her wrist. 'He'll be out in the back yard. He's converting the old stable buildings into holiday cottages. It isn't quite time for him to start preparing for tonight's dinner.' She gushed nervously on, 'He's been a busy man since Bill's accident. Have you any idea how he is? Bill I mean.'

'Still in a coma,' Matt said, tersely.

From his previous visits Matt knew his way around the hotel. He pushed through the door to the side of the reception desk marked private, closely followed by Beth, Alys and Ivor.

Startled, Penny called after them, 'Shall I tell Mr Llewellyn you're here?'

'No need,' Matt called back as the door swung shut behind them.

It seemed an age since Matt had spoken to Bill out by the bins, but in reality it was just over a week. So much had happened since then. Time had a strange way of stretching and contracting in one's mind.

Matt's nose twitched. Had Bill smoked to hide the smell of decaying food waste that hung in the air?

A short track led from the bin area to the yard where three single story buildings were in various stages of renovation. The sound of sawing came from a lean-to shed attached to one of them. Matt strode over to it, closely followed by Beth, Alys and Ivor.

Matt peered in through the open door. Huw was

inside, sawing a plank that was resting across a pair of trestles. The shed was lit by a single bulb dangling from a roof beam. The carcass of a partly constructed kitchen cabinet stood beside him.

Huw looked up as Matt's shadow dimmed the light from the doorway.

'What are you doing here?' Huw demanded. Suspicion clouded his face.

'Put down your saw and come outside, please,' Matt said. 'We need to talk.'

'What about?'

'Just come outside please.'

Huw put down the saw and wiped his hands on a rag. He wasn't a large man, but he was stocky and looked fit.

Matt stepped back from the doorway as Huw emerged into the daylight.

'Well?' Huw demanded.

'Huw Rogers,' I'm arresting you on suspicion of ...'

'What the hell are you lot doing here?' a voice shouted from behind Matt. 'You can't just walk in here without permission.'

The moment's distraction was all Huw needed. He leapt forward and, with a vicious uppercut to the chin, lifted Matt off the ground. As his arm came back, he elbowed Beth in the throat. She collapsed backwards into Ivor, before dropping choking to the ground.

Alys moved fast, grabbing Huw's wrist and kicking at his groin. He was too quick for her. Her boot glanced off his thigh as he twisted out of her hold. Only her agility prevented his return kick from shattering her knee, but she lost balance and fell over sideways.

Griff stood open mouthed in surprise. As he sprinted past Griff, Huw thumped him in the chest with the heel of his hand, sending him flying.

Matt struggled to his feet, reaching for his radio, dizzy and disorientated by Huw's punch and the mayhem that he'd wreaked. Alys scrambled over to Beth who was in a bad way, clutching her throat and gasping for breath.

Alys suddenly remembered her two PCSOs, waiting at the top of the drive.

'Quick, warn Fliss and Holly,' Alys shouted at Matt. Then, turning to Ivor, 'Look after Beth.'

Alys jumped up and sprinted after Huw.

*****

Alys yanked open the door, sending it crashing back against the wall with a bang as she dashed into reception.

Penny looked startled. A trio of elderly hotel guests shrank back as Alys dodged around them.

'What's going on?' Penny asked.

'Get a first aider up to the yard. Now!' Alys cut across Penny's voice as she ran through the building and out of the front door.

What would Huw do to Fliss and Holly if they tried to stop him? She'd already seen the damage he could inflict.

An engine started and Alys jumped back to avoid being knocked down by Huw's pickup. It rocketed off up the drive, disappearing around the corner. Alys heard the screech of brakes as she started sprinting up the drive. No sound of a crash. Distant shouts. Her heart was in her mouth.

Then the sound of an engine screaming, approaching.

Alys jumped back into the rhododendrons as the pickup shot backwards down the drive.

She scrambled out of the bushes and set off in pursuit.

The pickup screeched to a halt in a shower of gravel. Huw leapt out and ran for the coast path, leaving the pickup with its door open and engine running.

Matt and Ivor rushed out of the hotel just in time to see him go as Holly drove down the lane in Ivor's patrol car with Fliss beside her.

Alys jumped up onto a wooden seat to get a better view. 'He's running towards Madoc's Haven,' she shouted as she jumped back down.

Beth staggered out of the hotel clutching her throat, followed by an anxious Cassie with a first aid kit in her hand.

'I've radioed for backup. I'll follow Huw and arrest him,' Matt told Alys. 'You take Ivor and cut him off at the Madoc's Haven end in case I lose him.'

'You can't tackle him alone,' Alys said. 'You've seen what he can do.'

'I've given you your orders,' Matt said, grim faced.

'You two,' he said, turning to Fliss and Holly. 'Patrol the road between here and Madoc's Haven and make sure he doesn't cut off from the coast path across the fields. Don't get near him or try to arrest him. Just keep him in sight and let me know where he is. Understood?'

They both nodded. 'Yes, Sir.'

As Matt set off in pursuit of Huw, Alys turned to her two PCSOs.

'Take one patrol car each. If you see Huw, don't let him get close, radio it in and follow him. We're taking Huw's pickup.'

'Get in,' she ordered Ivor as she jumped into the pickup and slammed the door.

She hoped and prayed that Matt knew what he was doing. Huw had made mincemeat of the four of them. Now Matt intended to tackle Huw alone.

Not if she could help it. Once she and Ivor got to Madoc's Haven, she planned to run back along the coast path like the wind. Together they'd take Huw down. He wouldn't defeat them a second time. There would be no Griff to distract them.

CHAPTER 48

Huw's pickup truck was larger and heavier than Alys's patrol car but she hardly noticed the difference. All she could think of was Matt attempting to take down Huw alone, and Huw's lighting fast reactions and brutal violence. Where had he learned those skills?

She cursed as she met an oncoming vehicle in the narrow lane. She rammed the pickup into reverse as she was closest to a passing bay. She clenched her fists on the steering wheel in her frustration. The pickup didn't have a siren and flashing blue lights. It did have flashing orange lights if she could only find the switch.

She nearly crashed into Fliss in her patrol car as she came racing towards her. Fliss was quick off the mark, screeching to a halt before reversing back at speed to the where the lane widened.

Both Fliss and Alys squeezed their vehicles into the passing place tight up against the bank.

'What the hell,' Alys fumed, as the approaching vehicle slowed and pulled up alongside.

'It's Julie Bowen,' Ivor said.

'Hello Alys, what's going on? Julie asked through her open window. 'I had a call from the hotel. An emergency, they said.'

'Move on so I can get past. No time to explain. If you see Huw Rogers, shut your windows, lock your doors and don't let him get near you. Don't run into Holly, she's coming this way too.' Alys's words tumbled out in a torrent as she revved the pickup's engine impatiently and edged forwards.

As soon as Julie started moving, Alys went for it,

not caring at the scraping sounds as sticking out branches scored the passenger side of the pickup. She found the switch for the flashing orange lights and turned them on. She prayed that they wouldn't meet any more oncoming vehicles.

She was tempted to hop out and cut across the fields to the coast path, leaving Ivor to carry on to Madoc's Haven, but she didn't know how far Huw and Matt had progressed. If she misjudged, Ivor might have to confront Huw alone. She couldn't let that happen.

Several agonizing minutes later Alys screeched to a halt in the beach car park in Madoc's Haven, frightening off a scavenging trio of black-headed gulls that were fighting over a discarded scrap of food.

She jumped out of the pickup and slammed the door, waited while Ivor got out more slowly, then locked it. No point in presenting Huw with his getaway vehicle if he evaded them all.

'Follow me!' Alys shouted as she sprinted across the car park towards the steeply sloping path towards the cliff tops. She didn't wait to see if Ivor was keeping up and had no intention of slowing down if he couldn't.

Maintaining her pace up the path was a struggle, particularly when it ran out of tarmac and turned into an uneven stony track.

How fast had Rianna been running as she headed towards her death that misty morning? Was it only just over a week ago?

Alys was hot and sweaty in her uniform. The equipment on her belt bounced against her body.

Her breath became more laboured as she reached the top of the first headland. She scanned the coast path ahead. No sign of Matt or Huw.

She glanced behind her. Ivor was only half way up the path and not moving quickly.

Her leg muscles burned and she was panting from

her exertions.

I'm being stupid, Alys told herself. I don't want to be knackered when I confront Huw. I'll need every ounce of energy I can muster.

She slowed her pace to a steady jog, allowing her body a respite.

Please don't let any innocent civilians be up here on the path. Please don't let Cedric and Whiskey be out for an afternoon stroll. Was the vicar a creature of habit? It had been around the same time of day when they'd met up here the previous week

Alys continued to scan the cliff tops ahead as she kept moving forwards.

Would Huw spot her before she saw him? Could he be hidden over a wall waiting to spring out and attack her, just as he'd attacked Rianna?

Suddenly Alys felt scared and alone but she had to press on. She determined to help Matt if she could.

*****

I won't let him escape, Matt told himself as he pounded along the coast path after Huw. He can't have that much of a lead. How fit can he be?

Matt replayed the failed arrest in his mind, seeking clues. How had Huw overcome four of them? Matt's whole face ached from Huw's punch, but the adrenalin pumping through his body eased the pain.

The coast path dipped, twisted, climbed and fell, in some places hemmed in by barbed wire fences, in others right on the edge with no barrier to prevent the unwary from plunging onto the rocks and churning waters below.

Matt ran up an uneven flight of steps and scrambled over a stile at the top. No sight of Huw. Where is he?

What Matt needed was helicopter support, but the force's helicopter had been axed and the nearest one was based far away, over by Cardiff.

He ran on, hoping Huw was suffering as much as he was.

Where was the man? He could be hidden in a dip or hollow ahead, or had he cut off across the fields? What would he do in Huw's position? Make for the road and hijack a car, or keep going until he reached Madoc's Haven and steal one from there?

Matt hoped and prayed that none of the others confronted Huw and came to grief. He feared most for Alys with her determined streak. Would she have the sense to back off?

He caught a sudden glimpse of Huw emerging from a dip in the track up ahead, running away from him, two or three hundred yards ahead. Then further into the distance another figure came into view, running along a level stretch of cliff top towards them both. It was Alys. Where the hell was Ivor? Had she left him behind?

Fear clutched at Matt's heart. Which of them would reach Huw first? It was bound to be Alys. She was running towards Huw, closing the distance dramatically.

The path ahead swooped into a shallow gully. Matt stumbled on the descent and only just kept his footing. Alys and Huw were both hidden from view. A short wooden bridge crossed a rivulet that trickled over the cliff's edge. The path ahead looped out around a grassy mound. Until he'd circled it, the only view Matt had was of the sea.

Beyond the hillock, a gentle rise stretched up to the skyline, blocking sight of the coastline beyond. Matt sprinted on up to the top, his muscles burning. The ground in front of him fell away to a golden sandy beach, a hundred feet or more below him. All that stopped him from going over the edge was a low tangle of brambles and gorse.

He should have remembered, Baruc's Cove. The

beach was a gem, isolated from the nearest habitation but reachable from the coast path or by a track that ran down the valley from the narrow road that joined Madoc's Haven to the Madoc's Bay Hotel.

The coast path plunged away to Matt's left down a steep flight of irregular steps.

Then he spotted them again.

Alys was on the opposite cliff top staring down into the valley between them. She was at the top of a matching flight of steps, although the ones on her side of the valley looked steeper and more tortuous.

Huw was crossing a wooden bridge that spanned the brook in the valley bottom.

Matt willed Alys to stay at the top. There she had the advantage of height, about the only advantage she did have over Huw.

Huw looked up and his posture changed, his body stiffened. He'd evidently seen her. Then he turned to look back up the path behind him. He must have noticed Matt too, staring down at him. What would he do?

If he altered course and made off up the valley, he'd have both Matt and Alys on his heels and there was no certainty that he could hijack a car. He could turn back and tackle Matt, or go forwards and take on Alys.

Matt knew which he would choose. Alys was more slightly built and shorter than Matt. She should be the easier option.

Huw must have thought so too. He crossed the bridge and started heading up the steps towards Alys.

Matt leapt down the steps on his side of the valley, hoping Alys could hold off Huw long enough for him to reach her. The steps were steep, uneven and no two were of the same width or depth. If he misjudged and tripped he'd go tumbling down them. If he was lucky he'd crash into the gorse and brambles. Worst case he'd break his neck.

Once started, he couldn't stop. He took two, then three steps at a time. What saved him was the training he'd taken for a charity parachute jump two years before. He collapsed sideways and rolled as he landed on the broad pathway at the bottom. Even so, the impact knocked the wind out of him and the stony surface jarred his body.

Staggering to his feet he glanced upwards. Alys was standing her ground at the top of the steps. Huw had almost reached her.

'Don't come any closer,' Alys shouted.

Matt ran for bridge, fuelled by adrenalin and fear for Alys's life.

'Do not come any closer,' Alys shouted again.

'Get out of my way!' Huw shouted back.

Matt started up the steps. His whole body ached.

'I told you, don't come another step closer!'

'Get out of my way!'

Matt was still too far away. Must get up the steps. His leg muscles burnt. Glancing up he could see Alys holding out her arm at Huw, her fist clenched. At least another twenty steps before he could reach them.

'Spray!' Alys shouted urgently.

Matt's training kicked in. He shut his eyes and his mouth, pinched his nose and turned away. He wanted to breathe but knew he couldn't. He heard a hiss and droplets of liquid hit the back of his neck. Pain etched his skin where they hit.

'Watch out!' Alys shouted. 'He's falling towards you. Stop him.'

Matt turned and risked opening his eyes. Huw collapsed, clutching his face, screaming and swearing, coughing and spluttering.

Huw started tumbling down the steps towards him.

Matt's eyes were stinging, but he ran up and stopped Huw before he could gather momentum.

Alys stuck the spray canister back in its holder and

drew out her handcuffs as she leapt down the steps to join them.

Huw screamed, cursed and struggled, trying to fight off the pair of them. His eyes were half shut and streaming with tears, snot flowed out of his nose and he was gasping for breath.

Between them they grabbed Huw's wrists, wrenched them behind his back and cuffed him. Alys breathed out a huge sigh of relief.

'Thanks for the warning,' Matt said. 'I wouldn't have wanted to get that in my face.'

Alys collapsed onto the step beside him, flushed and breathing heavily.

'It's going to be a bugger getting him back to the road,' she said.

CHAPTER 49

Alys loved the shady lane that led from the coast to the mill. Primroses and snowdrops flowered in profusion on its banks. But Alys's mood didn't match the blue skies and the sunshine that had broken through.

'He still hasn't called?' Fliss asked, as they climbed out of their cars, 'after what you did?'

Alys shook her head miserably. 'Not a word.'

Birds flew between the bushes, tweeting. Alys recognised the calls of a blackbird, long-tailed tits and maybe a wren too.

Fliss put her hand on Alys's arm and pointed up towards the sky. 'Look!'

High above them a pair of buzzards circled lazily above the valley looking for prey, taking advantage of a sunny-day thermal.

The bell pinged as Alys pushed open the door and stepped inside the café. Joyce looked up from behind the counter and several customers turned around. One of them began to clap. Then Joyce and several more joined in. They were all looking at her.

Alys was embarrassed, perplexed.

'What on earth is going on?' she asked Joyce as she and Fliss walked over to order their drinks.

'It's not often we have a local hero drop by for coffee,' Joyce said.

She picked up a copy of the local paper and held it for Alys to see.

'Brave Female Cop Takes Down Cliff-Top Killer,' announced the headline. And there, beneath the headline, was her face smiling back at her. She recognised the photo. They'd taken it when she'd done an interview about the role of the police in tackling rural crime.

She blushed and wanted to hide. Instead she turned to the customers, smiled tentatively and held up her hand. 'Thanks, but it was a team effort.'

'Don't believe her,' Fliss said, smiling broadly.

'Traitor,' Alys muttered under her breath.

'Same as usual please,' she said to Joyce, before quickly heading over to join Julie Bowen at her corner table.

'It's like being in a movie or having a nightmare,' Julie said, after the other customers had returned to their own preoccupations. 'I always thought this was a quiet part of the world.'

'I can't think who spilt that story to the press,' Alys said.

'I'd guess one of your new admirers.' Fliss smiled. 'Matt's young DCs were almost coming to blows trying to get your attention the other day.'

Alys decided to take that up with Matt. If his DCs had been talking to the press, it was unacceptable.

'What are the villagers saying?' she asked, turning to Julie.

'About their new heroine?' Julie said, with a twinkle in her eye. Then, more seriously, 'It's all a bit much to take in. A few are saying that Rianna got what she deserved, but they can't understand Huw trying to kill Bill Symonds or stealing all those vehicles.'

'He hasn't been proven guilty yet,' Alys said, although she felt sure that he'd done everything he stood accused of, maybe more. 'Speaking of Bill Symonds, I'm going into the hospital tomorrow to get an update. They say people in a coma can maybe still hear what's going on around them.' She gave a shrug. 'I'll stay by his bedside for a while and try talking to him. It can't do any harm.'

'That's kind of you,' Julie said, resting her hand on Alys's sleeve, 'but I wouldn't go near Gemma for a while. First some policemen she'd never seen before turned up with a warrant, searched her house and took away a load of Huw's clothes and his computer. Then she saw that newspaper article blowing your trumpet. She was practically foaming at the mouth. Dylan's in a state of shock.'

'Any update on Meg?' Alys asked, partly as a diversion. She had no intention of discussing anyone who could still be a potential suspect.

'I've spoken to both Vicky Morgan and Caitlin Gray.' Julie smiled and took a sip of her coffee. 'I've persuaded Vicky and her husband to apply to become foster parents. They have Caitlin's support and she's confident that they'll be accepted. She's going to see if she can get their approval fast-tracked. Assuming all goes well, she'll recommend that they foster Meg until Dylan's situation is resolved.'

'That would be excellent. I'm sure that Dafi and Meg must be missing each other.'

CHAPTER 50

Alys's phone rang. She glanced at the screen. Hope, frustration and anger surged through her, leaving her breathless. Damn, how could just seeing his name do that to her?

'Sergeant Carey,' she said tersely.

She pulled into a gateway, turned off the engine, took a deep breath and exhaled slowly.

The bleating of sheep in the field filled the sudden silence.

She'd waited days for this call. Well, maybe it was only three.

'Sorry I didn't call sooner,' Matt said. 'The last few days have been hectic.'

No they haven't, Alys thought. They've been as boring as hell. You could have called my mobile anytime, day or night. Why didn't you?

'Hello? Are you still there?

'Yes.'

The tone of his voice changed subtly. He must have sensed her mood.

'I haven't thanked you properly for going up against Huw Rogers the way you did. It was incredibly brave of you.'

She wasn't going to let him off that easily.

'Just doing what I've been trained to do.'

Then she relented, just a little.

'How's Beth? There was a snippet on the news saying that an officer had been injured and taken to hospital. I'm assuming that was her?'

She glanced at the sheep in the field. Their flanks

were swollen. It was nearly lambing time, almost spring.

The last time Alys had seen Beth was when she'd emerged from the hotel, clutching her neck and gasping.

'Her neck and throat are pretty badly swollen and bruised, but the doctor doesn't think there'll be any lasting damage. They kept her in overnight, released her the following morning. She'll be signed off work for at least a week. That's why it's been so busy.'

A spike of resentment hit Alys as she remembered their parting at the Armel Arms.

'You should have had me attached to your team. Then you wouldn't be short-handed.'

There was an awkward pause in the conversation.

Alys watched as sunlight glittered off the waves rolling into the bay. Then they both started speaking at the same time.

'No, you go first,' Alys said.

'I called to give you an update on how the case is progressing,' Matt said.

Disappointing if that was the only reason.

'Huw's been remanded in custody by the magistrates' court,' Matt continued. 'He's in Swansea Prison awaiting trial at the crown court. That won't be for a while yet.'

'Has he admitted anything?'

'No, he's keeping quiet, but we've had a breakthrough with Rob Scruton. He's admitted to being Huw's accomplice for the Land Rover thefts. He's hoping they'll let him off with a lighter sentence. Better still, forensics have come up trumps.'

'I heard that they searched Huw's house and took away his computer and some clothes,' Alys said. 'What did they find?'

'It was what they found at the buildings Huw was working on at the Madoc's Bay Hotel that was important,' Matt said. 'A black hoody and a balaclava. The threads the SOCOs found where Rianna was murdered matched a rip in the hoody, and the lab found minute specks of Rianna's blood on the balaclava and traces of Huw's saliva around the mouth hole. He might as well give up and plead guilty. He'll never wriggle out of a murder charge now.

Alys breathed out a sigh of relief. 'That clears Dylan then. I was afraid that he was involved in the Defender thefts and that he'd killed Rianna too. That would be terrible, the thought of Meg growing up knowing that her father had killed her mother.'

'Agreed.'

'Still horrible though, especially for Dylan. According to Vicky, he genuinely loved Rianna. I can't imagine how it would feel, knowing that your father killed the person you loved.'

Matt finally pulled away from their dark thoughts.

'Have you heard the news about Bill Symonds?'

'Yes,' Alys said, smiling. 'I popped into the hospital yesterday. The doctors are hopeful that he'll come around in the next couple of days.'

There was another pause in the conversation. Alys waited hopefully for Matt to say something.

'We haven't had time to catch up on what we've both been doing since ...' Matt's voice tailed off.

'Since you left Madoc's Haven and went off to university,' Alys completed his sentence for him, but she added in her thoughts ...and we both gave evidence at the inquest into Hannah's death.

'We could meet up one evening,' Matt said, hesitantly. 'Do you know the restaurant at the Ty Gwyn Hotel? It's about halfway between Llanbrioc and where I'm living.'

Wow! Alys's heart rate spiked. Was he asking her out on a date? The Ty Gwyn Hotel and Vineyard was a five star hotel with a restaurant to match. It often appeared in the local papers as a wedding venue. Not the place for a casual catch-up chat between colleagues, a detective inspector and a uniformed sergeant.

'We'll split the bill,' Alys said, decisively.

'No, my treat,' Matt replied. 'A thank you for your part in the investigation.'

That poured cold water on Alys's exhilaration. Surely that couldn't be the only reason he was inviting her out for a meal there?

*****

Matt arrived early and sat staring at the hotel in a daze. He couldn't believe his eyes. It must have changed hands since he'd last seen it ten or more years before.

It certainly hadn't been a five star hotel then with floodlights illuminating its elegant gleaming white facade. They'd extended its name to the Ty Gwyn Hotel and Vineyard.

He gulped. He should have checked before he invited Alys here. He'd been in a rush and hadn't checked the website. He'd just asked a colleague if she knew the number, called it and booked a table. He wondered why she'd given him a strange look.

Stepping inside only heightened his nerves. It had been totally refurbished, while still managing to keep its distinctive character. After announcing his arrival and having his coat taken, he was directed to the bar. The walls and ceiling were painted white, setting off the pale brown hues of the wooden bar top and floorboards. The dark brown leather armchairs and settees surrounding low glass-topped tables looked comfortable and inviting. Several couples glanced up from their drinks and conversations.

'Welcome to the John Adams' bar, sir. If you'd like to take a seat and make yourself comfortable, I'll come over and take your order.'

Whatever would Alys think? That it was a date?

At that moment she walked into the bar, spotted him and smiled a radiant wide open smile. He smiled back, nervously. She looked stunning. She was dressed in a form fitting floral print dress that complemented her glossy chestnut hair. The background buzz of conversation in the bar stopped. Matt wasn't the only man in the room looking at her.

Shake hands or kiss cheeks?

Alys solved the problem by stepping forward. He hoped she'd repeat the hug that she'd given him when they'd met on his return. She disappointed him with a chaste kiss on the cheek, but the memory of that previous embrace lingered on.

She stepped back, leaving the scent of her perfume in his nostrils.

'You look beautiful,' he said and instantly regretted it as heat flushed his face. Was that too effusive? He was useless at complimenting women.

'Why thank you, kind sir,' she said as she sat down, but he thought that she was colouring up too. For goodness sake, they were like a pair of schoolkids on their first date, but was it a date? He was no longer sure what he'd intended.

'What's the latest on the case against Huw Rogers?' Alys asked in what Matt thought was a rather brittle tone.

That killed the afterglow of her touch. He hastily redirected his thoughts.

'Like I said over the phone, the case against him for murdering Rianna is solid. What I forgot to tell you is that the Port Talbot SOCOs recovered hairs from the driver's headrest of the Defender. We're waiting for the lab results. If any match Huw Rogers' hair, he'll go down for Bill's attempted murder too.'

Alys started to cross her legs, but obviously thought better of it given the length of her dress. Matt guessed she was more used to wearing jeans or her uniform trousers.

'So what made you come back?' Alys asked, after they'd ordered and received their drinks. 'I wasn't expecting to see you again after all this time.'

'A combination of circumstances. My elderly Aunt Nerys died and left me her cottage on the outskirts of Tenby. She'd been a widow for ages and her only son went before she did. I was her closest living relative.'

Matt shook his head and took a sip of his drink. 'Then when I was down for the funeral, I saw an advert saying that Dyfed-Powys Police had a vacancy for a DI, and that transferees from other forces would be welcomed.' He shrugged his shoulders. 'So here I am.'

He looked into Alys's eyes and felt a sensation deep in his chest, a combination of excitement and longing. Surely she could see it in his eyes?

'What about you?' he asked breathlessly. 'How come you're not married with a hoard of unruly children?'

Alys shrugged. 'The right guy's never come along. I've had relationships, but they've never lasted more than a few months. The longest was nine.'

Matt turned, suddenly aware of a waitress hovering nearby.

'Sorry to interrupt, but if you let me know when you're ready, I'll show you to your table,' she said.

'I think we're ready now.' He turned back to Alys for confirmation. He didn't want to know about her previous relationships.

'Then follow me, please.'

The waitress led them into a high trestle-roofed restaurant. It must have once been a large barn. The under surface of the roof consisted of wooden laths with white plaster in between. The walls were bare stone. White tablecloths, silver cutlery and cut glass gleamed on every table. The room was illuminated, partly by candles, partly by skilfully concealed lighting that reflected off the white plaster.

Alys linked her arm through Matt's, throwing him into further confusion. 'This is beautiful. Thank you for bringing me here.'

The waitress led them towards the far end of the room and pointed up to a wooden-railed balcony. She turned to Matt and smiled. 'Everything's ready for you up in the Nook, including a complimentary glass of bubbly from the management. Just go through that door,' she said, indicating a door to the right. 'It's at the top of the stairs on the left.'

Matt thanked her. His heart pounded. He racked his brain, trying to remember what he'd said when he'd booked the table. Had he absentmindedly agreed when they asked if it was a special occasion? They must have thought he was intending to propose!

*****

Alys wished her dress was longer and that she'd worn flats instead of heels. Climbing the steep stairs to the Nook was a challenge to propriety. She should have told Matt to go ahead.

At the top, a smiling young waiter clasped a bottle wrapped in a napkin. He held the door open for her.

The Nook was occupied by a single table with two chairs. The table was laid up with a white table cloth that glowed in the candlelight. Freshly poured fizz streamed bubbles and the silverware glittered. A single long-stemmed red rose lay on the table.

She was glad that Matt had refused her offer to go Dutch. The Nook and the meal must be costing him a fortune. Auntie Nerys must have left him more than just the cottage.

But Alys was puzzled, frustrated and excited. Matt was giving off so many conflicting vibes that she couldn't make out his intentions.

He pulled out a chair from the table. For a brief

moment she didn't realise that he was attempting old fashioned chivalry. They collided with each other as she moved to sit on the chair opposite and they ended up in an accidental embrace. She tilted her head back, lips slightly parted, expectantly. Damn, he'd better give her a kiss.

Epilogue

'It's disgraceful, Dylan's still not allowed back into his flat,' Gemma said angrily. 'I thought the courts were supposed to be about justice. Where's the justice in that?'

Gemma's voice could be heard above the general hubbub. Small clusters of Historical Society members stood talking, waiting for the meeting to begin.

Could it really be a month since the last meeting? A month since Huw killed Rianna? A month since Alys met Matt for the first time in ten years?

Gemma was putting on a brave face. Alys couldn't imagine what it must be like, having your husband awaiting trial for the murder of your son's wife. For many villagers, the attempted murder of Bill Symonds was the far greater crime. She had to admire Gemma for showing her face at the meeting. It couldn't have been easy.

'Ah Gemma,' Cedric's voice rang out as he walked into the room and joined Gemma's little group. 'These are testing times for us all. I'm so pleased that you've come.'

'I can't bear being in that empty house all alone', Gemma said. 'I'm hoping that Dylan will come back to live with me.'

Alys blocked out Cedric and Gemma's voices and tuned in to her friends.

'Any news on what's happening with Dylan and Meg?' she asked Julie.

Julie smiled. 'Vicky and Nick have said they'd love to become foster carers. They've filled out all the forms and I've persuaded the agency to fast track their application. Vicky's working through the online training and it's looking hopeful.'

Julie looked around and lowered her voice to make sure that Gemma didn't overhear.

'Vicky seems to have won Gemma over. She invited her around for lunch as a thank you for the cuddly toy she gave Dafi. Now Gemma adores Dafi and thinks that he's the perfect playmate for Meg. I think it's a weight off her mind. Seems she fell out with Dylan when she said she couldn't look after Meg. Now they both think that Vicky and Nick fostering Meg would be the best possible solution while Dylan gets his life back on track.'

Three loud claps silenced their discussion.

'Welcome everyone,' Cedric said in rich sermon delivery tones. 'We have a special guest speaker tonight, so we need to get the meeting started. I'd like to welcome Wendy Pryce, lecturer at Pembrokeshire College and the county's archaeology advisor. Please all take your seats and we'll quickly cover the minutes and matters arising, and then I'll hand the floor over to Wendy.'

As the session got under way, the minutes of the previous meeting and matters arising faded into the background. Alys tried to concentrate, but her mind kept drifting back to the Nook at Ty Gwyn.

She came out of her reverie with a jolt, just in time to hear that there would be a further update on the 'Rediscovering Ancient Connections' project at the next meeting.

Alys's mind wandered again as Cedric catalogued Wendy Pryce's qualifications and publications. It snapped sharply back into focus when Wendy told the meeting that the undergraduate student's supervisor had put in a formal application to have the Clebaston Manor site listed as a scheduled monument.

'If the application's accepted, the site will have interim protection,' Fliss whispered. 'The Llewellyns won't be able to do a thing unless they get the application rejected.'

*****

'Have you heard the latest on Bill Symonds?' Julie asked excitedly. 'He finally came out of his coma. They let me speak with him for five minutes this morning,'

'Wow! That is good news,' Fliss said, 'I'd almost given up hope.'

'You should never give up hope,' Julie said, frowning. 'You should come to church and pray.'

Julie turned to Alys, doubtless realising that her words were falling on stony ground.

'What's this I hear about you and Matt Vincent?' Julie asked, smiling. 'I heard on the grapevine that he took you on a date to the Ty Gwyn Hotel. Sounds serious. I'd almost given up hope of you ever finding yourself a man.'

'You should never give up hope,' Alys shot back at her. A warm glow spread through her body. How on earth had Julie learned about her supposed date? Matt would never have spoken about it; she certainly hadn't. She'd not recognised anyone at the Ty Gwyn, and she'd have thought the hotel was out of Madoc's Haven's gossip range. Spooky.

Alys looked around to make sure that Gemma couldn't overhear. 'It wasn't a date. It was a thankyou for my part in arresting Huw.'

Fliss grinned and shook her head. 'I bet that was just cover. Why are you blushing Alys? And why haven't you stopped singing for the last couple of weeks?'

Alys refused to be drawn. She'd pressed the red rose using sheets of kitchen roll and two of her father's massive old dictionaries.

She lowered her voice.

'I should really wait until it's definite, so not a word of this to anyone. A vacancy's come up for a detective sergeant in the Major Crime team. I've applied for it and Matt's given it his approval.'

'Oh Alys,' Fliss said, dismay plain on her face. 'What will we do without you? I can't see Ivor heading up the team.'

Alys thought the same. 'It's a shame you're a PCSO and not a PC. You'd make a great team leader.'

'Thanks for the compliment, Alys, but I love my painting and jewellery making far too much to want all the extra responsibility. I'm happy as a PCSO.' She put her hand on Aly's arm. 'I don't know if I told you, but I'm planning an exhibition at the tourist information centre. It's provisionally booked in for June.'

'That's excellent news, Fliss!' But Alys wasn't so sure. That meant Fliss wouldn't be up for extra overtime when she moved over to Major Crimes.

A bemused look furrowed Fliss's brow.

'How will you manage working alongside Beth Francis? How did she react when she heard?'

Alys grimaced. 'She doesn't know yet. Matt's telling her tomorrow.'

ALYS & MATT

WILL RETURN IN

FOREVER GOODBYE

A Pembrokeshire Murder Mystery
Book 2

Did you enjoy this book?
You could make a real difference.

Reviews are critical to
the success of an author's career.

Please take a few moments
to give a star rating and to enter a review
of 'A Final Regret'
on Amazon.

Many thanks!

ABOUT THE AUTHOR

I love Pembrokeshire and its coastline, which is similar in so many ways to Devon, the county in which I was born. I married a Pembrokeshire girl in a local village church.

My wife's aunt and uncle ran a country house hotel in West Wales. They had the misfortune to lose their chef due to illness at the start of one holiday season. Back then I was a chemistry lecturer and my college effectively shut down for two months in July and August, so I stepped in to help out in the kitchen. For the next few summer holidays my wife and I and our two young children slept in an old caravan and we divided our time between the hotel kitchen and the beaches.

Since those days my career has spanned university teaching, writing educational software, running courses for hospital laboratory staff, technical editing and leading a global knowledge management team for a computer software company. Now I'm an author and sing songs from the musicals with a choir.

My wife and I return to Pembrokeshire every summer to revisit its beautiful coastline and to meet with my wife's childhood friends and their families.

Printed in Great Britain
by Amazon